ALL COYOTE'S CHILDREN

ALL
COYOTE'S
CHILDREN

a novel

BETTE
LYNCH
HUSTED

Oregon State University Press   Corvallis

Library of Congress Cataloging in Publication Control Number: 2018014069 (print)

∞ This paper meets the requirements of ANSI/NISO Z39.48-1992
(Permanence of Paper).

First published in 2018 by Oregon State University Press
Printed in the United States of America

Oregon State University Press
121 The Valley Library
Corvallis OR 97331-4501
541-737-3166 • fax 541-737-3170
www.osupress.oregonstate.edu

To see the world and say it true
Means starting with loss.
But that's not what the heart wants,
That's not where the saying stops.

—Gregory Orr

Which story should I tell you, then? Aren't all stories about belonging if you look closely enough? Of course, most people don't. Most of us don't reach out and slow the story down, either—hold it a minute longer, tighten our grip on the part that feels off-balance, even if it grates aginst our rib cage when we breathe. It's better, or so we have been taught, to let it go. But sometimes a piece of story breaks off and rides the wind, and even if you close your eyes you know it's going to find you. You hear it coming.

1

The woman watching from the rock bluff hears the screen door bounce against the doorframe, loose on its hinges, and sees Annie emerge from the shelter of the arbor. She has cut her hair, reached around and sliced the braid off with a knife, by the look of it. And she's thinner, though she always has been slim, her step light as a girl's. She stops in the center of the narrow canyon and turns in a slow circle, scanning the cottonwoods, the old gateposts, the barn, and the rocky road leading up to what was once a hayfield on the bench beyond the rimrock. The shadow of the bluff leaning out over old orchard. Then the tangled maze of blackberries climbing up from where the river bends back on itself, and then the river, where the swimming hole has disappeared beneath the sweep of spring runoff.

Now she is looking back at the farmhouse, her fingers laced on top of her head, elbows out, the way children do when they've made a mistake they wish they could take back. But runners do it, too. Opening the cavity that holds the heart, filling the lungs, recovering. And now she is walking toward the house.

Yes, the woman thinks. Yes, good. She has come home.

⟡

One step at a time, Annie told herself. Kitchen, living room, their old room. *Yes, you can. You have to.*

The bedroom at the top of the stairs was the hardest. Jack's chair. His desk, his computer. The bed where they had slept the first summer he brought her to the ranch. Annie leaned on the sill for a long moment before she found the strength to push the wooden window frame up in its wobbly guide. In the yard below, the lilacs were already deep in shade.

There was something in this room. Something in the air behind her.

But of course there was nothing. Nothing but absence. You'll always have your memories, the counselors had said, meaning to comfort her. But even the good memories made it hard to breathe.

That first summer: two look-alike men gulping the last of their black coffee, matching stride for stride as they walked toward the barn; Jack turning in the swather seat to check something behind him, Roy waving a brief signal as the windrower edged up the narrow road that led to the high hayfield. Jack's hand, already callused, resting on one or the other of the geldings' withers as the horse turned to nose for a handful of sweet grass or wild apple. In spite of the stories Jack had told her about his father's distance, and his sternness, Roy had accepted her with the kind of courtesy she somehow associated with cowboy movies, even touching his hat that first day when he had emerged from the barn, squinting into the afternoon sun. And always "Thank you, Annie" every night as she started up the stairs. For the clean kitchen, she supposed, and the sun-brewed iced tea she served with supper, simple foods from the recipes she'd found in a pantry drawer, the salad greens fresh from her garden. What must it have been like to grow up here, she had wondered, as hand in hand she and Jack walked down the path through the blackberry vines to the swimming hole, where Jack splashed like a boy and her body felt free, all the heavy awkwardness of her pregnancy floating away.

They had only come, though, because Roy needed them. Needed Jack, anyway. "It's his heart," the neighbor who had called them said. "He'll never tell you, of course. And you know him. He won't leave that ranch. Maybe you can talk him into selling the herd, though, or at least cutting back. The truth is, he won't make it through another haying season on his own, and I thought you ought to know."

❧

They had met at college. That was the way Jack always told their story, and it was true in the way that truth has of lying below the flickering shallows of mere fact like bedrock in a river. She had been working in the campus cafeteria, blocked from view by the gray steel wall of dishwashers. Stacks of trays and plastic bins, plates, glasses, bowls stuffed with cracker wrappings and crumpled straws. If Jack could have seen past that wall, what would he have seen? In the Employees Only bathroom mirror, her hair, a plain brown like her mother's, lay flat beneath the mandatory netting; sweat left her eyebrows damp before it seeped into the corners of her eyes. Sleeves pushed to the elbow of her reddened arms, dry-skin cracks along her fingertips, that sharp throbbing in her thumb as she jerked the paper towel. *Remember, you are handling someone's food.*

It had been raining that afternoon, so she had tucked her library book beneath her jacket as she stepped out of the shelter of a campus doorway and into the current of students gathering onto the city bus. The one who sat down beside her stashed a heavy book bag between his feet, but he must have found some shelter for reading too, because he pulled a book from beneath his own jacket at the same time she retrieved hers, and their elbows collided. "Dammit!" Annie felt a jolt in the center of her chest. But the man was grinning. "I'm so sorry. You okay? No permanent damage?"

She nodded. The ease of that smile.

"It's the curse of us lefties. Southpaws. We're always jabbing people. My dad says I'm a menace." He tilted his head to read the words stamped along the spine of the scuffed library binding. "Tillie Olsen. You like her work?"

The first story was the only one Annie had had time to read as she ate her sandwich, and she wasn't sure if "like" was even the right word. It was the world she knew, and here it was in print. "I Stand Here Ironing."

"It's sad," she said, finally.

He nodded, unsmiling. Had she said the wrong thing?

"Mine's sad, too, I guess." His own book was thick, substantial. *A People's History of the United States.* "Zinn says people should feel inspired by what happened, but it's hard."

Inspired? Annie had a quick memory of her high school history class: the murmur of barely muted conversations, the rhythm of rap songs turned up loud enough to hear through the earphones of those boys in the back row. A huge white clock. That minute hand stuck in place, immobile.

"You're a lit major, then?" the man was asking. She shook her head, glancing down at her book. *Tell Me a Riddle.* "Don't tell me you're one of those smart ones, getting your degree in something practical? Something that will actually get you a job?"

Was it a lie, the slight smile she felt coming? Get a job. Yes, that was her, all right.

"I'm history, myself. Nearly as useless as English. Tits on a boar, to quote my old man." He turned toward the window, looking away from her. Something new in his voice now. "But we can't help it, can we? People like you and me." He turned back. "In fact, I'll bet you a cup of coffee in the cafeteria that by the time you finish that book of yours, you'll *be* an English major." He raised his hand as if to stifle protest. "No, no. It's written all over you. Well, I guess technically, I can only vouch for your face. The visible part." There was that teasing, slightly wicked grin again. Before Annie could react he stuck out his hand. "I'm Jack."

Would he have been able to see her if he had known then that she wasn't a student at all? He got off the bus before she did. He shared a place on Thirty-Ninth Street with four other guys, a dump, he had called it, but she didn't know if he meant the house itself or the state of any place inhabited by five male college students. What if he had stayed on the bus long enough to see the neighborhood where she and her mother lived? Would he understand that books like the one in her lap had been her shelter against what was happening just outside her bedroom door? Or beating on it, trying to break through.

It took her a long time to believe that someone like Jack could come into her life. That a man could be kind. That her life could change, that there were possibilities she had never let herself imagine. "Don't worry," Jack laughed. "I'll believe for both of us until you catch up." Tillie and Howard, he named the blue-eyed kittens he found at the Humane Society on her twenty-first birthday. They were living in Married Student Housing then, and she was an English major.

By the time Jack took her home to meet his father, his dissertation was nearly complete. She had graduated, too, and Riley was on the way. Jack had met her mother, of course, and he hadn't flinched at the sight of the rust-stained trailer, even the empties stacked in soggy cartons outside the door. But their wedding had been only a few words spoken in the presence of his housemates and a justice of the peace. The student special, they called it. After that they were so busy with classes and part-time jobs that her relationship with Roy had been limited to cards she signed at Christmas and on his birthday, and the awkward conversations when Jack handed her the phone. Jack wrote his father every month but their budget didn't allow long distance calls, and Roy, who didn't answer letters, phoned only rarely, usually to tell Jack the price his calves had brought or how the hay crop had turned out.

"You waited until you were sure I'd pass muster," she teased as they laid their jackets on top of the boxes piled in the back seat. "So your dad would know there'd be another generation of Fallon men to inherit his land."

"Damn right." There was something in Jack's voice, a tone she couldn't quite place, and she looked up quickly. But he was smiling. "You, my beautiful bride, are a genius."

⌖

Outside the open window, mourning doves were calling. Three short notes, then a cry. How could she live here, in this house, without Jack? "You're strong, Annie," Dennis had told her. Dennis, the good counselor. "Stronger than I think you realize."

But her legs were trembling. She sat down on the bed. This wash-worn quilt with its crochet-thread ties—each piece of fabric had once been part of a girl's dress, she thought. Or a man's shirt, a checkered kitchen curtain. Someone else's memories, stitched together as if that would make them last. Someone long gone.

Yet the quilt held her own memories, too. They had been lying side by side beneath it talking quietly that late August night, only a few days before they would return to the apartment where Jack would finish his dissertation and she would repaint the battered wooden crib they had found at a garage sale. "We'll leave long before sunup," he had been telling her. "Don't even think about getting up to fix breakfast. We'll just take a thermos of coffee and that big lunch you packed. We can work on that pretty much all day." They were bringing the cattle down from the high country. "Seventy cows and their calves. Dad's only going to feed a few head through the winter, he says. He still hasn't said why, of course. But all seventy are still out there on the summer range. It's timber country, second growth, which means underbrush. Windfalls. The cows will be pretty wild. They're the same cows that have followed the feed wagon like dogs every winter and will be doing it again by November, but they're spooky now. And there'll be trouble cows, the kind that like to head off into some brushy draw and hide like deer."

His forearm felt like stone. Well, it was hard work, bucking bales, hefting them up onto the flatbed as Roy inched the truck along in granny gear. But he wasn't responding to her touch; he didn't seem to notice her hand resting there, or even feel it brushing his hip, sliding down along his thigh.

"If you're lucky enough to find them, you don't dare wade through the brush to flush them out. They'll charge a man on foot. Defending their calves. We'll be riding Snip and Pete, and they're good cow horses, they've done it a dozen times. But it'll be an all-day job, especially without a dog."

"Why doesn't he keep a dog, do you suppose?" Their close bedroom walls seemed to have disappeared, fallen away. Even through the window she could see only darkness. "You grew up with a border collie."

"Lady was mine. Not his." He lay still. When he finally spoke again, she knew he was pulling himself back from wherever he had gone. "You're right, though, she was a big help. I don't know how we'd have made it without her." He turned toward her, lifting his weight on one elbow as he reached to cup her breast and then nuzzled her neck, his hand coming to rest on her swollen belly. "More to the point, I don't know how either of us would be making it through this without you."

Annie had spent the day with her harvest. Sweet onions and peppers, Early Girl tomatoes. When the salsa was simmering, she wandered back into the garden and lifted a tomato vine; until this summer, she'd had no idea tomatoes could smell like this. A pair of orioles flashed their quick dazzle of black and orange into the cottonwoods. Was it simply her pregnancy that made the world so suddenly alive? The birds of her childhood had seemed dirty, searching with fluttery desperation along the curbs and gutters as she walked by on her way home from the bus stop, a plain brown bird herself, arms aching from the weight of the food-stamp groceries and her library books. But here, hawks soared on updrafts. Swainsons and redtails, Jack had taught her; the ones that dipped and turned so gracefully over the hayfield were marsh hawks. Tiny rose-breasted nuthatches hung upside down on the apple tree's bark. Sometimes, hearing the song of a canyon wren, she turned so quickly to follow the sound that she felt dizzy. Until he left for college, Jack had wakened every morning to this land where sun rolled down the hills across the river from the farmhouse, lighting the pines as it went, and then the cottonwoods, and filling the pre-dawn shadowy draws with all those shades of green.

Long before Annie expected the men, she had a stew bubbling on the back burner; the beef, even the carrots and potatoes, sprung from this earth. The dozen pint jars of salsa cooling on the counter made her think of that first Christmas with Jack, when she had wakened to a shower of red and green M&M's. *It's not Holly, it's not Ivy, but it's all I can afford, I'm the luckiest man in the world, you're the woman I adore* .

But it was only Roy who would finally sit straight-backed at her table, though she could see he was exhausted too. Jack had brushed her cheek on his way upstairs, too tired even to eat. Outside the cattle bawled, the cows separated from their calves for the weaning. "I wish you didn't have to be here for that," Jack had already explained, "but there's no getting around it this year." Finally Roy stood, bracing himself almost unnoticeably on the edge of the table before he carried his dishes to the sink. "Thank you, Annie." The calves were desperate now, their mothers frantic. As she opened the bedroom door she could see Jack curled into a ball, his back toward her. When she slipped beneath the quilt, he pulled her arm more tightly around him, but he didn't turn. He was bracing himself, holding on. All night the cattle bawled, and they were still crying when she woke in the gray light before dawn. Jack was lying on his back, staring up into the dimness.

Annie leaned back, her elbows braced on the old quilt. Yes, it was still there. Tacked to the sloping ceiling above the bed where a tall man coming through the door would never see it, the only sign that a boy had grown up in this room: a faded National Geographic map of the world, the words along one border printed with a held-upside-down pencil. *The boundaries can change.*

↤

All night the house stretched its weathered bones: creaks from the ceiling joists, swollen window frames settling in their sashes as if to follow the moving shadows across their panes. A great horned owl called from somewhere near the barn. Annie lay on the couch, listening. Softly, from somewhere far away, an answer.

She had put fresh sheets on the bed this afternoon. But she couldn't sleep in their bedroom. Not yet.

Her bed at the hospital had been even narrower than the twin bed up in Riley's room. When she left the Stress Center, the part of the hospital known as Third Floor, she had slept on the floor with a blanket folded beneath her sleeping bag for padding. There had been a Murphy bed in that studio apartment, but its old mattress had kept the memories of so many strangers pressed against the wall that its sour, musty smell had made her gag.

Tonight it was enough to be here, lying as still as she could in the darkness of this house.

But she must have slept, because when a sudden gust of wind pushed though the door her dream had opened too, and there was Riley, coming down the stairs in his footed pajamas. "Mom?" So strange, that deep fifteen-year-old voice coming from such a little boy. It was trying to speak that woke her, sounds strangling in her throat.

She sat up and turned on the flashlight. Beyond the partially opened door a half moon hung above the canyon rim. Detach, Dennis had told her. Once she had watched the roots of a rain-loosened fir slipping into a river's flood water to ride the current. But how could she let go of herself? It went where she went, this hole she carried, the place where joy had lived, and wonder. It expanded to fill the dry walls of city rooms, rubbed along cement sidings and bricked foyers, reflected from lofty mezzanines and lobbies sleek with glass and plastic. Annie stepped out onto the porch. Moonlight filtered through the grape arbor and dissolved against her skin. They were all alive out there, the mice and owls, raccoons, the deer. Coyotes.

This afternoon in Riley's room she had buried her face in a gray sweatshirt he had tossed toward the closet. But of course his smell had faded.

⊸

Get the power turned on. The phone connected. Find a job.

Get Riley back.

None of it would happen if she couldn't get the truck to start. Annie was still leaning into the steering wheel in a pleading embrace, one hand on the ignition key. A pheasant cock called from across the river. She let go of the key and laid her head on her arms.

On your own. An expression of her mother's. *Out on your own.*

Except for them. They were always there, like shadows at the edges of her mind, the strangers sitting behind desks. Their faces blank, impassive.

Everything had to be justified to them now, things she didn't understand herself, would never understand. Explained to people she didn't even know. *If you and Jack were living such a good life with your son, why did this happen?* And Dennis had warned her: even after Riley had completed the treatment program at that place where the judge sent him, they would not release him to her care unless they could see that she had reached a place of acceptance. Jack was gone. Like a swimmer who drowns trying to save another swimmer who survives, he had plunged into a mountain wilderness in search of his lost son and disappeared himself. Though as it turned out Riley hadn't been in danger after all.

Acceptance. Things no one can change. Hospital words.

The pickup's battery was dead. That was all. But without a phone—yes, already she was helpless. Why should Riley's caseworker believe she could make a safe home for him here?

And what if she couldn't? They had lived here only in summer, when Riley was out of school and Jack between teaching terms, Jack researching his next book while she and Riley climbed the ravine or waded out to cast Roy's old hand-tied flies or just stood in the current letting the water-striders circle their knees. All three of them, and Riley's friend Alex too, lay in the August grass to count the shooting stars. "Really, they're meteors," Riley had whispered to her the summer he was ten. "Burning-up rocks." Sometimes, and of course this was nothing she could expect a social worker to understand, she had simply stopped on the trail to the barn or stood up in the garden and felt at home on the earth, at home on *this* earth, as if her body had grown out of the soil like the big Ponderosa at the top of the high hayfield, and remembering that feeling had given her more solace in the last few months than anything the counselors had said. But that had been summer. What about winter? Could she get the Toyota out of the driveway, or even navigate the county road, in the kind of snows Jack had told her about? Sometimes frozen pipes, too, he'd said. And you had to make sure the pump didn't freeze during those twenty-below cold snaps. *Chains required.* Putting them on, taking them off. She'd never even seen it done. Could she split and stack enough wood to last the winter? Days, weeks, it would take. She'd need a maul, and splitting wedges. Riley would help, of course. But what if he cut his foot? What if he fell and shattered his leg, like Roy? Or caught his hand in some machinery, or—God, that rattlesnake when he was little—

She closed her eyes.

Once, starting awake in the darkened hospital, she was sure her life with Jack had been a dream and it was time to get up, past time; she should be at work, washing other people's dishes, making their beds, cleaning their toilets, though she couldn't make the places where she lived with her mother completely clean, those streaks below the faucets etched into the enamel, not even ammonia strong enough to lift the grime from their own cupboards. It was embedded in the crumbled grouting, along the edges of the countertops.

"Leave that for housekeeping," Dennis had cautioned when he found her wiping a table in the occupational therapy room so the streaks of reddish clay from their craft projects wouldn't harden into an elbow-aching job for George, or for Maria, who worked the night shift.

Annie lifted her head, remembering. Someone had cleaned the kitchen counters. Wiped the road dust from the stove and kitchen table. And those sprigs of apple blossoms in their pink-sheathed buds had still been there this morning, rising from their Mason jar vase. None of it had been a dream, not even the yellow-eyed coyote watching from the lilacs beneath the bedroom window as she drove slowly past the buck rake and the old horse-drawn mower, years of grasses matted in thick-spoked iron wheels. Past the empty chicken house, the rock sled. Toward the house.

Who could have known she would be coming? And the floor, whoever it was had swept the floor. *Ask Jack.* The thought formed before she could stop it, filling her now like smoke, dry, swirling, crazed, a rising dust-devil of silence.

She sat up, arms stiff against the steering wheel. Outside the pickup cab, the coyote's ragged coat, nearly the same color as the stalks of last summer's yarrow, was already dissolving into cheat and yarrow and the fallen branches of the cottonwoods. But it had been there again, watching her.

Annie hugged her knees. The river swirled and eddied around the dark roots of a storm-fallen lodgepole trapped on the gravel bar. The pine was new but otherwise everything was as she remembered it, the cove sheltered by a half-circle of vine maple and syringa, leaf-mottled sunlight shimmering on the water. She had followed the path along the river and dipped between the wires of Roy's barbed wire fence. "It's easy if you know how," Jack had told her that long-ago first summer. "You just don't let it stop you." Each of them had had a place that pulled at them like gravity when they needed a moment alone. Jack's was the shelter of the big pine; Roy's had been the barn. This was hers, though it was not on their land. *Her* land. Not on *her* land.

Maybe it would help to think of it as Riley's land.

She had closed her eyes again, so she didn't know how long the woman had been standing there. A small woman, with the sleeves of a blue chambray shirt rolled midway over slender forearms. Dark hair, yet somehow older than that black hair made her look. An Indian woman. It took Annie a moment to see the jumper cables in her hand. "I was on my way down the trail, so I went back and drove around the long way." The woman's voice was so quiet it was almost swallowed by the current. "Looked like you needed a jump."

Annie's mouth opened, but she couldn't make words come out.

"I saw you trying to get your truck started this morning."

Annie was still shading her eyes, looking up.

"Our place is on the other side, up Iskuulpa Crick." The woman smiled. "The trail's a whole lot quicker than the road."

"You're the one. You swept the floor." Annie was conscious of a tingling warmth climbing into her shoulders and then filling her arms. "Leona?"

The woman nodded, still smiling. "I couldn't think where you'd be, and then I remembered. Mary used to come here, too." She raised the jumper cables. "Want to get that truck started?"

"You knew her? You knew Jack's mother?"

"Oh, yes." The woman was already picking her way across the smooth rocks, her free arm out for balance. "We grew up together."

Leona. "I hadn't seen her for so long," Jack had said last summer. Annie had just come back from town; he was helping her unload the groceries she'd bought for their Fourth of July picnic. "And there she was, coming through the orchard. Leona. Auntie Ona. I'd forgotten all about her. But her voice—it's coming back, Annie. Some of it is coming back. She was part of my childhood, I know that."

Leona's vehicle was a pickup too, a battered Ford with rusted fenders and a missing tailgate, and she had to climb onto the bumper to attach the clips to the battery posts. "Let's see, now. Positive to positive?" She grinned around the Toyota's hood, then disappeared again. "Okay, start it up." The motor came to life.

"There you go."

Annie was still gripping the steering wheel as Leona unhooked the jumper cables and climbed into her truck. "Might want to ask the guys at Les Schwab to check it for you, though." She twisted to look behind her, one arm thrown over the seat. It took Annie a moment to realize she wasn't just backing away. She was leaving.

Wait. *Wait!* There was so much to—"What was she like?"

Leona was already turning the corner by the barn, but Annie heard the words as clearly as if they had been borne across still water. "Jack. She was like Jack."

2

All Annie knew about Jack's mother had come from his memories of her. He was six, not yet in school, when she died. "For a long time I didn't understand what had happened," he had told Annie. They were lying in bed, lights of the passing cars streaking the walls of their first student apartment. "When I heard people say I had lost my mother, I thought she had gotten lost up on the mountain because I wasn't there to show her the way home. I used to have nightmares about her being out there somewhere, cold and scared."

"And your father?"

"Wouldn't talk about her. Or couldn't. Maybe he couldn't."

"So she hadn't been sick?"

"Her heart stopped. Apparently it was some kind of defect, the kind of thing that's been there all along and you don't know it. Dad drove her to the hospital, of course, but she was already gone. When I woke up that morning it was because Lady was in bed with me licking my face. She was still only a pup; she'd never even climbed the stairs before. The house was empty. I thought Dad must have asked Mom to help him in the barn; I remember I was feeding Lady my Cheerios when I heard his truck coming. He turned off the motor and just sat there. For a long time. A long time."

"He didn't come in and tell you? Talk to you?"

"Roy?" It was the first time Annie had heard bitterness in Jack's voice. But when he spoke again, he sounded like the Jack she knew. "I'm pretty sure he was different before Mom died. I remember—I think I remember, it's all so muddled. They used to sing sometimes in the pickup on the way to town. She sat next to him so I could see out the side window, and once he reached behind her back to muss my hair. I must have said something. She was laughing, I remember." Annie lay quietly. "You know, it's funny," he said after a while. "In high school, when everybody else hated history, memorizing all those dates, battles—it was pretty boring, the way Turner taught it—even then, when all the other guys were down in the gym shooting hoops, I'd be sitting on the floor between the library stacks with some book I'd pulled from the history section. I couldn't have explained it even to myself, but somehow I always had this feeling that there must be a way to find out what really happened. All the things they weren't telling us about. The stories. The *people*."

"What did he say? Your dad? When he finally came in?"

"Your mother's gone, Jack. It'll be just you and me now."

"Was he crying?"

Jack was silent. Finally he turned to her, held her close. "Oh, Annie," he said. "Men don't cry."

That first summer on the ranch she had found the recipes that must have been Mary's, and the weedy garden plot. Jack had laughed at her expression when she saw the deer fence he put up while she was in town getting groceries—yes, honey, it really does need to be that high. In the root cellar were canning jars, a blue enamel kettle. Mary had touched these things; now her own hands were the ones smoothing garden dirt over cucumber seeds and washing the warm, slippery jars. Was this part of what Jack meant by history? One morning, at the back of the top pantry shelf, she found a pair of small leather work gloves, softened with wear. After that, nothing. What about Mary's parents? A sister? Surely a friend. Maybe there were family photos in an album somewhere, probably in Roy's closet; there were none on the walls or on his bedside stand. In the brief glimpses through the doorway, his room looked almost as sparsely furnished as Jack's: a double bed, one chair. And a mirrored bureau where Jack's mother must once have laid her hairbrush, bare now except for the small bowl where Roy kept his keys.

Then Riley was born, and right from the beginning, from that phone call Jack made from her hospital room just as the baby's tiny features contorted and he started to cry, things were different. "Dad says that's no John Ryan you've got there, Annie," Jack told her over the receiver. "That's one riled-up Irishman, and you might just as well call him Riley and be done with it." That summer, when their heavily laden car turned off the country road, Roy was waiting for them at the gate. "So where's that boy, then? He's a*sleep?* At this time of the day?" But Jack was already lifting the baby from his car seat, and then Roy was reaching, cradling the baby's head in the crook of his elbow. He was wearing a new pearl-snap western shirt. "Well, we'll have to fix that, won't we, Riley?" He pulled the baby against his chest, tucking his chin to peer down at the dark, blinking eyes. "A man don't sleep when the sun's up, does he? Not a rough tough customer like you!" The baby smiled one of his quick happily-startled-by-the-world smiles and ducked his head into Roy's shoulder. Jack was grinning.

"First thing I've done right," he whispered against her neck as they lay in bed that night. "And you did most of it, at that."

Breakfasts that summer were as quiet as ever, but the evenings were different. By late July the baby could pull himself forward on his blanket and then he was crawling from his father to his grandfather and back again. Roy liked to bounce him on a crossed foot, holding a giggling Riley's outstretched hands for balance. His first horse, Roy said, though he had already sat the baby on Snip's back, and Riley had leaned forward to feel the horse's wide neck with both hands when Snip shifted his weight and the muscles quivered. Annie moved an old wooden rocking chair out to the porch. "You've Got A Friend," she and Jack sang to their son as the summer air cooled. Or they leaned together on the porch steps as Roy rocked and sang "The Strawberry Roan," "Little Joe the Wrangler."

"Been thinkin' I might sell the rest of the herd this fall," Roy said over the top of the sleeping baby's head one night. "Summer a few head of Gus's cows, maybe, just pasture the place. I've probably put up enough hay for one lifetime." Jack nodded. "I'll have to keep the horses, though. The boy'll be wanting to ride."

"Can it be this easy?" Annie whispered as they lay waiting for sleep. Jack didn't answer. She lay listening to his breathing until he turned to her again. "You, you, you," he said, nuzzling her neck.

But the next summer, and the one that followed it, were even better. Jack was an assistant professor now, a tenure track position at the campus across the river in Vancouver, with students lining up early to register for his courses, hoping at least to get their names on a waiting list. She spent the days at home with Riley, but two evenings each week she taught a writing class at the community center. She and Jack were sharing a new kind of security. Not financial, Lord knows; they were still paying off their student loans, and scraping together even a down payment on a house of their own seemed impossibly far away. But familial. That was the closest word she could find for it, this feeling she had of being at exactly the right moment in time, a man and a woman with this beautiful little boy growing between them. Roy was part of it, too, wasn't he? Jack's summer work on his father's ranch was lighter now, so every afternoon he was immersed in his research in their upstairs bedroom while Riley followed Roy down to the barn, begging to sit on the old saddle Roy had strapped to a low beam, or scrambled up the hay bales to wrap both his arms around the big gray barn cat, his "bestest kitty." Then it was Jack's turn again, laughing at Riley's stiff-armed rock throwing, the two of them counting the skips of Jack's smooth pebbles across the swimming hole—"one two three BUNCH!"—or Jack was explaining the world of ants and field daisies, sharing the taste of braided pine needles, both of them blowing as hard as they could to scatter the seeds of a heady salsify. The wishing weed, Jack called it.

"It must have been like this before your mother died." Annie was talking directly to the stars as Jack lay beside her on the grass. "Mmmm." On the porch a tired Riley was still fighting sleep, and they could hear Roy's low voice, a song about a Tennessee waltz. Had her mother ever rocked her to sleep? Annie pictured a desperate young mother walking the hallway of their first tenement, jiggling a colicky baby. Once, she remembered, her mother had pulled her down onto her lap, her breath smelling only faintly of beer. "We need a Daddy Warbucks, don't we, Annie? And I haven't found him yet. But at least you're not growing up in foster homes the way I did." Well, she was in Alaska with the fisherman now, according to the postcard she had sent that Christmas. Or not. Why was she, Annie, the lucky one?

"Let's just sleep here in the grass," Jack whispered.

"Let's spend the night on the moon," she whispered back. It was just coming over the canyon rim, an amazing light.

The next afternoon, on the hottest day they'd had in the canyon, Riley sat in the shallows at the edge of the river talking his way through an ongoing story of boats and "peeny fishes" while she read, cooling her feet in the water. Jack had just finished his work upstairs; she had heard the bump of the back door's screen, which meant he was probably standing in the shade of the apple tree and looking up at the canyon wall, letting his mind re-enter this moment, this day. In a minute he would join his family and they would wade out into the deeper current, Riley trailing his legs out behind his father's shoulders the way he loved to do. And here was Roy, too, coming down the path. He was whistling, something her mother used to sing. "The Yellow Rose of Texas." She held her open book over her forehead like a hat brim, shading her eyes to smile up at him. "Hey, there." Riley lifted his chin. "Look, Granddad!" Roy bent down to inspect the network of rivulet-canals and when he stood up he was holding Riley, one hand beneath the boy's back and the other beneath his legs, swinging him back as if he were about to toss him like a sack of potatoes. "'Bout time *you* learned to swim, pardner," she heard him say, and then her son's small body was airborne above the swimming hole and splashing down into the dark green water. *Riley!* But he was gone, her son had disappeared. A train was roaring through her ears, her legs were thick dead sticks churning into the river in the impossibly slow motion of dream; then Jack was passing her, his body stretched into a dive, and he was lifting Riley from below. She heard a small, sputtering cry, but already Jack was tossing Riley into the air. "Up he goes!" He ducked, keeping Riley's chest above the water. "And down! And UP he goes!" Again, and again, until she heard Riley laughing, that near-hysterical giggle she knew from the times when he "got too wound up," as Jack always put it, times when the run-and-tussle games got out of hand. When she turned, unbalanced by the current, Roy was still there, his face a tight, flat sheet. Was it the sound coming from her own mouth that suddenly twisted his? She stumbled toward him, falling, splashing forward on her hands and feet, but by the time she reached the shallows he had turned and was walking up the trail. She was going to be sick.

Jack waded back in, Riley in his arms. "Let's dry off, Buddy," he said. "Mom, can you bring us a couple towels? I gotta see what our boy's been building here, looks like canals and docks and is that a *submarine*?

Annie could only nod. She was still bending over, ankle deep in the silt of the river shallows, her hands braced on her knees.

Back in the house, she kept one arm around the boy who leaned against her, drowsy now. She would never let go of him, never. The men's voices rose and fell again into a pool of silence, too far away to let her distinguish words. Roy must have gone on through the barn and into the corral. Jack would have followed him no matter how where he went. They would go home. They could leave tomorrow. Keep Riley away from him. She felt the nausea rising again. Jack's voice climbed angrily above his father's as she turned another page in Riley's *Little Bear* book. Her own voice was dull, mechanical. Or maybe it sounded calm, steady, the way she wanted to be. For Riley. For this boy.

Through the open door she saw them coming, Jack leading the way. Roy went into his bedroom without looking in her direction. She heard the latch click. Jack sat down on the other side of Riley and laid his arm across the top of the couch to touch her shoulder. But when Riley reached toward the page—"Read!"—he rocked forward, burying his face between his elbows, hands on the back of his head. "My God," he said. "That poor sonofabitch."

"Son a bitch!" Riley laughed. "Son a *bitch!*"

Jack sat up and gathered the little boy onto his lap. He shook his head. "Oh, no. No, kiddo. You've still got some time."

"What was he thinking?" Annie had kept her voice low but now she felt it breaking.

"Same thing he's always thought. *Make a man of you, boy.* And now he says—oh, never mind. Enough. Enough."

Riley wriggled free and wandered out onto the porch, plopping down amid the scattered plastic farm animals. Annie reached for Jack's hand. "Jack, did he beat you? Were you abused?" The words had come out almost in a whisper. Why had she never asked?

"No, that wasn't—" Jack looked away. "No. Not yet. Not so far. And not, by God, today." He pulled her up from the couch. "Let's go find some shade."

And get out of this house, Annie thought. Yes, let's.

It was Riley who brought them back together, climbing into his granddad's lap after their silent, cold supper to beg for a story. Roy stood up and let Riley slide to the floor. "You wait right here. I've got something for you." When he came out of the bedroom he was carrying a battered child's cowboy hat, black with what had once been white lacing around the brim.

"Your daddy used to wear this when he was about your age. Suppose you're big enough to fit it now?"

Riley stood on tiptoe, reaching with both hands. "Big enough! Big enough!"

"Well, let's try it on for size. Yup, fits just right. I thought it might." Riley pulled the hat down over his ears. "Now, did I ever tell you about the time your daddy caught the biggest fish in the whole river? No? Well, he was wearing this very hat, I remember."

Jack looked at Annie and shook his head, what can you do, but she had already seen the flicker of relief in his face. And something else, too. Jack loved his father, of course. Yes, and she did too. Look at him. He meant well. He must have meant well.

Riley was still so young they couldn't be sure if he remembered this moment or if he had simply heard them tell the story of his cowboy hat until it became a memory he could claim. Roy's fall from the barn loft that next winter had left a ragged spear of femur protruding through his jeans, but it was exposure, not shock or pain or even his heart, that killed him. He had dragged himself almost halfway to the house, Gus said, when he found him on that bitter January morning, one arm beneath the drifted snow still reaching as if to pull his body forward. "I should have come by," this old neighbor told Jack at the funeral. "Two miles. It was only two miles, but his place was upriver and I didn't—"

Jack had brought Gus's handshake closer and wrapped an arm around the older man's shoulders. "No one could help him, Angus. That's just how he was."

3

This time Annie saw Leona coming. She had been watching, scanning what she could see of the ravine as she passed the window above the kitchen sink. Now that the electricity was back on and she had a few groceries in the house, she would be able to offer a real welcome. Coffee. She should put the coffee on. But already she was out the door and starting up the trail, and Leona was laughing, holding out a paper bag marked by dark streaks. "You must have smelled my fry bread! But you know, it's even better with coffee."

Annie laughed too. When had she laughed? And how long had it been since anyone came to see her? Neighbors, her fellow teachers in Portland— even Sue, who had left a message at the hospital desk, *if there is anything I can do.* Of course, she understood. They had families of their own, and pain like hers might be contagious.

"Yes, and jam, it's real good with jam." The kitchen was warm, quiet. Outside, the mourning doves called to each other. Leona's voice, too, was feather-quiet, a comforter of sound. Annie kept feeling her scalp prickle. Once—yes, her mother's hands gently combing her hair, her mother had been singing. Was this moment with Leona real, or a waking dream? But she had already poured the last of the coffee. Leona liked milk in hers. And sugar. Three spoons. And she was dividing yet another piece of fry bread. "Especially huckleberry." The wrinkles around her eyes fanned wider as she smiled. "But I'm all out. The kids get into it. We'll make some more this summer."

We.

Leona reached across the table and laid her hand on Annie's. "Fry bread may be bad for the heart, like they say at the clinic, but you know, it always makes my heart feel good."

No. Not now. *No.* But it was coming. Stop it, she had to make it stop. Leona might leave again. Even in the hospital, Annie hadn't cried. And afterward, all those nights in the apartment. She had just been so numb, so numb. For a long time she had thought she might be dead, that she had caught death like an illness no one else could understand, and this was why she had been unable to speak. Even breathing took too much energy.

Leona's hand had closed on top of Annie's. She was humming a quiet and almost tuneless song. Annie heard herself trying to talk.

"I don't—it happened so *fast.*"

"Ahhhh."

"But how could everything be gone so fast? So good, we had such a good life." Annie lifted her face. "And for no reason. They told me there had to be a reason and I just wasn't—"

"No. No, they didn't know."

Annie laid her head on her arms. The table might not be strong enough to hold her. She felt heavy, so heavy.

Leona had begun to hum her song again.

Finally it was over. Annie took a deep, shuddering breath, and then another. She had been so afraid. If she ever started, it would be like falling into a bottomless blackness, falling and falling, never again able to catch up with her breath. But she was stopping. She had stopped. In the silence she could feel the room around them, the walls, the very air holding them together. Leona had closed her eyes; outside, the spring frogs had taken up their chorus. And birdsong: swallows. The violet-green swallows were back. Her body was rocking slightly on the kitchen chair, but Leona wouldn't care. She was looking past Annie now, intent on her own inner vision. "They say fry bread came from Basque Redondo. The place where the army kept the Navajo people after the Long March."

"Jack said—" Annie's voice sounded strange in her own ears, an amplified but wavery sound, as if she were standing in the middle of an empty auditorium. "It was like a concentration camp."

"Yes. People died there. It was a place of sickness. And so many were already gone. They'd been killed, shot." Leona was silent for what seemed a long time. "Or died on the March. People starved, or froze." Her face shone with her silent tears. It was happening in her mind right now, Annie thought. Like Jack, and Riley, even Roy, it happens and happens. *They are alive and well somewhere*, Walt Whitman had written, but this was different. "Nothing would grow there, the earth was just alkali and dust. And the army gave them only flour and lard." Leona looked at Annie. "So they learned to make fry bread. That's what we taste now when we eat fry bread. How they survived." Her face glistened, but she was smiling. "Tastes real good, doesn't it?"

From the open field across the river the notes of a meadowlark's song rose and fell and lifted again, piercing the kitchen air. Leona wiped her cheekbones with the heel of her hand. Had the old linoleum shifted beneath them? They were spinning in a slow eddy of fragrance, fry bread, the smell of dark coffee. Dust motes floated in the beam of afternoon sunlight, rising, sinking back. If only she could ride one long enough to follow to its journey's end. *What is it?* she had asked Jack. *What is it that we're missing?* Jack had felt it too, even though Northwest Native history was his field. "The more I know about Indians," he had told her after his first book was published, "the more I realize I don't know."

Riley's summer playmates had all been Indian children, older cousins shepherding the younger ones, like that group of girls she had seen once on her way into town, their arms linked, walking in the water. Alex and Mouse and Lee, Jesse, Evie, Marissa, families living up and down the river. But there was something else, a nagging emptiness she had never been able to shape into a question. Before she met Jack, the Indians she knew washed dishes and cleaned other people's bathrooms just like her, or hung out on Burnside looking as if they'd slept under the bridge or maybe in someone's car the way she and her mother had to do that time. On her first trip to Eastern Oregon a sign out on the freeway reminded her she was ENTERING THE UMATILLA INDIAN RESERVATION, and by then she knew that Roy's land was one of the small white squares dotting the reservation map. CTUIR: the Confederated Tribes of the Umatilla Indian Reservation, Umatillas, Cayuse, Walla Wallas. The peoples native to this place. Jack had told her about land allotment, how reservations had been divided into individual acreages to force an end to the tribal way of life, and how the

Umatilla Reservation was one of the first places where it happened; the 1885 Slater Act, he said, was a trial run for Senator Dawes' Allotment Act two years later. But even he didn't know the exact history of his own family's acreage, whose allotment it had been, and whether it had changed hands more than once before it was sold for taxes. What had happened on this soil before anyone "owned" it? These were the questions that he had started to explore last summer.

Leona knew, though. About this land. Jack's mother. And about their family, too.

Annie had stopped rocking. "Leona," she said. The word seemed to open in her mouth. "Why hadn't I seen you before?"

Leona tore off another corner of fry bread and held it out to her. "They're looking for teachers for the summer school program. I told Dorothy about you. It's that small building between the longhouse and the Tribal Police."

On her way past the reservation project housing and into Mission, even as she turned left at the four corners intersection, Annie watched for Alex. No sign of him, of course. Maybe he had gotten off easy. The reservation courts were lenient, or could be, unless the juvenile officer was out to prove his worth or simply had a grudge against the family, and then Alex might be locked away in some youth facility too. The highway rose toward the view of the distant Blue Mountains, and as the Toyota crested the rise she saw it all again, the bull lying on the asphalt as if it had been dropped from the sky, both front legs corkscrewed into amazing shapes, the gray tongue hanging from the side of his mouth, eyes staring into the glare of a white August sky. Marissa bleeding, Jesse holding his arm. Riley shivering, even in that heat. Alex sitting on the edge of the asphalt with his head between his knees.

Then Riley in those too-short Juvie sweatpants, castoffs for outcasts, trying for a joke. "My first DWI. Driving with Indians." And then, "I'm sorry, Mom. I'm sorry."

"There was beer in the car, Riley," Jack had said.

"I know. Alex's uncle left some cans under the seat."

"Were you drinking?"

"They were warm. I guess otherwise we might have been."

Jack had stood, and Riley stood, and Jack pulled Riley tight against his chest, and then loosened his grasp to include Annie in this hug. "It'll work out. It'll be okay." Riley's voice breaking. "Dad, I'm really—"

"You weren't drinking and driving, kiddo. That's the main thing." Jack hesitating. "Of course it's still an MIP, minor in possession—"

But Riley knew. "It's the bull, isn't it?"

"Yeah." It was a confession, the air pushing out of Jack's lungs as if he were the one who had been driving the car. "It's the bull. Property damage." Jack had looked at Annie. "Jim Casey's property."

"Carload of Indians Kill Prize Bull. Carload of Indians and One White Kid, Driving." Riley's ankles thin below the elastic of the faded orange sweatpants. Fragile. At fifteen he had still been part child; she could always recognize his giggle coming from the dark corner of the movie theater where he sat with his friends. But thoughtful, too. And he had a courage rare among the kids she had worked with in the after-school program at the community center, something beyond adolescent daring or bravado. His eyes, like his father's, did not look away. "We were just heading into Mission for Cokes, Alex had some money, and then there it was and I hit the brake." He was rubbing his forehead. "How's Marissa? Is Jess okay?"

Her hand, reaching.

Stop it, Annie told herself. Think about today. Today is what matters.

The freeway dipped into Pendleton. Burger King, a trailer plant, the old mental hospital a state prison now. Then the highway climbed Reith Ridge and settled into the long sweep of wheat fields and sage steppe. Annie stretched her arms over the steering wheel, flexing the knot behind her shoulders. A pair of hawks was sharing a power pole; steam spewed from the potato processing plant as she passed Hermiston. Her mother had done that kind of work, stood for hours bent over conveyor belts, forbidden to talk to the women whose elbows brushed her own as they sorted peas, asparagus. Potatoes. The smell of her mother's T-shirt, damp and sour, then the liniment that always made her own eyes sting as she stood on the chair beside the stove, stirring. "Is it soup yet?" Her mother's voice already blurred.

They had thought they were good parents, she and Jack.

"But Annie, what's the alternative?" Jack had argued as they left the Juvenile Detention building that day. "Riley loves the wilderness, you know that. This LifeQuest thing would give him a way to get the smell of Juvie out of his lungs."

"I can't," Annie said. "I can't." She stopped in the middle of the parking lot.

"Two weeks, and then all this will be off his record and he'll be home with us. I can get Will to meet my first classes if I have to, or you could wait here for Riley. And we'll figure a way to pay for Casey's bull. Take out out a second mortgage. Something."

Now she was passing the Army Depot, row on row of nerve gas bunkers stretching north as far as she could see. Sarin, mustard gas, God knows what else beneath these mounds that looked like children's forts, houses for gnomes, with something like a chimney protruding from each one.

"But why?" she had demanded. Demanded, as if Jack could change what had happened. "For money? *Property*? They're not thinking about the boys. And Alex. What's going to happen with Alex? Jack, they're children. They're kids. Kids make mistakes. Though for that matter anyone could have hit that bull, you don't have to be a kid to hit a thousand-pound bull in the middle of the road!"

"I know, I know. Yes, it's about the money. And worse: they look at a carload of brown-skinned kids, even kids Marissa and Jesse's ages, and see gangs. I know it isn't right. *Christ*, Annie, of *course* I know it isn't right." He looked away. "Casey, of all people. You may not know what that means, but I do." His hands were jammed in his pockets, his elbows locked. "Annie, you heard what Tara said. It's the best way to get him out of this."

Tara. Riley's caseworker with the thick stack of folders on her desk. She had glanced down at Riley's before she said his name. (Riley? Rory? Ray?)

Annie remembered an image: she was a mother bear, huge, ferocious; her son and his childhood friend were huddled like cubs in the cave behind her outstretched arms. She would let nothing past her. Nothing that could hurt these boys.

"Riley's tough." Jack had pulled his hands out of his pockets and now he reached for her. "He's strong, like you. He'll get through this."

They don't love him, Jack!

If she hadn't cried then, in his arms. If she had been stronger.

At Celilo Park she left her shoes in the car and walked across the grass to stand in the shallows of the river. Out on the wide, flat water windsurfers swiveled and dipped, pitting their strong young bodies against the wind. Once, on their way back to Portland, she and Jack had stood together at the edge of these same shallows. Behind them lay the village of Celilo, a longhouse and a huddle of splintered shacks, dirt yards sprawling with the clutter of poverty: all that remained after the rising waters of The Dalles Dam had flooded their ancient fishing and trading site. "They say you could hear the falls from miles away," Jack told her. "And the mist rose so high that those dry bluffs across the river stayed green all summer."

A place of acceptance. Dennis had always smiled when he spoke these words. A good counselor, offering her peace, or trying to.

Had he ever seen Celilo Falls? Even in photographs it was a sacred place.

No, what had happened didn't have to happen. But it had.

↔

Annie stopped at the Memaloose rest area to change. She had to get this right. It would be so easy to say the wrong thing, or the right thing but not in exactly the right way, and if they didn't let her bring Riley home today, she—no. No. She had to. She had to, and she would. She looked fine, she told herself. Competent. Capable. A good mother.

A good mother who was about to see her son for the first time in six months.

Yes, she had written; they let her send one envelope a week. But she hadn't seen him. Even after thirty days in the hospital, when she was still right here in Portland, she had been barely able to function enough to clean guest rooms at the Motel 6 on Stark Street. It was work that felt familiar, even comforting, as one by one she left each room restored to readiness. She didn't have to talk to anyone. And it paid for a place to stay while she was getting her Aftercare counseling. The McLaughlin Center was just across the river. The staff didn't encourage visitors, but how could Riley understand why she hadn't been strong enough to push past that barrier?

She didn't even want him to be able to understand. She wanted the boy he had been before the accident.

There was no one at the desk, but Annie could hear voices, someone laughing. A boy clattered down the stairs and stopped short. "Oh, hi. I'm Alfie and it's all my fault." He held out his hand. Curly hair, dimples. A charmer.

"Chores, Alfie." The man who had appeared behind Alfie was wearing cargo shorts and an AC/DC T-shirt. Maybe she hadn't had to change clothes after all. "Sorry about that." The man offered his own hand. "Dan. You're Riley's mother? Annie?"

She nodded. Remember to smile.

"The kids have housekeeping duties after lunch. Riley's upstairs finishing his, so let's just get you settled." Dan led the way down a hallway past a cramped office and a bigger room—games, a Ping-Pong table without a net, a stack of plastic bins. "Here we are. There's still coffee, I think. This one's hot water, and the tea bags are here somewhere. Yes, here. Good." Annie took the empty Styrofoam cup he offered. Six metal folding chairs in a half circle facing a flip chart. Outside a car alarm was honking. "Just make yourself comfortable. It'll be a few minutes."

Think of it as a ritual, Annie, Dennis had told her. You're not on trial. They're just doing their jobs.

A job, yes. Well, she had one too, thanks to Leona. And a place to live. She filled the cup with water. Chu'ush: Leona's word. Water. What we need to be alive.

She was here. His mother had come for him at last. He couldn't look at her. Riley followed Dan into the room where the others were already settling into the metal chairs: Jennifer, Justin, Dave. And Brian, still shaking her hand. Brian the Professional. Allison was there, of course, standing between him and his mom like a steel shadow.

"Oh, Riley." She had taken a quick step toward him before Allison put a hand on her elbow.

"Let's give him some time."

Time. Yeah. That's what he needed, all right. More time. He tried to focus on a square of tile, the pattern of brown lines like worms drying on a sidewalk.

Was she okay? She looked so different with short hair. And pale, like a sick person trying to look well. Well, he probably looked pale too; he felt like a ghost sometimes, his skin yellow-green in the fluorescent light. Out of the corner of his eye he saw her sitting down in that metal chair, her back rigid. Had he ever seen her hands folded in her lap like that? And her clothes. Some kind of dressy sandals, and slacks, the kind with a crease down the front. She had ironed her blouse, too. As if this was a job interview.

Which it was. He was the job.

"It's been eons, Riley," she said. "At least two."

His head came up. Their family safe-word phrase had been "a couple of eons." His dad's idea, a little history joke. But serious, too. Don't get in a car with someone you don't know unless they say it, son. So what was she trying to tell him? *Don't worry, it's safe to get in the Toyota with me?* A couple of eons. Exactly how long he'd been in this place. Maybe she meant *It's taken me this long to come for you because what happened was your fault.*

But the interview had begun. Yes, her job was part of a summer program, she was telling them, but the director had said she might need her for the after-school program this fall, and the tribal charter school was scheduled to open soon. And there were several neighboring towns within driving distance, with substitute teachers always in demand. Yes, she could arrange for family counseling at Mental Health.

Counseling. With Mom. No way, no way in hell.

The circles Dave had been drawing around the stick figure representing Riley were dark. He filled them in on the flip chart with a black marker, one by one: no siblings, no aunts or uncles. Grandparents deceased or simply absent. Riley felt his grip tightening on the edge of the metal chair and made himself let go. Yes, his mother was saying, she did understand that she would be her son's sole source of support. Yes, she'd had some trouble, but she was well now. She was ready. "We need our family back."

"Our focus here at McLaughlin Place is on accountability." Brian looked up from his notes. "And Riley has struggled with accepting responsibility for some of his choices. It's in light of that that we're concerned about his returning to the reservation and the company he was keeping there. If you don't want to slip, stay out of slippery places. It's a recovery cliché, but it's still good advice."

At first she looked baffled. Then Riley recognized a trace of indignation. How else would she react? These people were obsessed with gangs, and of course his mother wouldn't know there were gangs on the rez. Wannabes, anyway. Kids desperate for respect, mostly.

Be careful. It's a trap.

"We had hoped Riley could return to his neighborhood in Portland. His classmates, his old friends." Dan stood. "Can I get anyone else a coffee?"

She still hadn't said anything.

Dan sat back down, turning his Styrofoam cup in his hands. "Maybe you could explain why you chose to return to the reservation, Annie."

Her chin came up. Good. She wasn't going to fall for their crap. "Jack's colleagues helped me contact a rental agency to get our house leased," she said. "They knew there was no income coming in, and with no insurance settlement, they wanted to make sure I wouldn't lose it. I'm grateful to them, of course. But it means the Portland house won't be available for at least a year. Jack's family's ranch is ours, rent-free, and our income will be more limited now." She smiled. Calm. In control. "And our neighbors along the river have always been supportive."

"Riley?" Allison's tone was confrontational, but his mother hadn't blown the job interview and he wasn't going to, either.

"No gangs."

"What?"

So he turned to meet Allison's eyes. "I said, I don't like gangs."

"Are you denying that there are Native gangs on the reservation, Riley?"

"No. No, I'm not denying there are gangs on the reservation."

He could feel his mother's eyes. Why did he feel suddenly protective? *Don't scare her,* he wanted to say. *She's been through enough.*

"And how do you plan to avoid them?"

Now he leaned forward, keeping his voice quiet. "The same way I would the ones in Portland." The same way I always have, he wanted to add. But he had been caught in the spin cycle of this argument too many times.

The counselors looked at each other. Dan checked his watch. "Well, Annie, Riley, there's a lot of work ahead of you. No use pretending otherwise. And we've all been tiptoeing around the question I have to ask you, Annie. But I'm sure you've thought hard about it, too. So how will you help Riley deal with his guilt?"

"*Guilt?*"

Riley felt his heart clench. Here it was, at last.

"I know it's confusing." Allison was smiling, her hand resting on Riley's shoulder as if she thought he was about to get up and run. "The difference between accountability and guilt."

This time there was no confusion on his mother's face. That set smile was gone, too. Yes, she had changed, but not as much as he had imagined, not like in the nightmares. It was her, all right; this was the face he knew. And even though she was speaking to them, she was looking directly at him. "I don't know why Riley walked away from LifeQuest that day, and I don't know why Jack disappeared in those mountains. He loved the wilderness, and he was an experienced hiker. I don't even really know why I wasn't able to be here for Riley until now. I always thought of myself as a strong person. But I know, I *know*, that none of us has ever deliberately tried to hurt anyone. Certainly not Riley. Riley has a good heart. His father's heart. His father was a good man. An amazingly good man." Tears had filled her eyes and were starting to spill over, but her voice was strong. "There's a difference between regret, even the kind of profound regret Riley and I feel, and guilt. I will help him understand that, if I can."

No one spoke. Dan looked down at his clipboard.

His mother stood up. "We have a long drive ahead of us."

Riley felt Allison move, but he was no longer watching the counselors' reactions. He was out of his chair and walking toward his mother. And then she was holding him, pulling him close, and he didn't belong to these people anymore.

4

He slept all the way to Arlington. When he felt the pickup slowing for the freeway off-ramp he jerked awake. "What—?"

"Sorry," she said. "We need to stop for gas. Even Old Blue can't make it home on fumes."

He yawned. "Fumes. So that's what I've been smelling."

Pathetic. No future in stand-up for either of them, apparently. Maybe they could try sign language. They'd have to talk to each other somehow.

When she pulled into the Shell station he got out and stretched, then crossed the street and leaned against the handrail above the city park. The train over on the Washington side of the Columbia looked like a delicate green toy. He had loved this place when he was little. Ducks, grass and sand, and water. Even a bright yellow caboose. They always stopped here on their way to Portland.

That was a long time ago, though. Someone else's life.

His mother drove the Toyota across to the parking lot and rolled down the window. "You hungry?" He nodded. She lifted the small cooler from behind the seat and turned back for the blanket, but he was already halfway down the steps to the park, swinging the cooler as if it were a child's lunch box. He wolfed a half sandwich as she spread the blanket on the grass. Another, and then another. Half a dozen brownies. Finally he lay down on his back, knees up, staring into the leaves.

It used to be so easy. Talking with Dad. Or Mom. Even the two of them together.

He heard her take a deep breath. Then another. "Riley," she said. "I'm sorry. I can't—"

"Don't, Mom. Please. Just don't." He closed his eyes. Sleep. Avoidance behavior. They'd taught him all about that at McLaughlin. Say it, then. "We both know it was all because of me. I'm the one who screwed everything up."

She didn't answer. Wasn't she going to face it? She'd have to, if they were going to talk.

"Son," she said at last, "those people at the treatment center were wrong."

"You mean today? What they said today?" He sat up and reached for one of the Cokes she had brought from the gas station's mini-mart. "Yeah, that thing about Indians and gangs just about drove me nuts." The Coke was ice cold. She used to buy him juice instead of sodas. "And that was just one piece of their so-called wisdom. Talk about a power trip—everything in that place was a privilege. *Breathing*, according the Allison, was a privilege. Which you earned by going along with whatever load of *crap* she happened to be dishing out." He drained the soda can and set it down. "I hated it. Being there. Sometimes I hated you. If you were still at home, the judge would have given me some community service hours and probation instead of sending me to long-term treatment. That's what I told myself, anyway. I was pretty sure he knew I didn't actually have a drinking problem."

She looked as if he had punched her in the stomach.

"But then I'd feel worse than ever. Because no matter how much I fought it, the counselors were right about one thing. I did it. I'm the one that made you sick, and Dad—"

Jesus. Now he couldn't even say it.

"No, Riley, you—"

"Yes, Mom! Yes! He's dead because of me, because I walked away from that stupid LifeQuest thing and he went looking for me, of course he would, I should have thought of that, I should have stayed no matter what that guy—*God*, Mom, I should have stayed, I should have stayed!" Then she was rocking him in her arms. As if he were a goddamn baby. And he was letting her.

Beneath the siren of his grief Annie could hear a sound like swarming bees: her own voice, spreading its thin hymn of human comfort. But her arms weren't strong enough. Could she hold her son together? The heart, keep the heart inside.

Finally it was over. Still on her knees, she laid him back on the blanket and pushed the hair away from his forehead. His dark eyes were glazed. She brushed his tears with the heel of her hand and reached into her pocket for a Kleenex.

"Some picnic." He bent his other elbow across his eyes.

"Riley." When he didn't move, she lifted his elbow and then urged him up until they were both sitting cross-legged. She wanted to touch him, hold him again, but she put her hands on her own knees. "I need to tell you something. Please. I'm not trying to spare you. I'm not just being Mom." She saw his head tip slightly, though he was still looking down. "When I said I don't know why your dad disappeared into the wilderness, I was telling the truth. He knew you could find your own way out of those mountains." Riley shook his head. "Son, when he showed me the place in the LifeQuest brochure that said, 'We put young offenders in the middle of nowhere, so there is no other place for them to go,' he laughed out loud. It was the exact opposite of everything he had taught you. In fact, he thought you'd be so at home in the Eagle Cap—that's where they told us you'd be going—that you'd actually enjoy the two weeks in the wilderness with LifeQuest. I think he pictured it as pretty much the same as our backpacking trips."

The sound he made was a choking half-laugh.

"I know," Annie said. "I know. But then when you came home you wouldn't have to deal with court and probation. He thought the wilderness trip was a way of helping you not feel like a criminal, or be treated like one, when you didn't deserve to be."

"No?"

"No, Riley. You didn't deserve it. I know you've had months of people preaching 'accountability,' but think about it. You made a mistake. A mistake anyone could make. You weren't able to stop a car fast enough to avoid hitting a large animal. If I'd been driving I would have hit that bull, too. You weren't speeding. The sight distance just didn't allow enough time to stop. Yes, there was beer. It didn't belong to you or any of your passengers, and it was unopened. You didn't even know it was there until you were halfway to town, did you? Legally, you were a minor in possession of alcohol. In reality, you were a fifteen-year-old boy with a fifteen-year-old's judgment—a perfectly healthy fifteen-year-old's judgment—who had the bad luck to have an accident that killed an expensive animal."

"With Indians."

"And with a limited license. A learner's permit, with no adult in the car." He was looking at her now. "If you had been stopped it would have meant a ticket. Maybe just a warning, on the reservation. Maybe nothing."

"But Dad went in after me, Mom. There's no way around it."

"No. No. But Riley, there's more to it. He didn't—" Annie looked out across the water, waiting until she was sure of her voice. "He didn't even call me. Tell me he was going."

Riley looked at her and then quickly away, as if he had inadvertently witnessed a moment of intimacy between his parents. "He'd driven back to Portland for in-service week while I stayed at the ranch to wait for you. You'd been gone a full day before the LifeQuest people reported you missing, did you know that? They thought you were hiding, of all things. Giving them a bad time. By then we knew they had taken you into the Wenaha-Tucannon Wilderness, not the Eagle Cap—but Riley, he'd shown you how to read the land anywhere you were. Remember all those games out in the mountains? Find your way home? The sheriff's office told me Jack was coming to join the search and rescue posse and I should stay by the phone." Annie paused. "But they never saw him. They don't even know where he left the car." Riley was watching her. "I've gone over it and over it, trying to answer all their questions—the police, the sheriff, even the insurance investigators—and it just doesn't make sense. He didn't change out of his street shoes, I found out later. All his jackets were still in the closet. Pack and canteen hanging on their pegs in the garage. Does that sound like him? There's something missing, son. Something we don't know."

Riley looked down. "I wondered, too. None of what they told me sounded like Dad. But Allison and Dan—God, *Dan*. 'Denial: it's not just a river in Egypt.' He must have that tattooed on his ass. Ass*hole*. That'd be even more appropriate." He looked up. "Sorry, Mom."

"Sorry? You don't ever need to say that to me again. You'll never catch up with how—" Tears choked her throat. Keep going. Swallow. Say what he needs to hear. "How sorry I am that you had to be in that place for so long."

He looked away.

"I can't even explain it. It was as if I were some other person. How could it be me crawling through brush, sweeping the grass with a stick and shining a light into the holes left by uprooted trees as if I expected to find your dad taking a nap on the ground, or caught like some animal in a pit? They'd put you back in the detention center, and I couldn't bear to think of you in there alone, not even able to help look for him. Then that storm hit us—three days of wind and rain—and then the first hard frost. Exposure, hypothermia. I knew. When they finally called off the search, I—trauma does that to some people, they told me. I just shut down. I couldn't move. For a long time I couldn't even talk. And then, well, you could probably tell from my letters. When I left the hospital I was still having a hard time. That's why I didn't—"

"But now." Riley was looking at her, his face open.

"Yes. Now I'm like you. Finding the way back. And so glad to have you with me that I may start crying all over again."

He pulled his knees up closer to his chest, forearms on his knees, then reached down to pick a dandelion blooming at the level of the mowed park grass.

"I even have an official seal of approval from my counselor, who was a whole lot nicer than yours. And Leona. She seems to think I'm okay too, though sometimes I wonder if she keeps coming around just to make sure."

"Leona!" Riley's eyes widened.

"She's a—do you know her?"

"Yeah, she's Mattie's grandma. I've been up to her place a couple of times. She wrote to me once in the treatment center." He picked up the empty Coke and rolled the can between his palms. "She comes to see you?"

"She had the house swept for me when I got there. And apple blossoms in a jar."

He smiled. "Sounds like her."

⟿

Mattie? Annie wondered as they climbed the stairs up to the parking lot. Mattie was not one of the friends she knew about. And Leona, writing to Riley? Even as she was getting her son back he was moving away from her; he had been growing away from her even before—yes, but that was what they wanted for him, that was what being a parent meant. "We're like the edges of a swimming pool," Jack had said one night as they lay together on the blanket watching the moon rise. "We're the wall for him to push off from when he swims out into the deep end, and the steady place he can reach back for when he needs support."

Be that steady place, she told herself. Be as steady as you can.

She needed her son, too. Maybe it was wrong to need Riley as much as she did. Night after night swallowing those meds, rinsing her dry mouth with chlorine-tinged water in that small, stained sink in her studio apartment, until at last her doctor had found the right one, the one that would help her keep drawing breath. It was the image of Riley that had kept her going through those long weeks, days when getting through her shift at the motel was all she could do. When she had still been too shaky to see him, or let him see her.

But the thread connecting her son was still fragile. Like the tungsten filament in an old-fashioned light bulb, brilliant but breakable. So it wasn't until they were winding down Reith Ridge into Pendleton, the Blue Mountains folding into their evening shadows beyond the valley, that she loosened her grip on the steering wheel enough to turn the music down. "Riley, you started to say something earlier. 'I should have stayed no matter what that guy—' What guy? No matter what that guy, what?"

"The one who was taking me out for my so-called Vision Quest, the overnight-alone thing. Darrell. On the way up the mountain he said something about Mattie. I can't repeat it, Mom. Especially to you." He looked out the window. "He'd asked me who I hung with, what my friends were like, and I'd told him about her. He said there were safer ways to get laid than with an Indian girl. Only the way he said it was a lot worse. A whole lot worse."

Annie couldn't speak.

"I thought, I can't stay here. With these people. I'll just go home and take whatever the judge wants to give me for driving with beer in the car and killing Casey's bull. But it took me a while to walk out." He shook his head and turned toward the window. "Profound regret. I guess that's what Dad would call an understatement."

Annie pulled off at the exit and stopped at the edge of the freeway ramp until her eyes, suddenly blurred, could clear. "You really do have your father's heart," she said when she could talk. "I meant that too."

5

The coyote was trotting along the fence line, coming toward them. When Riley got out at the gate it stopped, watching as he pushed the post away from the tight wire loop. "Hey," he whispered, and it looked back over its shoulder as it slipped into the dusk. He dragged the gate across the gravel. "I'll walk on down," he told his mother. She drove through the gate. The first faint stars were barely visible above the barn. He shut the gate and stood there, hands in his pockets, looking up, until he heard the pickup door closing.

Until a light came on in the kitchen.

Even the air had changed. It was heavy with lilac, like the night air around their Portland house in early May. He had somehow expected syringa, which wouldn't be blooming for another month. The month they had always arrived. He lifted his head. Yes, he could smell the river, but it was different too, still high with spring snowmelt. Sometimes, waiting for sleep in the treatment center, he had tried to remember the sharp, bitter odor of yarrow, and summer-dry grasses, as if he could step outside and be back in that late August day before any of it happened.

Right here. Here, by this gate. What was he, three or four? *C'mon up, kiddo*, his father had said, hoisting him onto his shoulders. *Let Dad carry you for a while.*

He should go in. She would worry.

Well, let her. It was her turn now.

And then, immediately, he felt guilty. Feeling his way toward the path along the fence line as his eyes adjusted to the dimming light, he saw the swirl of current and then the barbed wire, stretched wide where people had dipped through. His mother, mostly. *If you can't find her, son, here's where she'll be.*

It was going to be harder than he had imagined. Better than going back to the Portland house, though. This was where he had left his father. Here. On this place. This land.

Across the river an owl called, and from somewhere in the night another answered.

They had all meant well. He knew that. Even Allison had meant well. They were trying to help him. It's just that the counselors were fighting the wrong enemy. Like a mirror image: they had everything backward.

He had waited so long for this moment. But now that he was here, how could he go forward? One step at a time, his father said. That time on the trail up to Maxwell Lake. And Ice Lake, all those switchbacks.

After a long time he made his way across the river rock and dipped a double handful of water to splash on his face. It seeped into the corners of his mouth, almost the taste of home.

⟜

It had been dark for over an hour. Annie had warmed her black-bean chili, his favorite, and heaped two bowls with cheddar and chopped Walla Walla sweet onions. But she had not watched from the dark side of the house, or stepped out into the shadows to look for him. "Live alone in the bee-loud glade," she was murmuring as the door opened. Her eyes were closed, her hands flat on the table. "And I shall have some peace there—"

"Hey. Chili."

"What would you like to drink? Milk? Or juice? There's some V-8."

"Could we have some coffee?" He slumped over the table, elbows sheltering his steaming bowl. Coffee. Well, things would have changed in all these months, anyway. Annie circled her own mug with both hands.

"Good to be home." His voice was not quite so husky now.

"I know it's hard, Riley. Maybe it would have been easier if we could have gone back to our house in Portland."

"I didn't leave anything in Portland, Mom." He sounded tired. Riley's old, Annie thought. At sixteen, he's already old. He stood to carry his empty bowl to the sink. "Dad was—well, as far as I'm concerned, this is home." When he turned he was a boy again, if only for a moment. "Think we could try and find Alex tomorrow?"

"Sure. And Mattie, too." She paused. "The whole gang. So to speak."

There. Finally, that grin.

Annie smiled, too. But how far would humor carry them?

Always before, Alex had just appeared a day or two after she and Jack and Riley had returned from the Valley. She would look out the window and there they'd be, down by the river, two dark heads bent over something in one or the other of their small hands. Always it was as if they had never been apart. Alex lived with his mother, but sometimes that meant staying with one of several uncles or an older cousin. In the summer he lived mostly with them, the brother Riley couldn't take with him when they returned to Portland in the fall. And the friend she would have chosen for her son, if mothers did the choosing in these matters.

Riley looked toward the stairs. "Guess I'd better go on up." He took a step, hesitated. But no hug. "'Night, Mom."

Annie listened to his footsteps climbing, pausing at the landing. Then going on.

Tonight she would sleep in the double bed, the bed she and Jack had shared. Her bed.

Funny how having a child with you could make you feel braver, or at least act braver. Buck up, as Roy used to say. Get some backbone. *Girl, you need to swallow a lump of starch.* Who? Oh, yes, the cook. They had lived above a café part of the year she was in second grade. The old cook used to say that, even though it was always a slice of dry cake or a broken piece of pie, not a lump of starch—whatever that was—that she had carried to the cracked-plastic booth where Annie sat slumped over her subtraction homework, chewing her pencil and trying not to look up at the hands on the pale yellow clock pointing like long black fingers past the time her mother should have been home.

The Red Badge of Courage. In Portland, at the community college, she had taught that book as if she knew what courage was.

⊷

Alex was standing just outside Mission Market, and at first Annie wasn't sure he recognized them. She turned off the key and reached to touch Riley's arm. *Go slow*. But he was already sliding out, leaving the Toyota door open behind him. Alex didn't move. Annie shut her eyes and opened them again. As if this were a movie with the camera panning back to show how far he had to go, the distance between the two boys seemed to have lengthened. She watched as Riley's steps slowed. Alex looked away.

Then Riley called something, some sound she couldn't quite shape into meaning, and held out his hands, palms up. Alex leaned slightly forward, and in an instant Riley had closed the distance and was pulling his friend's shoulders into his own chest and then wrapping his arms around Alex's back. "Thank God," Annie heard him say. "Thank God."

"I looked." Alex's voice sounded different. A low, liquid sound. "I looked fr'im."

"I know. I knew you would." Riley shut his eyes. A group of young men came out of the store but Riley hadn't loosened his grip on Alex. "Hey, Pockets." One of them was walking backward as he spoke. "Fallon. You back for a while?"

Riley let go at last and turned to nod.

Annie saw the man point with his lips toward Alex, who had slumped against the wall again, his head tilting oddly to one side now. "That's good," the man said. Riley looked toward the truck and she nodded, yes, yes! and he turned again to Alex. They crossed the parking lot together, the balancing support of Riley's shoulder nearly imperceptible. Annie remembered their faces sticky with marshmallows in the light of a bonfire, their two skinny little-boy bodies glistening in the river. "We can talk without words, Mom," Riley had explained when he was, what, nine? "It's like we're always thinking the same thing."

Riley had to boost him up into the pickup. Alex didn't look at her, but he laid his head on her shoulder before he closed his eyes.

Riley had been treated for this problem, she thought as she rolled down the window, even though he didn't have it, and neither did Alex, then—but maybe that meant, somehow, yes, Alex would be okay, because Riley—

Dear God. Could she do this? She was barely strong enough to stand upright herself. And Riley. He'd been through so much. But Alex was part of their lives. He always had been.

"Home?" Riley had reached around Alex to touch her shoulder.

"Home." She turned the key. They could call Alex's family from the house. If there was anyone to call now. Things could change.

"Can Alex live with us?" Riley didn't understand what a sleepover was, Annie had thought that day, the first summer Alex stayed with them. But as it turned out, Riley had asked exactly the right question. Ruby was still too young in many ways to be anyone's mother, and her brothers were all drinkers. "These things aren't as black and white as they might seem, Annie," Jack had cautioned when she sat down beside him that night. She had bathed the boys before tucking them in, Riley in his twin bed and Alex in the trundle bed beside it; she could still smell the sweet soapiness on her own skin. "Alex has a family. They're just trusting us to be part of it."

Riley had scrunched into the outer corner of the front seat, one arm still wrapped around Alex's shoulders, his eyes focused on the road. Annie took a deep breath. Tomorrow she would have to leave them while she met with Dorothy, and by Tuesday she'd be away all day. Riley motioned with his free hand: a pair of mule deer with their antlers still in velvet, picking their way up from the river through a swirl of cottonwood fluff. Annie slowed as the deer stared, frozen, then bolted across the road and up the bank, clearing the barbed wire fence at the top. Alex had opened his eyes. "Brothers," he whispered before his eyes shut again.

How old had the boys been when they found the treasure? Seven? No, eight, the summer they had climbed as far up the ravine as the trail would take them and then crawled on their hands and knees, Alex making a stirrup for Riley's foot and Riley pulling Alex up beside him until they could wedge one after the other through a crevice where yellow monkey flowers were blooming above the cool seep of moisture from the earth. And behind that crevice, something wonderful, the seep widening out into a sandy hollow surrounded by ferns, and though they could look up through the overhanging branches of tall pines and see the sky, sometimes even a hawk flying over, they called it their cave, and they were sure no one else knew about this place. Jack had come for her one afternoon, his eyes smiling, and led her up the trail until she could hear not words but the shape of words, their voices soft as small birds settling for evening. "I'm glad he has Alex," Jack whispered, kissing the back of her neck. "It's so much better to share it with someone."

Jack had showed her this place one evening while Roy was rocking Riley to sleep out on the porch. But he hadn't told her about what he had left there so long ago, the coffee can he had buried in a rock cache behind the screen of ferns, so when the boys pulled her up the trail to share what they had found,

Annie felt almost like a child herself, as if she too had been there when they pried off the brittle lid. "Some of them were mine," Jack later explained, "but most of them were Mom's. Dad was getting rid of all her things, so when I found some of her keepsakes in a coffee can down by the river, I hid the can in my secret place. In case she came back, you know?" A squirrel skull. Two owl pellets, an obsidian spear point. Pheasant tail feathers. Petrified wood. A leaf fossil engraved on flat sandstone, three marbles flecked with gold. A Roy Rogers jackknife, rusted shut. A beetle encased in amber, and a ring.

And his son had found these things. His son, and the boy who was like a son to him.

"Is it diamond?" Riley whispered.

"Amethyst, I think," she told him. "It's beautiful."

"It's somebody's treasure, Mom." Riley was still whispering. "But whose? Who was here?"

Annie had put an arm around each boy's shoulders, the three of them on their knees in the damp silt. "Your families have both lived here," she said. "Yours, and Alex's. You remember Granddad, Riley? And his father lived here before him. Maybe his father too, I don't know. And Alex's family were here a long time before that."

"Right here?" Alex's eyes were big. "In this place?"

She lifted one arm to point up at the sky and swept it in a circle. "Here, everywhere. The mountains, the rivers, everywhere. Your family lived here for thousands of years."

"Did *they* leave this coffee can?"

"Well, you know, I don't know who left it. It's a mystery. Maybe your dad would have some ideas, Riley. You boys have discovered a treasure, for sure."

Leona, Annie thought now. After Mary died, Leona must have left the can by the river for Jack to find. And she knew just where by the river Leona would have left it. *This is where she always came.*

Why had Leona been missing from their lives for so long? She had just appeared in the old orchard that day, Jack had said, and handed him the letter. To help with his research, he thought.

⌇

When his mother turned off the ignition they sat without speaking. Alex had slumped against him; if he opened the pickup door he was pretty sure

Alex would topple over. Alex had grown, too. He was heavier. What if he dropped him?

"Go on in," he told his mother. "I'll just sit here a while."

She nodded. "If he needs it, later—if he gets agitated, I still have some—"

Riley shook his head. He didn't want to hear what they had given her. Or why.

She was right, though. Some of the kids had said detox was the worst part. Wouldn't have made it through detox, they said, without help. Boy, do I wish I had some Ativan right now!" Dylan. Third-time-around Dylan.

Alex wouldn't be like that.

Through the open window he could hear mourning doves, and some other bird he didn't recognize. His mother closed the driver's side door softly. "Call if you need an extra shoulder. I'll be listening."

He smiled at her—*reassure her, she'll need reassurance*—and closed his eyes. The sun felt warm on his arm. He heard the motor ticking, and then the sound of the river. A kingfisher scraped his way upstream. Noisy bird. Alex's weight was squeezing him tighter against the door. His chest was not exactly deep, and now it felt as narrow as a shadow. The Vanishing American, Alex would say. Would have said.

It wasn't much of a plan, was it? Just sit here and wait for Alex to wake up and be Alex again.

It was even harder to leave them than Annie had imagined. She had knocked lightly before she pushed open the bedroom door, but they were still curled toward each other like parentheses in the twin and trundle beds as if they fallen asleep talking and neither of them had moved. They had slept late yesterday too. Her meeting with Dorothy had taken only an hour or so in the morning; Riley had been spreading peanut butter on his toast when she got home, but Alex was still upstairs, and he hadn't come down until late afternoon. He and Riley had spent the evening out by the swimming hole. "It'll be okay, Mom," Riley had whispered last night before he followed Alex up the stairs. Would it? Neither she nor Riley could know. Alex had hardly said a word, at least in her hearing. Had he eaten anything? He looked so pale. But his skin wasn't clammy, and she hadn't seen his hands trembling.

This summer school class wasn't part of a remedial program, Dorothy had already explained. The kids wouldn't be coming because they had failed a semester of English and needed to make up a credit. It was just extra help, she said, to keep the Native students from falling behind over the summer, or to catch up if they were already behind, which many of them were. "Our dropout rate is the big reason we're here. We need to stop that leak. When we lose our young people, we all lose."

Voluntary summer school? "Well, we sweeten the pot," Dorothy laughed. "Most of the summer program is recreation. The swim bus leaves for the city pool every afternoon at two, and we do traditional skills and games too, atlatl contests, art. And we're recovering our languages. We make it fun. And it's something to do."

Annie pulled into the parking lot and sat with her hands still gripping the wheel. She had always been nervous before starting a new class at the youth center, and later as an adjunct at the community college. "Yup, this is it," Jack had teased her at breakfast one morning. "This is the term they find out you're a fraud!" But he wasn't here to help her remember what a good teacher she was. Or had been.

Act as if, Dennis had told her. As if you can do this. She took a deep breath and opened the pickup door.

Learn their names, Annie told herself, though she didn't recognize any of the kids who drifted in, small schools of fish grouping themselves around the tables. Get the names right.

"You're Pockets's—Riley's mom?"

Pockets. Riley's cargo pockets bulging with rocks and snails and mosses the summer he was ten had earned him this nickname. She smiled. "Yes. I'm Annie Fallon. You can call me Annie."

"He back too?" Makayla, wasn't it? And now another boy. Cecil. She added his name to the list and looked up.

"First, can we push a couple of these tables together so we can sit in a circle? Or as close to a circle as tables can make?" There was a moment when she thought two girls weren't going to move, but they did, smoothly in fact, sliding into chairs at the end of the tables. "Everybody good? Okay. Yes, Pockets is back. He's been home for a couple of days. You'll see more of him this year, if you know him, because he won't be going back to Portland in the fall. We live here now, Riley and I."

They were all looking down, or slightly away. She could feel the heat rising to her face. They all knew what had happened. "I wanted us to sit in a circle because stories need listeners, and listeners need stories. It's a circle. Stories connect us." They were looking at her now, at her burning cheeks. They would know about her breakdown, too. Or some version of it. What story had they heard? She had to force the words out. "Some of you probably know my story, Riley's and mine. It's an ongoing one, and we're in the middle of it, just like you are in the middle of your stories." She touched the stack of books on the table beside her. Maybe they wouldn't hear the quaver in her voice. "These writers found their stories in the stuff of their daily lives. I'd like us to try that, too."

Makayla again. "What if nothing's ever happened to us?"

The boy named Sammy tipped his chair back, one finger touching the table to keep from falling over. "Don't know about you guys, but *my* life's an action-packed adventure!"

"Yeah, right. Super Sam." But they were smiling. They liked him.

"Sherman Alexie has a poem about waiting in the car outside a tavern while his parents are drinking. Every so often they come out with Pepsi and chips, but then they go back in." She looked at them. "I've been there. Maybe you have too."

The room was so quiet it was as if everyone had stopped breathing.

"And I've always loved Elizabeth Woody's story about Buckskin, a '76 Galaxy 500 she calls an Indian car, a War Horse. I got to hear her read that story once, in Pendleton. Buckskin's windshield wipers fall off in a downtown Portland rainstorm and her transmission linkage pops out in a Seattle traffic jam, but she carries the whole family to powwows and rescues them from all sorts of injustice."

No one said anything. Leann, Cecil, the boy who reminded her of Mouse. Everyone joked about rez cars. Hadn't she reached anyone?

"So that's what I mean when I say claim your own lives, your own experience. It's funny, you might think nobody wants to hear the details of our ordinary lives, but that's exactly what we do want to hear. Broken windshield wipers. Pepsi and chips."

It was Alex who had taught her not to be afraid of this kind of silence. Alex. How was he—and Riley—but she was here now. With these kids.

And they weren't buying it. Well, what did she expect? A white woman, teaching Native literature to Native students? They knew Riley, but they didn't know her. It was one thing to share these books with Jack, reading her favorite passages aloud, but—

"Are those books *all* by Indians?"

"Native." Sammy was serious now. "Native American."

"Yeah, well, whatever. We were on the Umatilla *Indian* Reservation, last time I looked."

Sammy shook his head, but he was grinning. "Okay, be all politically incorrect. Just don't say I didn't try to save you from yourself."

Annie waited until they were ready. "These books are from the Native lit class I got to take at Portland State." A girl leaned closer, trying to read book titles. "That was a few years ago, though. Now there are so many Native writers that I can't even keep up with them. These two are from the Northwest—they may even have relatives on this reservation."

"That Buckskin has cousins here, for sure."

"Are you gonna read us those stories?"

"Do we have to write about family stuff?"

Did the relief show on her face? They were talking, and all at once. They were with her after all. "Yes, we can read these stories, and no, you don't have to write about family. I guess I've just been thinking about family myself." The girls looked at each other. Her face had flushed again, but now she knew she could keep going, riding the wave of fear and elation that she always felt when she was teaching. "There's a bigger family, right?" she said. "The life around us? The deer, the salmon, the mountains. The river. It's time for you to be heading off to your language classes, but tomorrow let's start by writing about the river. It's your river. You have watched it, waded in it, swum in it, listened to it. So tonight, think about that river. You might even go down to the river. But don't fall in, it's still awfully high." Cecil grinned. "Maybe you'll remember something, or something new will come to you." She looked at the clock. "Okay, see you tomorrow. With paper and pencils! Or pens!"

Sammy waved a backward acknowledgment over his shoulder. Annie let herself slump in her chair, her heart finally slowing. She had made it through this class, the first since Jack had died: somehow the fragments of her life had been compressed into a shape that could pass for the teacher she had been before. Not the fragile, desperate mother whose foot was still jiggling under the table. She wanted to lay her head on the stack of books and close her eyes.

"Annie?" The girl's voice behind her so quiet that at first Annie thought she had imagined it. Dawn? No. Matilda. Tillie, to her friends? The girl reached out as if she were going to shake Annie's hand, a gesture of respect on this reservation, really more like gently touching someone's hand than shaking it. But Matilda was putting something in Annie's palm: a small bag made of buckskin. "Could you give this to Riley?"

Such a slight weight, and the girl's voice so soft. Annie felt suddenly light-headed. Matilda. Of course. Not Tillie. This was Mattie.

6

The sounds came almost in unison: two sharp cracks separated only by seconds, then a tearing and splintering. Annie dragged the gate across the driveway and stood listening for a moment before she understood what she was hearing. Loose gravel whispered beneath her tires as she turned past the barn. There—the arc of the splitting mauls, Riley closest to her, Alex a shadow only a few feet behind him. No, not a shadow but a mirror image, because it was Riley's left hand and Alex's right, sliding up the maul handles and back down as the heavy blades met the round blocks of wood. Like a butterfly's wings, she thought, and then she thought, my God, look at their faces. They were grimacing, not with effort but with anguish, a mixture of fury and desperation.

She had stopped to buy ice cream. Their favorites, chocolate and strawberry. As if they were still little boys.

But Riley looked up at her, then tilted his head toward the house. Leona was sitting on the edge of the porch, hands at her sides, swinging her feet.

When Annie sat down beside her she was still cradling the bag of groceries. Her own feet touched the ground. "I'm glad you're here."

Leona smiled. "James brought wood."

"I wondered."

"He hasn't been drinking, you know. Since it happened."

"That's good, I guess. But the accident wasn't his fault. He didn't know the boys were going to take the car, and they didn't know about the beer cans."

Leona nodded. "It's his nephew." She leaned back on her hands and looked up into the vines roofing the arbor. "James wants to help."

Of course. Alex was detoxing. Could Riley lead him back across that tenuous bridge from those months of heavy drinking to his old self? She had left Riley with a job she had no idea how to do herself, a job no one in Alex's family had been able to do either, apparently, but that didn't mean they didn't care. Even those young men at the Market yesterday had hoped Riley would be the one, and what they had offered her son was—what? Permission? Approval? No. Gratitude.

He was everyone's best hope, but he would need all the help he could get. From James and Ruby, from herself. Leona was here too. Still swinging her feet. "Better not get a dog until that coyote quits coming in so close. He'll stay back once he sees you're okay."

A dog. Yes. Yes, a dog.

Maybe a border collie.

"So you've met Mattie."

Annie looked down. The bag's buckskin string was sticking out of her shirt pocket.

"She asked me to give this to Riley."

Leona nodded. "My granddaughter. She's been living with us for a while."

"Riley wants to—Riley mentioned her name." Annie pulled the medicine bag from her pocket. "It's very light."

"Don't open it."

Annie looked up, startled. "No, I just—"

But Leona was laughing. "Let's not let that ice cream melt. I'll help you start supper. Those boys'll be real hungry."

⟳

It wasn't just Alex who was different. *He* had changed, too. Everything had changed.

They were awkward with each other. That was the worst part.

But of course it wasn't the worst part. Not for Alex, anyway. It wasn't even close. What he, Riley, was doing was easy. By comparison.

And what if he failed? What did he know, really?

Mattie's gift had felt good in his hand. Soft, soft buckskin. Like a promise. Riley swung the maul. Hope is the thing with buckskin. Or inside it. The bear claw meant something, too. He didn't know what, but it must be something good. Weird how his blisters had stopped throbbing after he hung the bag around his neck.

He had to take two or three swings to split a round of tamarack, but at least he could hit it in the same place now. Even so, sometimes he had to pull the two halves apart by hand. They made strange, squeaking sounds, as if they were crying in protest. He heard Alex's maul crash through a round in one blow, then the two pieces tumbling away from each other. When he turned he saw Alex leveraging the blade out of the chopping block.

"Think through the wood, son," Riley's father had taught him. "Don't focus on the surface." That had been in Portland, though. Wood for the Christmas fireplace. Nothing like this.

Whatever else it meant, Mattie's gift meant she was out there, waiting. He swung the maul again.

⊸

It took a week to split and stack the wood. "The sweat cure," Riley called it. He was lifting the lid on her big soup pot. "Spaghetti sauce. Yeah, spaghetti's good."

"Sweat without the sweat, more like." Alex had come in so quietly Annie was sure neither of them had known he was there. It was the first time she had seen him smile. The sweat, what some people called the sweat house, was for healing, cleansing, prayer. Coyote's gift, according to the old story. Coyote, iSpeelyi, sent by Creator in the time of the Animal People to prepare for the coming of human beings. Men sweat with men on this reservation, and women with women.

One afternoon Annie came home to find Ruby helping James unload more stove-length rounds from the back of an old truck. She stopped the Toyota and got out. James met her eye and she thought he might have nodded, but the brother and sister didn't break the rhythm of their work, James bending and then handing the wood to Ruby, who turned to toss the round onto a growing pile. Where were the boys?

"I wondered how we'd get enough wood to last the winter." Annie had come closer as James jumped lightly down from the truck bed. Ruby sat down on the tailgate and pushed herself off with both hands. "I don't know how to thank you."

James glanced at Ruby.

Was she supposed to pay? Annie wondered. People made ends meet by cutting wood. Next week when she got her check she—but maybe that was wrong, maybe they would be insulted. The wood was probably a gift. They were doing this for Alex, they were doing this to thank her. To thank Riley.

Ruby and James turned at the sound of the screen door. Riley held a glass in each hand, whatever was in them sloshing over the rim as he walked. "Guess I got them a little full."

He wiped his hands on his dirt-stained Levis. "It's lemonade. We made it this morning."

"Eeeww." Ruby made a face and held her glass out at arm's length. "You guys ever hear of sugar?"

"Sugar. Well, okay, sure, we can take that into consideration." Riley grinned. So much like Jack that sometimes—

"Where's Alex?" James's voice was almost as quiet as Mattie's.

"In the barn. He's working on the rototiller. Good thing one of us knows something about motors."

"What's wrong with it?

"I don't know, it just won't start. We were hoping to get the garden tilled up today." Riley looked at the mound of unsplit tamarack. "This is good, too. Thanks."

James nodded. He handed Riley back the empty glass. "Not too bad for a first try."

"They'll get it right," Annie said. She had seen the flicker of fear on Ruby's face when Riley had pointed toward the barn. Fear, yes, and anguish, and guilt; Ruby, too, was a mother separated from her son. Watching them leave, though, again Annie wasn't sure she had said the right thing. But they had both shaken her hand, and Ruby lifted a slight wave as the truck turned onto the county road.

"You up for some of this?"

"Absolutely." Annie rested her hand lightly on Riley's shoulder as they turned toward the house. "Oh, sorry. I forgot." Last night she had rubbed Tiger Balm into both boys' shoulders, their back muscles so sore that even her touch was painful.

"No, it's okay. We're getting tougher, I guess." He smiled, but glanced back toward the barn before he motioned her toward a seat on the porch steps. "I'll bring you out a glass."

"This is a big thing you're doing, Riley. A hard thing."

"Not much choice."

But when he pushed the screen door open with his elbow and she reached up to take the full glass from him, his hand was shaking. "I just hope it works." He sat down beside her, looking toward the barn. And listening.

"Was today—"

"Yeah. Today was harder. I think because we got stopped. It's better when we can move."

"Do you talk? The two of you?"

Riley looked away.

"I'm sorry, of course you talk."

"Yeah, but you're right, it's not the same. You've seen how he is."

Annie put her arm around her son, this time deliberately. "You're doing everything you can, Riley."

For a moment he let himself slump against her. He felt small in the circle of her arm, the slender silhouette of a boy. When he pulled away and leaned forward, though, hands on his knees, he was a young man again. "I saw enough in that place—McLaughlin—it's a tough thing to kick, Mom. Especially if it's in your family. Some of the kids were there for their second or third time. It's supposed to be genetic, some chemical thing that happens in the brain. And Alex's family—Indian people, all the statistics—oh, I don't know."

"You know my mother was an alcoholic, don't you?"

"No." Riley glanced toward the barn.

"Was, or is. If she's still alive. All I know is, she suffered, and she drank to ease that suffering. And her drinking made everything worse. What makes some people get caught in that cycle? I'm not sure anyone really knows."

He rubbed his forehead. "I knew there was some problem, but I guess it all seemed so far away."

"I think you're giving Alex what rehab could give him and more. You're standing by him while he gets through the physical withdrawal from the heavy drinking he's been doing, but the main thing is he knows you'll be there when he needs to talk."

Riley looked toward the barn again. Annie pushed him gently off the porch. "Call if you need me?"

He nodded. He started toward the barn but turned, walking backward, his forehead wrinkling. "Could you make, like, a double batch of brownies?"

Annie wanted to smile but didn't let herself. "You got it, kiddo."

Riley stopped. Then he walked quickly back and pulled her into a hug almost as strong as Jack's. Maybe he really had forgiven her.

7

Mattie wasn't the only quiet one in Annie's class. By the second week Cecil had yet to speak, though he had smiled when Virgil called him Hawk. A private joke? There was so much she didn't know about this community.

Her community, now. Or was it? She lived here. Maybe that was all.

Try starting with an epigraph, she had suggested this morning. A line from a song or a poem, a sentence from a news story, something that stirs your own ideas. She had brought Ojibwe writer Louise Erdrich's poem about the captivity of Mary Rowlandson in 1676 as an example of where an epigraph could lead. *He* (my captor) *gave me a bisquit*, Rowlandson had written all those years ago, *which I put in my pocket, and not daring to eat it, buried it under a log, fearing he had put something in it to make me love him.*

"A love potion! Ayyy!" Sammy again. The others were silently reading ahead.

"Oh my God, he dragged her by her *hair*!" Cecelia's voice climbed mid-sentence. Makayla touched her friend's elbow, a tiny movement, almost imperceptible.

"It sounds terrible, doesn't it?" Annie said, keeping her voice calm. "But they're fording a stream, water so swift and cold she thinks she might be sliced in two. You've seen how fast a high-water current can take someone? Well, I hope not someone, but some *thing*?"

"So you mean he drags her 'from the flood' by the ends of her hair because—"

"Because he barely caught her." Cecil's voice, at last.

But Cecelia's head was down, her long hair a hanging curtain for privacy.

"What's this worry about recognizing his face, though? 'I could distinguish it from the others'? Well, yeah, I should hope so!" Makayla's instinct to use laughter as a poultice was failing her. "And then she says sometimes she even understood his language—*feared* she understood his language, which by the way was 'not human'? Was not *human*?"

The room tipped into silence the way a lake swallows a rock.

"It's a painful poem," Annie said quietly. "Sometimes to write honestly you have to be willing to take big risks."

But they deserved more. No matter how hard it was to say.

"Mary Rowlandson has been taught that Native people *are* less than human." Makayla was still looking at her. "You've probably seen that picture of Columbus planting his flag on the beach and claiming the New World for Spain? That was because the Pope had divided Africa and the Americas between Portugal and Spain—as if they were his to give. Any place that wasn't already Christian was considered empty land. Unoccupied. Just waiting to be 'discovered.' Actually the idea went all the way back to the Crusades. People who weren't Christians were considered the enemies of Christ, and it was the Church's duty to eliminate them. Or enslave them. Or convert them."

Mattie looked at Annie. "But—not *human*? How could anyone believe that?"

"I know. It seems impossible. How can one person look at another and see something other than a human being?" Annie braced herself against the edge of her chair. "And here's what's awful: we've done it too. We haven't attacked a sleeping village or forced Jews into a gas chamber—or enslaved people based on their skin color—but I'm pretty sure we've all seen someone as less human than we are. Migrant workers. Felons. Those men down on the levee."

"Suyapo." The derogatory word for whites. Someone snorted.

"That too. No one's completely innocent." Annie looked directly at Virgil. "I'm guessing everyone in this room knows what it feels like to be put down, seen as 'less than.' Though 'takes the fat' does have historical context, right?" She let herself smile. "Let's get to the love story. It's beautiful, isn't it? The way she describes the love scene without describing it at all? She tells herself that she will starve but she does not starve. 'He gave me to eat of the fawn.'

It's almost Biblical language, the kind she would associate with beauty. And it's an unborn fawn, 'so tender, / the bones like the stems of flowers / that I followed where he took me.'"

"Wooo! And no mistaking what comes next," one of the boys said. "Even if it is PG-13. 'The night was thick. He cut the cord / that bound me to the tree.'"

"There's no happy ending, though."

"Yeah. After she's 'rescued,' she says she 'sees no truth in things.'"

"What's all that stuff about her husband driving a thick wedge through the earth?"

"It's a plow, dork."

"Hey, *my* people are not agrarian."

Cecelia's head had come up at last. *Thank God*. Annie had been so focused on the love story that she hadn't foreseen all the dangers of sharing this poem. The last stanza might offer comfort, though. "The speaker says the earth 'shuts' to her husband, year after year," she said. "Why do you think she sees herself as she was when she was with her captor, 'outside their circle,' begging the earth to open, 'to admit me as he was'?"

"'And feed me honey from the rock.' Whoa!"

"She's hungry *now*, ennit?"

"So she's a Wannabe! See it here, folks, step right up to Annie's Amazing Summer School and meet the one, the only, the original Wannabe!"

"Be serious, you guys," Mattie said. "She's begging the earth to open—'to admit me as he was'—but he's not *buried*, he's not in the earth." She frowned. "So it's a metaphor, right? But is she speaking for herself or saying something about all white people? Europeans, I guess I should say." It was the sound of chairs being pushed back that made her look up.

Sammy put his hand on her shoulder. "Early language class today, remember?"

Mattie blushed. She had entered the poem so completely that she hadn't noticed what Annie knew the others had already seen, the tears she could feel rising, threatening to spill. She had led these students safely past the snares of their own pain only to fall into the waiting pit of grief.

How long will a man lie i' th' earth ere he rot? While she was still in the hospital, Annie had heard the voice in the midst of group therapy, or as she walked down the hall to the dining room. It's a memory, she told herself. It's only an echo of a voice. Once, in the tiny apartment, she almost caught the shadow of a face in the white glare of her journal. Derek Jacobi, wasn't it, the actor she had first seen playing Hamlet? The BBC production. She had watched it on her mother's black and white TV. Sometimes at night the vision jerked her up from a shallow sleep, the dream-Hamlet still mottling the dark ceiling above her, asking and asking his terrible question.

"Some things are unbearable, Annie." Against all the rules one morning as the Aftercare group was breaking up Dennis had reached across the table and taken both of her hands in his. "Somehow we bear them," he said. "We bear them."

"Where *is* he?" she had demanded. How could she find it, this place of acceptance Dennis wanted for her, without knowing? And if this was to be her place, this place of acceptance, where was Jack's? How could he be in the earth if his body had never been buried? Yet he was not on the earth either, the searchers had found nothing, not even a shredded piece of shirt or fibers from his jeans, his cotton socks.

"Annie, do you believe he left you? That he walked away from you and Riley and he's alive, somewhere?"

"No, I told the insurance people, Jack would never—"

"You *know* he didn't. That's something you do know. In all this mystery, that's something to hang on to." Dennis's knuckles were wider than Jack's. There was hair on the backs of his fingers. "It would be easier to bear, I know, if there were some trace. Something you could see, or touch."

"There has to be, doesn't there? Somewhere? People don't dissolve into thin air!"

Dennis had kept gripping her hands. "No. They don't. But the searchers don't always find anything. We don't always have a skull to hold, Annie. People fall into ravines, their bodies can be hidden under brush or buried by rockslides. I'm going to be blunt here, because it's important. Human bodies can be scavenged by animals. Bones get scattered, even worn away by rodents. Clothing rots, or it's simply never found. You've read about those children lost when they're out cutting a Christmas tree with their families, or working cattle, or hunting. Hikers vanishing without a trace. It happens every summer in Yosemite. Montana. Idaho. People get lost and are never found." He let go of her hands. "You don't know what happened. What you do know is what didn't happen. He didn't leave you."

She nodded.

"In fact, he was trying to bring his family back together."

"Yes."

"That's what you have, Annie. It's all you may ever have. But it's a lot."

"He thought the earth was alive," she had said at last. "Not just in some symbolic way. Really alive. He told me he wanted to belong to the earth in a way that was different from his father's."

"And did he?"

"I don't know. I thought so. All those summers, from the time Riley was a toddler, Jack was showing him grasses and rocks, feathers. He took us all backpacking. In the Blues, in the Eagle Cap Wilderness. Everywhere we went he taught Riley and Alex how to *see* the earth, how to see the drainages and ridges and the relationship to the sun and stars and the animals, and food and water. How to be at home wherever he was. Jack loved it all, the mountains, rivers, storms, but—but Dennis, all those days I sat there waiting the way they told me to and sure enough, Riley *did* find his way out, he was hungry and tired but he was safe, when the police called they said he's safe, your boy's okay, but Jack—"

"That's the part we don't know, Annie." Dennis sat back in his chair and then leaned forward again. "What happened, or why. The things we *have* to know. We *think* we have to know."

Annie had just looked at him.

"It's unbearable, Annie. But you bear it. I don't understand it, either. How do we do it? But we do. You do. You are, and you will."

"That thing Jack said about the earth," Dennis had said at last. "Hang on to that."

But how? What was there to hold on to? An idea, Jack's idea, yes, but *not* Jack, not his voice or his eyes or his shoulders, his chest. No body to hold in her arms but her own, this brittle rib cage beneath her own crossed arms, no real respite from this grief that felt like a boulder pressing on her chest, crushing her lungs. Annie leaned forward, her head touching the table in her empty classroom. How would she ever draw another breath?

And should she, even if she could? Somehow it was wrong, it was all wrong, all this going on, this we becoming I.

Riley. Riley, and Alex. She had to. For them. For Leona, even, and Mattie, for these kids. Her students.

Would it matter, really? Having a body? Some trace of him, some explanation? "There must be a way of finding out what really happened," Jack had said. He was a searcher. A historian. He would have kept looking.

But nothing anyone found could change what she already knew.

So was this the place of acceptance Dennis had wanted for her? The jagged edges of grief would never erode. Jack was gone. He was dead. And the weight of that truth could crash down from the clearest of skies, splitting her heart, her belly, as if for the first time. How could it be otherwise? Maybe this was all she could hope for.

8

They were coming down the trail single file, first Leona, then Mattie, then the dog. Like women serving at a First Foods feast, Annie thought, watching them come. That line of women circling the longhouse. These two were carrying something, too, their forearms held out ahead of them the same way the longhouse women bore the plates holding roots and then the bowls of huckleberries and chokecherries. Leona had reached the switchback. A small woman, the girl who followed small too, like a thin-trunked aspen moving in a constant dance of leafy grace, even in still air. Matilda. Then the dog, a half-grown pup. Black and brown and white, with the ears and tail of a border collie but a body strangely spotted, a coat more like a horse's than a dog's. An Appaloosa, or even a pinto. Or a paint: the puppy's eyes were light. Whatever she was, she seemed to know where she was going.

Which was straight to Annie. Leona and Mattie were still ducking between the low branches of the apple tree on the slope behind the house as Annie knelt to receive her.

By the time they set their packages on the porch, Annie was sitting cross-legged and the puppy had curled into her lap, alert and calm.

"Has the coyote been back?" Leona was already smiling.

"No, I guess he hasn't. But of course Riley and Alex have been making so much noise."

"She knows you."

Mattie knelt beside Annie, reaching to touch the dog's ear. "I hope it's okay. She's for you."

For a moment Annie felt light, as if she weighed nothing. Only this gentle weight in her lap held her on the earth. For Riley, a small buckskin bag; for her, warmth, and these gray eyes watching with her, looking up from the center of her body.

"Are the boys here?" Leona was shading her eyes, looking in the direction of the barn.

It took Annie a moment to answer. "They took the wheelbarrow down to get some of that manure from the old pile below the barn."

"It's good to have a garden." Leona was still looking. Listening.

"Mattie," Annie began, but couldn't finish. Finally she tilted her head toward the barn. "Riley will be happy to see you."

They watched her walking down the trail until she disappeared behind the big cottonwood. The puppy's eyes closed. She sighed. Leona sat down beside Annie, legs out, and leaned back on her hands. "She's a healer, our Mattie."

"I wondered. That buckskin—"

"Yes, that was to help Riley." Leona sat up again. "And it seems to be working." Alex was coming up the trail from the barn. He threw open his arms; then his head tipped back and he whooped. "I'm not sure she can heal herself, though." Leona's words were quiet.

Then Alex was here, reaching for Leona's hand, holding on.

"Sit down, Alex. You got too tall!" Leona squinted up at him. "But first, bring that picnic lunch over here. We'll get started on it before Riley and Mattie come back. You need some filling out, boy."

Alex turned away, still grinning. But he stopped midway to the porch to do an exaggerated fancy dance, dust rising in small puffs from beneath his sneakers.

"What was in that medicine bag?" Annie kept her voice low. "Can you tell me?"

"I will tell you, Annie, yes. When there's time to explain."

"And Mattie?"

"Yes, we'll talk about that too."

Annie looked down at the sleeping puppy. "Does she have a name?"

"You'll find her name. She's yours." Leona stood up now to take the box from Alex. "There's no blanket, but I don't guess we need one if we're already sitting on the ground." Alex was peeking into the box, sniffing. "Yes, little porcupine, there's jerky. Mattie smoked some salmon, too."

"Fry bread!"

"And fry bread. You sound like you haven't had fry bread in a while."

"Too long, Auntie. Way too long." Alex looked directly at Leona, then looked down. But he raised his eyes again, this time to Annie. "Annie, I—I didn't mean to—"

"Save some for Riley, now. And Mattie!" But Leona was already helping herself.

Alex looked away. "Oh, they can live on love," Annie heard him say, but his voice had caught with the effort of speech. Then she watched as he realized his joke had been a slip. Did Annie know?

"Love and *brownies*, maybe." She touched his shoulder, a mock punch.

There. Yes. He was grinning again. Blessings, Annie thought. On this food, on—Leona had even brought lemonade. The puppy was awake now, her ears pricked.

"I loved that coyote, though."

The voice—her voice! had startled her. She hadn't known she was going to speak, much less out loud.

"Yes." Leona chewed. "Who made this jerky? Must be from some old bull."

Alex looked up at the sky and laughed. Is he really back? Annie wondered. He had changed, of course—Riley had changed too—but just now he seemed to be Alex again. Cross-legged on the earth, he licked his fingers like the boy she had always known.

But where was Riley? Oh, yes. He was with Mattie. Somehow he seemed to be here and behind the barn at the same time. She lay back and closed her eyes, the strange-looking pup curled tight against her ribs.

⌐⊙

"It's compost." Riley had planted his shovel in the loosened pile, leaving it standing upright. "Really, by now it's just compost."

"Yeah?" Alex picked up the handles of the wheelbarrow and started up the one-wheeled track that snaked toward the garden. The wheelbarrow wobbled again and he flexed his knee to right it. "Well, I call it horse manure. Whatever it is, you've got some on your forehead."

"Horseshit!"

Would he laugh? Things were so much better between them, so much more natural. Riley could almost let himself believe Alex was okay now.

But Alex had set the wheelbarrow down, his back still toward Riley. "Watch your language," he said softly.

What?

"Don't want her to think you're uncouth, do you?"

Her? Yes, at last: it was Mattie, the top of her head visible beyond Alex's shoulder, black hair reflecting the sunlight. Riley felt his heart leap. He pulled off his gloves and stood rooted in the barnyard, his jeans streaked with whatever this was, call it compost or horse manure, a rich smell, he had been thinking only a moment ago, the smell of the earth full of promise.

She had come.

Alex stopped beside her for only a moment before he turned and waved. Was it a signal, a sign of some kind? Then he continued up the worn path to the house.

"She's the first girl you've had feelings for," the counselors had warned him. "That's all she is. And she has family problems, you said? Don't count on her, Riley. By next summer she may well be long gone."

"What's it to you?" he had asked. "Why's it so bad to love somebody?"

"Relapse. *Relapse.* Do I have to spell it for you?" Allison. Lovely, unloved Allison.

Mattie was holding out her hands. Riley twined his fingers into hers. She looked down, and when she raised her eyes again she was blinking away tears. Yes. He had known without knowing. "Oh, Mattie. I'm so sorry." He pulled her close, one hand on the back of her head. "It'll be okay," he heard himself saying.

"Maybe now it will," she said after a while.

Riley felt the light touch of her breath on his arm. Her hair smelled like sunlight. And something else. Lavender? She must be—oh, Lord. He released her and took a half step backward. "Sorry. I forgot how I must smell."

Mattie reached for his hand again. "You smell okay to me."

He stood there, looking at her. He had waited for this moment for so long. Dreamed it. Say something, he told himself. But what? Things had happened to everyone else while they were keeping him on hold in McLaughlin. Ever since he'd come home he'd felt as if he was trying to get into a car that was already moving.

But Mattie was the one; nothing would ever change that. Dad said it had been that way for him, too. *From the first time I saw her. Your mom.* He'd been older, of course. He must have dated other girls by then, maybe even had sex with—

Riley's mind skittered away from that thought.

Now she was leading him away from the manure pile and into the cool shade of the cottonwoods, pulling him down to sit beside her on the fallen white branch. There was just enough room. "You first," she said. "Tell me everything."

It was the dog's movement that woke her. Alex and Leona were sitting on the edge of the porch, Leona swinging her feet, both of them looking toward the barn. Annie sat up. Mattie and Riley were coming up the trail together, Riley walking in ankle-high grass beside the narrow track. They were holding hands. It wasn't until they were closer that she could see their faces glowing with the strange, anguished radiance she recognized as love. *Look, Jack!* Was their boy that old, already? And they had both been crying.

9

The smell of open earth rose up around her. Annie wrestled the rototiller into yet another turn. The manure-pile compost had all been tilled under and the soil felt soft beneath her soles, but she didn't stop. Behind her, sweet dirt, powder fine, slumped to fill the indentations of her footsteps. Finally she steered the tiller toward the garden gate and pushed down on the hand grips, letting the bare tines bump forward onto the grass outside before she shut the motor off.

Now the rake. Raking was as much about rhythm—pull, then skim the surface with a push, then pull again—as it was about smoothing the surface of the ground. "Zen gardening again?" Jack had teased her once. "I know, I know," she had shot back. "You'd come in here and show me how it's done, but someone might drive by and see a rancher doing farm work."

Outside the fence the pup stood up from her blanket, shook herself, then turned in a tight spiral and lay down again, nose resting on her paws. Annie marked off mounds for squash and cucumbers and a circle for pole beans, then spaced the old gray-weathered stakes at measured intervals. Tiller-width rows for peppers and tomatoes, onions, potatoes. And corn, Riley had said. Let's plant some corn. She stretched the thick white cotton string between the stakes. The garden looked so—what, innocent?—at this stage. Pure: that was a better word. Like a sleeping child, full of promise. The sun felt warm on her shoulders. It was late to be planting. But the main thing was to do it. Plant, and harvest whatever she could. Her hands smoothed dirt over a shallow furrow where she had scattered carrot seeds.

She was on her knees spacing the dry peas two inches apart when she heard a car slowing to turn into the driveway. A big car, cream-colored, maybe even white beneath that layer of road dust. It wasn't anyone she knew. The pup's head came up.

"Might want to think about a locking gate," the telephone company man had said. "You're pretty far out, here."

Was it Jim Casey? The rancher had blocked her cart with his in the Safeway produce aisle last week. "It's gonna take a hell of a long time to pay off that bull if you keep sending me those piddlin' checks that won't even cover a sack of chicken feed."

But it was Roy's old friend Angus who was getting out of the car, and Audrey, too, leaning on a cane. "H'lo there!" Gus called. "Got the coffee on?" The puppy ran to meet them, wagging a welcome that began in her midsection.

"And who's this little lass?"

"She doesn't have a name yet." Annie brushed dirt from the front of her jeans and paused for a moment, one hand on the top brace of the garden gate. She had been dreading this meeting. Gus and Audrey without Jack? But when Gus wrapped her in a bear hug and she felt Audrey's free hand on her shoulder, tears came to her eyes. "It's good to see you."

"We wanted to give you a while to get settled. But this morning, when Audrey pulled these cinnamon rolls out of the oven—"

"I should have called," Annie said. "I've been meaning to thank you for draining the pipes, winterizing everything." All the chores Jack had always done at the end of every summer. "I just—left, I was . . ." She hadn't even thought to worry about these things until Audrey's Christmas card found its way to her apartment.

"No need for that, now, girl. We've always come by to check on the place."

"Make sure nobody's moved in uninvited, you know? We're real picky about our neighbors." Audrey was still wiping the corners of her eyes, but she was trying to smile. "Bet you didn't know us, without the truck. Got so climbing into it was hard for me, so Gus traded it in last fall."

"Where's that boy of yours?" Gus asked.

"He and Alex went to town. They're supposed to be looking for tomato plants."

"Alex."

"Ruby's boy," Audrey told him. "You remember, he was here a lot in the summers."

Gus reached down to pet the puppy's ears. "I saw him a time or two last winter. Looked like he wasn't doin' too well."

"He's better now, though," Annie said. "Getting better, anyway. Riley's been helping him."

Gus looked at Audrey.

"And they've both been helping *me*. I lost track of how many wheelbarrow loads they brought up from the manure pile. They did the first tilling, too."

"Somebody's split some firewood, that's for sure." Audrey motioned toward the car. "Bring those cinnamon rolls up to the house while they're still warm, will you? Annie and I'll go on in and get some coffee going."

"Now you're talking."

"He's got nothing against Alex," Audrey said when Gus was out of earshot. "He just wants things to work out for you."

"I know," Annie said. She had always had a soft spot for Gus. Even after he sold his own herd and was no longer using their old hayfield for pasture, he had found excuses to come by. A dozen fresh eggs, an extra box of staples if they were out tightening the fence wires. Once it was an ice-cold watermelon, which he'd deliberately let bounce around in his pickup bed until it broke in pieces that had to be eaten "right now, folks. 'Fore it goes to waste." They had stood in a half-circle around his dusty truck, all of them dripping watermelon juice.

They had finished the rolls and were on their second cup of coffee when Annie said, "Alex has been like a brother to Riley. Part of the family. What happened hit him as hard as any of us."

"I know." Gus cradled his coffee cup in both hands. One of his nails was blackened. Weathered hands, tender and rough at the same time. Like Roy's hands, Annie thought. When Gus looked up, his eyes were glistening. "Fact is, there's a whole lot of people grievin' with you."

"And wanting to help," Audrey said. "Wishing they could."

"This helps. Your being here." Annie motioned toward the cinnamon rolls they had saved for the boys. "And these. Jack always said your cookie jar was what turned him into such a sweet guy."

"Jack." Gus lifted his cup and put it down again. "Listen, I didn't mean—"

He looked at Audrey, who had pulled out the Kleenex she kept tucked inside her sweater cuff and was using it to wipe the corners of her eyes. "I'd be doing the same thing," he said. "For the boy, I mean. Alex."

"He helped a friend once too," Audrey said. Gus was looking down into his coffee cup. "Yes, you did too. You did everything you could."

10

Mattie was leading the way up the trail, Riley following her so closely Annie wondered how he kept from stepping on her heels. She and Leona lagged behind. Alex wasn't with them this morning; he had pulled Riley's old bicycle out of the barn and ridden off, his knees sticking out as he pedaled, to visit James and Ruby.

The puppy leaped at a swallowtail butterfly. Already she had darted off the trail after a chipmunk, lolloping back only to stop abruptly and roll on her back in a patch of damp seep grass, wriggling and stretching her legs. But now as the trail steepened she settled into Annie's shadow, quiet and alert. "You'll find her name," Leona had said. But nothing she could think of seemed to fit. Phoebe? Fiona? Most of the dogs she had met on her morning walks in Portland had been called Maggie or Max. Molly, sometimes, or Lily. Or something gently mocking: Barkley, Mr. Churchill. One man had called his round, brown bulldog Bronx.

She had been up this path so many times she couldn't count them, wandering off on the narrower game trails too, even belly-crawling under ninebark brush sometimes, or sliding down a scree of crumbled rock on the seat of her pants. How could she have missed a clear trail to Leona's place? "Come on, then. We'll show you," Leona had said.

It was only when they reached the rose thicket that she understood. Wild roses, Woods Rose the natural history books called them, had spread so thickly where the land began to slope upward from the basalt cliff that this part of the trail, already fading in all this rock, simply disappeared. But Riley and Mattie had somehow vanished into the tangled mass. Now Leona slipped into the only crevice Annie could see and held the thorned brush open like a tight-sprung door to make room for Annie. Turn sideways to step left, another step, one more, and then the light opened. Someone had cut a straight path through the maze. Beyond the thicket Annie could see the trail, clearly visible all the way to the place where it edged around a turret of basalt. Beyond it, the bare slopes of the next canyon wall. In a minute they would be looking down at the drainage of Iskuulpa Creek.

But where was the dog? She had been right here, her nose touching Annie's calf every few steps. Leona laughed and led the way back through the brushy passageway. She'll be digging into an abandoned badger den, Annie told herself, or cocking her head to watch a beetle crawl. Please God, not lost. Disappeared. But there she was, curled on a sun-warmed flat rock at the very edge of the rose thicket, her strangely mottled coat a perfect camouflage. Annie dropped to her knees and pressed her cheek against soft fur, breathing in the puppy smell. When the dog wriggled away, tail wagging, Annie saw what she had been lying on: block letters scraped and gouged into the rock.

Behind her, Leona said something Annie couldn't hear.

"Mom?" Riley too had followed her back through the narrow passage.

Annie reached up with one hand to pull him down beside her. "Oh, son, there's so much we don't know. Mary died when your dad was small; only six, he never—"

"Dad's mother?"

"It must be her. He thought her body had been cremated. That's what Roy wanted for himself. Your granddad."

"So Dad never showed you this place? He never brought you here?"

"He didn't know. I'm sure he didn't know. Your granddad was—"

"A monster, it sounds like." Riley pressed his palms against the warm, flat rock. "His own wife? His son's—his little boy's mother?"

"No." Leona seemed suddenly tall. They both looked up, blinking against the high June sun. "He wasn't a monster. You mustn't think that. He was just hurting. Roy was badly hurt."

Annie was tracing the letters with her fingertips the way a blind person might feel another's face. "Somehow I almost felt as if I knew her. Because Jack and his father were so different, I suppose. I wished we could have been friends."

Mattie was emerging from the narrow gap. "Have you've found her name yet, Annie?"

Rose. Mary was buried next to the wild roses. The dog's name was Rose.

"Lady Rose?" Riley's hand was trembling, almost imperceptibly. The puppy's ears pricked, but of course she wouldn't come to any name but her own.

⌁

Leona's table was a long one flanked by benches so old they had turned silver. There was a wood cookstove and a woodbox overflowing on one end with newspapers. From outside came the sound of children's voices.

"Good one, Lance!"

"No fair, you had a head start!"

Leona was already making coffee on a hotplate. She pointed an elbow toward the woodbox. "Old news." Beyond the beaded curtain a man with thin white braids lay sleeping on an overstuffed red couch. Leona's father? The man was snoring so lightly that at first Annie had thought she heard a cat purring.

"Your dad was so amazing." Mattie was rummaging through cupboards for something to offer them with coffee. "He's why I—" She stopped, her face flushing.

Annie smiled. "It's good to talk about him, Mattie."

"Yeah, it helps," Riley said. "Especially this way."

Mattie ducked her head into the cupboard. "Pringles. If you can believe it. Not even real potato chips!"

"Oh, you know your uncle. Spike's terrible that way." Leona sat down sideways on the bench, glancing back at the percolator as she spoke. "Jack came to Mattie's class once, in Vancouver."

Mattie set the bowl on the table and sat down next to Riley, who immediately pushed a Pringle into his mouth and grinned at her. "No' as ba' as you might think," he said around the chip. "Kind of like me."

Mattie shook her head, *such a boy*. But her moment of embarrassment had passed.

"He told us about Centralia. Most of the kids had driven by it on the freeway, but none of us knew it had been founded by an African American man. Or about the Armistice Day Massacre that happened there in 1919, a gun fight between the International Workers of the World and the American Legion. One of the Wobblies was hauled from the jail afterward and lynched."

Leona nodded toward the hot plate and Mattie rose. She set the mugs in front of them. Spoons for sugar. "Sorry, Grandma, there's no milk."

"Those kids." Leona laughed. "There's not enough milk in the world for that bunch."

"He said history's about people. Their stories. And Grandma, you always say stories are how we know things. So I started reading, everything I could find, his books—"

"Dad's books? You've read his books?" Riley hadn't read his father's books yet, as far as Annie knew.

"Yes, both of them. It was pretty exciting."

"But he wrote about the Whitmans, didn't he? And Yellow Hawk? The Marias massacre? I guess exciting isn't how I thought of it. I don't know how he stayed so cheerful, thinking about that stuff all the time."

The kitchen door opened just wide enough to reveal a small face, but Leona shook her head once and the child backed away, pulled the door shut quietly.

"And people were constantly wanting to argue with him. Mascots, the Redskins, whatever. The worst was Dr. Jamison—remember, Mom? 'They were primitives, Fallon. Still living in the Stone Age. What we were supposed to do, starve while we waited for them to evolve?' I used to wish just once Dad would lose it, punch him in the mouth. Shut him up."

Annie wanted to reach across the table and hold him so tightly that none of it would have happened. None of it. They'd all be together at the river, Jack would be flicking water at his son's face, grinning. No wonder Riley's voice was shaking. If no one had insulted this girl, his father would still be alive. Sitting at this table with them.

"I know," Mattie said. "It's hard. But he said something that day that really helped me. He was talking about how history is about time, and how most people think of time as a straight line, beginning, middle, end, but some cultures see it as a circle. And then he pulled a beach ball out of his backpack blew it up. He stood there holding it—this dorky-looking pink and orange beach ball. 'What if it's a sphere?' he said. 'What would that mean?'"

The kitchen was quiet. There's no clock, Annie thought. Nothing ticking. Riley was staring at Mattie.

"If it's a sphere—" he paused, feeling his way.

"Then everything is always touching everything else. Like the air in a beach ball, or the water in a glass. Or a lake. The ocean, even."

"So everything that's happened—"

"And what's happening now, it's all connected. It *can't* be separated. And if that's the way time is, then there's a good reason to learn about the Whitmans. All those massacres, those hurtful things you were talking about. If we don't—I know we can't change them, we can't change what happened, but we can heal, at least. If we realize that *not* acknowledging the past is making us sick *now*."

"But acknowledging it?"

"Well, you're right, it can be painful. Like that poem you showed us, Annie."

"You were real brave, Mattie said." Leona squeezed Annie's hand.

Annie looked at Riley. "Brave," she said. "I'm not sure that's the word for me."

"But there has to be forgiveness. Doesn't there? I mean, if *everything's* connected to the stuff that's happened in our own lives—"

She stopped, suddenly embarrassed.

Riley broke a chip and offered her half. "Go ahead. I'll forgive you if you like it."

"You!" But she was smiling.

When the two young people wandered outside, hand in hand, Rose stood up from the blanket by the woodstove and stretched, arching her back to lift her hindquarters. She's going to follow them, Annie thought. Make sure they're okay. But the dog was coming to her. She laid her head in Annie's lap. In the other room, the old man purred steadily.

Leona picked up a Pringle and took a small bite. "The trouble with junk food is that you eat it anyway."

"Maybe they put something in the biscuits to make us love them."

Leona laughed. "I liked that poem too."

The kitchen was quiet. Annie lifted her chin, listening. Where had the children gone?

"Spike took the kids down to the river," Leona said. She leaned forward, resting on her forearms. She was wearing the faded chambray shirt. "It was a bear claw," she said. "In the medicine bag. Just a small one, but bears—every animal has a certain power. But a bear's power is special. Bears—they disappear, you know. Dig themselves a grave, you could say. They know how to turn their bodies off to survive hard times. They don't eat, nothing passes through. They hardly breathe. Their hearts stop. All but stop. Their bodies get real cold. But then, when it's time, they come back. They climb up out of that dark hole, and somehow they've multiplied. Little ones follow them out of that den. A bear's power is real strong, and it's a healing power. But not everyone—well, bears, you know, there's danger there. Most people shouldn't touch it." Leona glanced toward the beaded curtain. "But Mattie wanted to help Riley. She loves him, you know. And Alex—nobody had been able to reach Alex. He had a real hard time with it, everything that happened."

"Is Riley strong enough?"

"To touch the bag, you mean? Oh yes. She knew he was. He's a healer too, in his own way. But she wanted to help him with Alex. And other things."

"She gave me Rose." It was a question.

"Mattie thinks we need to know everything." Leona sipped her coffee, though surely it was cold. "I hope she's right. But I trust her. She's smarter than I am." Leona looked into her mug again. "There was a baby."

"What?" Annie's head was full to overflowing.

"But she lost it. While Riley was away."

Annie felt as if she were slipping sideways, her foothold on the earth somewhere far below. A baby? Her baby? When did he—but he was barely past puberty.

"She hadn't been with us long, our Mattie. She'd had such a hard time in Vancouver. Her dad was real bad then. Poor kid was weaned to Ramen noodles. Dry ones. There was no one to—'course, she learned to cook as soon as she could read. Three or four. She had to stand on a chair. For a while he had a woman, but that didn't last."

Annie shivered. "Your son?"

Leona nodded, once. "One of the lost ones. So when Mattie and Riley—they met at the river, I think, and they hadn't known each other very long, but Riley had already helped her so much, just being Riley, you know. He was the only one she told."

Annie felt as if she had tumbled backward, somersaulting into Mattie's lake of time. Late-summer days before the accident, evenings filling with the sound of crickets, laughter, Jack and Riley, Riley's friends. "So it wasn't—"

"No, no. It wasn't Riley's baby. The father wasn't anyone she wanted to remember. She could hardly think about it, even. It was someone who came home with her dad. He had a knife." Leona's voice had faded to a whisper. Then she smiled, remembering. "All Riley knew was that she was pregnant. The baby was a gift, he told her. Every baby was a gift. He wanted to help. He had a pretty good mom and dad, that Riley. I think you two made raising a child look easy."

"I didn't know, he hadn't even told us about—" She couldn't finish. Leona stood up and came around to sit beside Annie, her back to the table.

"They were too young. That's all." She looked sideways at Annie. "Don't worry. It'll be okay."

11

It was Alex who guessed Jack's password. Annie had been standing with her back against the door frame, listening. Rose had curled into puppy sleep on top of the old quilt. The room was warm. Late July, already. She closed her eyes and opened them again. Their two dark heads were still leaning together above the keyboard. They really could be brothers. Twins. Umatilla twins were considered an evil omen and usually left to die, according to the caption on the old Moorhouse photograph. It was a rare photo, then: the two round-cheeked babies laced into cradleboards propped side by side, looking suspiciously, Annie had always thought, toward the camera. Of course none of it was true. Even the Whitmans had recorded a set of twins. But it helped make the photo famous, and Moorhouse had sold 150,000 copies. "The Vanishing American," Jack had said. "Even before TV, we knew how to make a buck. *'Tis but the story of the race / Vanquished by too great odds. / Its members now sleep soundly / In the shadow land of God.'*" He had come down from the bedroom that afternoon looking drained by his day's work.

"Local history is personal history," he told her one evening not long after that. "People don't always want to know." They were sitting on the porch steps, watching the bats flicker like shadows above the river as stars burned their way back into a summer-lightened sky. She had been leaning against his shoulder, feeling the vibrations of his voice.

"Usually it's something simple." Alex frowned. "And he only had the computer set to password because he was doing research. He knew we wouldn't try to hack in. The password was just to keep us from accidentally losing his work if we forgot his computer was off-limits and started screwing around, playing video games. So why not make it something easy to remember?" Alex was thinking out loud, a soft spider-thread of sound. "But it's not your name, or your mom's, or mine—or his pet, lots of times it's a pet, but we've tried Lady. Of course there could be numbers or signs, but this file wasn't connected to his school's system, so I'm thinking—"

"It could be dates, though." Riley's lips whispered, counting back. "Let's try his birth year. Oh, I know, my birthday. No. I wonder—maybe the year he met you, Mom. 1983?" He had turned to look over his shoulder. Such a sweet thought.

"Eighty-four."

But that wasn't it, either. Alex pushed his chair back and stood up, stretching. Then he sat down on the bed. "We've tried Mary, and his dad, we've tried Roy. And John, that was his grandfather's name." He lay back, one arm around the sleeping dog. Then he stood up on the bed, steadying himself against the ceiling's sloping side as he tipped his head to read. "Try 'Boundaries.'"

"Nope."

"Lowercase?"

"No. Why 'boundaries'?"

"It's printed on this map. Looks like a kid's writing. 'The boundaries can change.'"

"Boundaries," Riley said. "It does feel right, doesn't it? Maybe we *should* add numbers."

"Eighteen eighty-five." Annie was surprised by her sudden confidence. "That was the year of the Slater Act. He said he was researching the changes on the reservation after the first allotment act."

"That's it! That's it!" They leaned closer to the screen. "And here's his most recent file: 'shadow land.' He named the file 'shadow land.' I wonder why?" Riley turned again. "You should be the first to see it, Mom."

Annie felt the grain of the old doorframe against her palms. Had she been holding herself up all this time, or was it only now that her legs couldn't support her? Could she really sit here at Jack's desk, her fingers touching his keyboard, to read what he had left behind?

"Print it out?"

"Good idea."

"Let's back it up first." Alex's long, slender fingers touched the keys. Alex, whose hands had understood how to bring even that old tiller motor back to life. Annie let go of the doorframe and walked toward the desk, bending to wrap both boys in an embrace.

"Riley," she said. "Alex. Thank you. Thank you."

"This calls for some *serious* chocolate, Mom," Riley said in his best mock-threat voice. Sheets of paper were coming off the printer now and settling into the tray like offerings. Page after page, all that remained of Jack. But bodiless. Bloodless. Almost as weightless as words.

Alex had turned away. "It's not much, Mo—Annie." When he spoke again his voice was hoarse. "It's the least I could do."

Riley caught her eye and shook his head. Not now.

Guilt? Profound regret? Whatever she chose to call it, it stretched over all of them like the bluff's afternoon shadow. Even Leona had said she had something to tell her, soon. Yet as far as Annie could see, no one had done anything so terribly wrong. Unless existence was wrong. Just being human. Being here.

Or maybe it had to do with their being *here*. Was that it? Where do we belong, then, Jack? Annie wanted to ask. Where do we belong now, Riley and I?

The printer had stopped. Riley picked up the stack and squared the pages on the desk before he set them, top side up, on her outstretched arms. They were still warm. She pulled the stack against her chest.

There had been no secrets between them. But last summer was the first time Jack had not come downstairs eager not only to rejoin her and the boys for supper and a swim, but also to share some small bit of his research. Something that had excited him, or made him laugh. Something that would give people like Mattie hope.

"Grandma told me a story," Mattie's poem had begun. Yesterday—no, Thursday. The last day of summer classes. Annie's students had been reading their work aloud for several weeks; quietly at first, paired knee-to-knee, and then in small groups, leaning in to listen to each other. Finally, though there had been no conscious decision as far as she knew, they had simply begun to read to everyone circled around the tables.

She said I might not understand.
Just think about it, Grandma said. Keep it
in your heart, this story.
Someday you might need a story
like this one.

The words had seemed to float like wisps of clouds, bathing Annie's cheek with sound that almost wasn't sound. "Listening is a skill," her own teachers had said, offering lesson plans to help her pass this skill along to others. But listening, she saw, was more like breathing.

It was about a boy who tried to please
his father. With his small bow
he followed the small birds. Rabbits.
Food for his mother's pot. "Oh, I killed
far more than you
when I was a boy," his father said
though the boy was good, he was a good boy.
And he became a good young man.
A hunter. Every day
he brought meat for his family
and for the old or injured.
Deer, and elk. Fish. Salmon.

But nothing he brought home
was enough
to please his father.

Sammy had closed his eyes. Virgil stared across the room, his eyes unfocused.

In a bad mind then, the young man shot and killed
a herd of elk. Another herd. Another. All five herds.
His weyekin, his spirit—it was an elk spirit—
led him down beneath the water
where the bodies lay. "See

what you have done to my people?
Now I will leave you."

The young man went home—
his father was laughing, talking—
and lay down on his elk skin.
"You wanted too much," he said.
"My spirit has left me, and I die."

The father was alive with grief
my grandma said.

I cried when I heard this story.
My grandma cried a little too.
It's a hard story to understand.
Sometimes I wonder
if I really want to.

"Ahhhh." The sound had come from everyone at once. But no one spoke. "Greed," said Cecil, finally. "It's about greed." Again, then, silence. "I wonder about greed, though." Cecil's forehead wrinkled. "I mean, everyone knows where it leads."

"He who dies with the most toys wins," said Dawn. "My dad said he saw that on a bumper sticker once."

They shifted now, smiling. "You win, then, Sam—your car's a toy, for sure."

"Hey, it's a Big Wheel. What more do you want?"

Cecelia, though, had something more to say. "Mattie's poem's about greed, but it's about fathers too. Isn't it?"

"And Mattie, that last line, what did you mean? Aren't we supposed to try to understand the stories?"

Mattie glanced at Annie, then looked away. *Mattie thinks we need to know everything.*

"Sometimes, to understand, we have to know things we wish we didn't know." This time Annie's voice had not betrayed her.

Leann nodded. Yes. Okay.

"Have fun with the rest of your summer," Annie had told them when class was over. "And please, you guys, be careful."

"Okay, Mom." There it was, that grin. But he was the first in line to touch her hand on his way out the door. Sammy, the irrepressible.

⌐⌐

When she opened her eyes again, the boys were gone. Rose lifted her nose and Annie sat down beside her on the bed with Jack's manuscript in her lap.

The first pages were notes from his research. The Slater Act, the Dawes Act. The Burke Act of 1906—that was the one that did it, Jack had told her. The allotments were in trust to the United States for the first twenty-five years to keep them from being sold for back taxes, but now, if the owner was declared "competent and capable," his land became what they called "forced fee-patent" acreage. Taxable. Whether he knew about this change or not.

Competent and capable. The same words she had repeated like a mantra on that long drive to the McLaughlin Center.

Heirship Acts, 1902–1916. July, 1902: Surplus Treaty Boundary Lands. Skimming, Annie lifted the pages one at a time. None of this material had been new to Jack. He was still in high school when he discovered that the ranch he had grown up on had been a forced fee patented allotment, his grandfather's low bid at the tax sale only possible because it wasn't farmable land. Whatever it was that had made him so quiet, Annie thought, must have been something more. Some part of this story he hadn't known.

Or maybe it was simply the cumulative effect of all this history, so close to home. On the next page she found the story of the land rush when the reservation was opened to non-Indian settlement. April 1 to April 30, 1891, speculators arriving by train from Portland; one of them, an E. J. Horton, had paid someone to bid for him while he diverted other potential bidders by staging a mock gunfight.

And on the next page, a single sentence. "By 1914 salmon were extinct in the Umatilla River."

"Mom?"

At the bottom of the stairs Riley stood waiting with a glass of iced tea. "We figured you'd be ready for a break. Alex is about to get into the sandwiches big time, so if you're hungry—"

On the table downstairs was a plate piled with sandwich halves, cracked wheat bread and rye. Lemon slices on a white saucer. Mary's sugar bowl.

"You guys," Annie said.

Alex pulled out her chair and stood waiting, oddly formal. When they had all sat down, one on each side of her, the boys reached for her hands and then across the table to take each other's, closing their eyes. This had been Jack's habit, his way of silently thanking the plants and animals whose lives were feeding theirs. It was important to remember them, he said. And of course to thank the people at the table for being there.

"Besides, it gives me a good excuse to hold your hand," he had said on their first date.

"Thank you," Annie said. "Thank you both." Riley's hand, rough from splitting wood, was only a little smaller than his father's; Alex's hand felt narrow, his fingers longer.

Why had she let this go?

Alex reached for the sugar bowl and began spooning sugar into his tall glass. Riley offered her the plate of sandwiches. "Gourmet peanut butter. Chunky. Or tuna, with pickles. *And* sprouts."

"This is lovely." Annie lifted a sandwich and then laid it down on her plate. It wasn't fair to make them wait. "So far it's just his notes about allotment, the Slater Act and—"

"Yeah, I figured." Riley chewed and swallowed. "I'm pretty anxious to see it, Mom. It's the last thing he was working on, all that. But we talked it over just now. We think you get the first turn."

"Keep in mind, he hasn't read his dad's other books yet." Alex stirred his tea. "You ought to make him start with Volume I and work up."

Riley tossed a lemon slice at Alex, who ducked sideways. "I didn't have to, you know?" He looked at Annie. "He told me everything."

They grew quiet. Annie finished her sandwich. "I'll take the tea upstairs with me."

"Take your time," Alex said as she stood up.

Upstairs again, Annie set her iced tea glass on the battered desk and laid the salmon-sentence page face down. Here. Here was what she had been hoping for: not notes, but Jack. Jack's writing.

But it wasn't his academic voice. Had he started a journal of some kind?

I had been sitting on the bottom step a little while before he knew I was there. I wasn't scared, I just wanted to be with him. Before Mom died he used to hold me on his lap sometimes before I went to bed. Nuzzle me with his whiskers, that kind of thing. He was leaning into the circle of lamplight on the table, writing something on the tablet of lined white paper Mom used for letters and sometimes even grocery lists. I remember the sound of the pen. Then he stopped, and there was nothing but silence. He had felt me there. And I knew, I could see it in his shoulders before he turned, he had no more words for me. All his words were going into that tablet. He looked at me and pointed with his chin. Get back upstairs.

All this time, the story's been right here. Out of sight, yes, but here. She kept him alive to raise me, and somehow she made sure I survived him.

But on the next page, more notes. Morehouse. "The Utter disaster." Notes on the next page, and the next. She turned page after page, quickly now, looking for her name, for—what? A map? Directions to his body? She had to press both hands against her face to stop their trembling.

Then she heard voices coming from somewhere outside the house. There were the boys, standing on the bank above the swimming hole, and Mattie, walking slowly toward them. The dog pushed a cold nose under her elbow and then turned toward the door. Annie stood up. Leona was here, too, sitting in the shade of the lilacs beneath the opened bedroom window, her back toward the house. The screen door bumped gently against its frame and Rose trotted around the corner. She's eager to greet her, Annie thought. But the dog simply laid her head in Leona's lap, and Leona bent forward, one hand on each side of Rose's neck. Mattie had stopped walking. She lifted her chin until her face was open to the sky, but neither of the boys moved. Then Riley hurried forward and pulled Mattie tightly against his chest, the two of them stood swaying in the slow dance Annie recognized as grief. Alex was swaying, too—no, he was falling. Crumpling. His legs seemed to dissolve into the earth.

Afterward, Annie wouldn't remember running down the stairs and out the door. She flew across the brittle summer grass as fast as Jack had run that day when Roy was still alive, but there would be no rescuing of children this time. Sam—Alex's cousin Sam, her own Sammy—was dead. Listening to his earphones as he walked along the tracks, he couldn't have heard the train.

Or might not have heard it. It was all too common on the reservation, suicide by train. So many young people, just last year—that billboard, "Tell Someone," and the suicide prevention workshops, even a special summer camp—

No. Not Sam. Her Sammy. Wisecracking, funny Sam.

But of course he wasn't her Sammy. What did she know of his life outside the classroom? Alex lay curled on the ground, unmoving, Mattie and Riley on their knees beside him. Then Leona was there, lifting the boy's head and shoulders to pull him onto her lap, and she and Alex seemed to merge into one being, a leaning, rocking whole, a universe of grief, their pain rising in a high wailing song whose language Annie did not understand.

12

He wasn't alone. But Mattie had stepped so quietly across the smooth rocks that Riley hadn't heard her coming, and the words could just as easily have come from him, he might have said them out loud. It was all he could think about.

"They want Alex to help with the dressing."

He bent down to pick up a rock and threw it as hard as he could. They heard the splash on the other side of the river. Another. And another.

"I didn't even know him," he said at last. "Somebody this close to Alex. I might have seen him a couple of times when we went in to Mission, but I'm not even sure. He'd grown up mostly in Warm Springs, hadn't he?" He looked back toward the house.

"Leona's with him. And your mom." She knew what he was thinking. "It can't all be you, Riley."

"I know, but—" He couldn't imagine it. Dressing a dead body, any dead body. And this one had been hit by a train.

"He won't be alone," Mattie said. "There'll be others. An elder. That helps. And you'll have some time with him afterward, because the Washat service won't start until at least seven. Then we'll all be with him."

"When does the burial happen?"

"At sunrise."

Mattie's voice caught and Riley reached for her hand. "Mattie, I'm so sorry. You did know him. He was in your summer school class, Mom said?"

She let herself lean against his shoulder. Swallows were skimming low over the river, scooping minute drinks of water into their open mouths. "Resistance is futile," she said after a while. "He could get a laugh with that line every time."

"*Star Trek: The Next Generation.*"

"The next generation," Mattie whispered.

"What was he like?"

"Smart. Funny. Of course that'll be turned against him now." She brushed tears from the corners of her eyes. "Kind. He was kind. He knew what people were feeling."

"He sounds pretty great."

"Yeah. He was."

Riley skimmed a flat rock out over the river, counting the bounces. Three, four, five. "People said it about Dad, too."

"What?"

"That it was probably suicide."

"Why? Why would they—?"

"Because he didn't take any gear with him. Not even a sleeping bag. And I didn't know this until I got out of McLaughlin, but he didn't talk to Mom first, either."

"Still, suicide? Why couldn't they think he was just rushing up there to—" Mattie stopped, and knelt to examine the river rocks.

"I know. It was like they couldn't think of enough bad things to say about him. As if that would help."

She picked up a smooth, flat rock and rubbed her thumb across the surface. "I guess it's like probing a wound," she said at last. "People think if they can wrap their minds around it, understand what happened—"

"Then it won't happen to them? Nothing bad will ever happen to them?" Riley tossed another rock out into the river, this time not so hard. "I don't know, Mattie. I hated when people talked about it. It seemed—dirty, somehow."

Mattie handed him her flat stone and he skipped it out across the water.

"But the truth is, I want to know too. What happened to him. I mean, beyond the obvious. He went looking for me, and he's dead. So why is it so important to know? What difference would it make?"

Mattie was looking across the river toward the railroad tracks, beyond the tracks, her eyes unfocused. "You know something?" she said at last. "I learned this from one of your dad's books. They could have built the railroad down Wildhorse Canyon like the tribes wanted, instead of Meacham Creek. It didn't have to go right through the reservation. People were worried about the damage to the river, and of course the danger to their kids, and to the animals. The game."

Riley looked at her. "Dad wrote about that?"

"I think he understood."

"Resistance is futile, you mean?"

When she turned away, Riley put his arms around her, pulling her back against his chest. It was like holding a small bird; yes, like waiting for a small, stunned bird to fly.

"It's true, you know," she said at last. "About the suicide rate. They have all kinds of fancy labels: 'historical trauma and unresolved grief' passed down in families, and 'disenfranchised grief,' the loss of land and culture and language and any possibility of being who you really are, or were, or would have been. Or just the same old, same old: alcohol, drugs. Depression. Abuse." She put her hands on Riley's. "I don't know what happened to Sammy. But when I look out at those tracks, I think: if they weren't there, no boys would be hit while they're walking on them. Nobody would drive up Wildhorse Creek to die that way."

☙

They were all tired, but Annie knew that this morning they needed each other more than they needed sleep. Mattie's eyes were red. Riley was holding her hand, but he was still watching Alex as if his friend might vanish, disappear into the earth like water. Or like Sammy in that wooden box this morning. But difficult as they had been, these three days of mourning together had been a gift. Something she and Riley hadn't had in the first days of their own loss. She closed her eyes, remembering the light of sunrise as they left the longhouse.

Leona was making coffee, as much at home in the kitchen as she must have been when Mary lived in this house. Leona must have sat here, at this very table. Mary's kitchen table.

She missed Jack. For a moment it was just that simple. Then the old anguish was back, that weight in her chest. The black, unanswerable question: How could this be happening? Her life going on without his?

"Survival is hard sometimes." Leona said. The smell of coffee was filling the room. "But it's all we have."

"What if someone else doesn't survive because of you?" Alex's voice climbed. Now it cracked. "What then?"

Annie frowned. How could Sammy's death be Alex's fault? Alex had been here with Riley, he had been helping her find Jack's password. All summer he had been pulling himself back from the edge where he had so nearly been lost himself. Not now, she thought. Not now, when you've just made it through—

"Alex, no! It was me, anybody can see that." Riley was breaking down. "You have to know that. Everybody knows it."

Annie couldn't make her vision focus. Nothing was making sense. Maybe she was slipping again. Dissolving.

"Alex feels guilty for being here."

"With us?" Annie and Riley had turned to Leona at the same moment, incredulous. How could Alex not know he was wanted? Needed. They *needed* him, now more than ever.

Leona smiled as if she were explaining something difficult to a small child. "Well, yes, but I meant just *being* here. Being alive."

"Don't!" Riley's cry startled even himself. "Don't say that! He's already—I *need* him to be alive!"

Alex looked up. "Oh, Rile—I would—I couldn't do that to you. Drinking was bad enough. I was pretty close to, I know I—Jesus, Riley, you've helped me so much. It's still hard." Alex looked at Mattie and then down at the table, pushing the heels of his hands against his forehead. "But you know it's true. If I hadn't lived with you, if my family hadn't been—or at least my uncle— but really, it wasn't them, it was me. If I hadn't wanted so badly to be part of *your* family. Your mom and dad were so—"

"It seemed like you had a perfect life, Riley," Mattie said. "Everybody wanted to touch it, be part of it. I did, too."

"And my family—I love my mom, I love them all, but—"

"I guess I just don't understand," Riley said, finally.

"I do," Annie said. "I think I do."

"Mom?" Riley's look was anguished.

"No, son, I don't mean I think Alex is to blame. For anything. And neither are you. I just—until I met your dad, Riley, I felt—well, I guess "guilty for being here" is exactly how I felt. No father, and my mother so—she was a drinker too, Alex, an alcoholic, and we always lived in such terrible—it was clear nobody wanted us around. People like us. We were—we weren't good enough." Both boys were looking at her. "We were the wrong people. We lived on welfare, or we had the wrong jobs. The kind of work poor people do so the other people, the people whose lives are valued, can do other things. I remember feeling like we were supposed to stay out of sight. We were ugly. Dirty, even, at least in their eyes. We offended people. We wore the wrong clothes, and we said the wrong things." Annie lifted her coffee and set it down. *Careful,* Jack had grinned. *Whole damn place might implode, you keep telling the truth like that.* She had never talked about these feelings with anyone else. "Of course I was angry about it, too. I knew it wasn't fair. And there didn't seem to be any way out of it. We moved so much I was always behind in school, and when I did do better than the others, the teachers seemed—offended. It threatened them. Their view of things."

Leona stirred sugar into her coffee.

"The worse part was the double message. I wasn't good enough, but I could make myself good enough—or almost good enough—if I pretended to be someone else. Covered up who I was. Change the way I talked and dressed and—felt about things. Pretended I didn't know other poor people. Didn't make anyone feel uncomfortable by doing things like saying 'Thank you' to the waitress, or the garbage man."

"Assimilated," said Mattie.

Leona sipped her coffee. Annie couldn't tell what she was thinking. "Well, that's pretty strong, Mattie, but I suppose in a way it's the same thing. Similar, anyway." She looked at Alex. "And then, just like you, I guess, Alex—I hadn't thought about it that way, but it's true—I met Jack. And he saw me as I was. Not who I could be if I tried hard enough, but who I was." Did Alex know this was how they had felt about him? How could she find the words to explain? He was a gift, he had always been a gift. Not a stray, an orphan to be rescued from his own family.

"You went to college," Mattie said.

"But not to become someone else. College helped me be more of who I already was. Who I had always been. Jack helped me see that." Alex was still watching her. "We have always been grateful for you," she told him. "And grateful to your family for sharing you with us. Yes, we need you now. But we needed you then, too. From the very beginning, we needed you."

"You needed me?"

"Every summer, you were here waiting for us." She stopped. "I don't know exactly how to say this. You made me feel like I belonged here. At least that it was okay to be here. You wanted us to come—Riley, and his dad and mom too—me, a city woman with blue eyes. I still wasn't all that used to being wanted, except by Jack and Riley."

Alex nodded. "I know the feeling." His smile was weak, but it was there.

"And Jack told me—oh, Alex, we knew it wasn't fair, we couldn't ask you to come back to Portland with us, but we all missed you so much. Remember that spring break you spent with us? When we went to the beach? You boys loved that octopus at the aquarium, you spent a whole hour with your hands in the tank, trying so hard to be good. Don't pet the octopus, the sign said. She doesn't like it. Remember the kite that got away? And roasting marshmallows in that big driftwood fire down on the beach? You had so much fun. But it wasn't just for you, or even you and Riley. On the way home from the airport—and you were so brave, flying all by yourself—Jack said, 'I'm selfish, Annie. I've made him miss the BAAD tournament, and the spring powwow. Maybe the root feast. Who knows what else. I know they had fun, and he got to see the ocean, but the truth is, I couldn't wait another week to see him, much less three more months.'"

Riley had been staring at his mother. "Wow. There's so much I didn't— but I did know I was lucky, Mom. Having this place to come to in the summers, and you and Dad. And Alex, and then Mattie. All my friends. Right up until—Dad, and then you, Mom—and it was like, a double shock, I guess, because things had always been so good. I was the only kid in that whole treatment place whose family had been anywhere near happy." Riley shook his head as if to clear his vision. "But when I saw that grave, my grandmother's grave so far up on the hill, and you said Dad didn't even know it was there, well, then I knew. Something was wrong. And it must have been wrong for a long time."

Leona picked up her coffee. Her voice was quiet. "You know, we're all in this together."

"And that's a good thing," Mattie said as if to reassure herself.

"A very good thing. But it's hard sometimes." She set the cup back down.

Riley was trying hard to smile. "That's the same thing you said about survival."

Leona's head dipped. When she looked up again, her eyes shone with a film of tears. "Yes, itt."

Riley looked at Alex. "Nephew," Alex said quietly. He looked better, Annie thought. Or maybe just different. Older. But maybe better.

She had a sudden image of that stack of pages still waiting for her upstairs. Whatever story Jack had left behind, they were all going to be part of it. Maybe they had always been part of it.

⌒

How much can we know? An even better question, Annie thought that night as she lay waiting for sleep, might be how much can we bear knowing? Yet not knowing was unbearable.

And yet, somehow, we bear it, Dennis had said.

Had Sam's death been an accident? Maybe what mattered to his family was what they believed. Or maybe none of that mattered. Only that he was gone.

She reached for the bedside clock. Three-thirty. Rose lifted her head as she sat up, feeling for her slippers in the darkness. No moon, and the big dipper already settling into the canyon. Oso. The bear.

Would Mattie's bear claw medicine heal her, too?

But she *was* better. On the surface, at least, she was a sane, functioning person. She was a teacher, a mother. She had found a friend.

She hadn't had a chance to tell Leona about Jack's manuscript.

The night was warm even for early August. From the porch steps Annie listened to the river, its current low now, barely audible. Had her eyes adjusted to the darkness, or was that first light already lifting the eastern skyline? Rose had settled back into the blanket, so Annie was alone as she started down the path, making her way past the buckrake and the old chicken house as if she were walking through the living room at night, knowing the position of each chair, the couch, the woodstove. The path smelled of dry weeds and ancient dust. Old wood. And something sweeter: elderberries? Though their bunches wouldn't swell into dusty purple ripeness for another month. The only sound was her own steps, the hour too close to morning for the chorusing of crickets that had almost pulled her into sleep.

When she reached the fence Annie untied her robe and let it fall to the ground, then bent to dip between the barbed wires. A breath of air stirred in the cottonwoods and touched the open throat of her light summer nightgown. Annie felt a shiver ripple along her skin. She had been a child, not much more than a toddler, still too young for school. Could it have really happened? Had her mother rubbed her back to help put her to sleep? Not after she had been old enough to carry home a can of soup and heat it on the stovetop. But in the caress of this night air Annie had felt the sensation of the soft circles traced by her mother's fingertips

Had her mother wanted to be there for her, too, the way she had thought she would always be there for Riley? Forgiveness, Mattie had said. It's about forgiveness.

Her hands behind her on the driftwood log, Annie had been leaning back for a long time before she knew he was there, not ten feet away, his coyote head tipped up as if he too had been wishing he could swallow the night sky, let the Milky Way slide down his throat to cool the ache that burned inside his rib cage. Annie caught her breath, and the coyote lowered his gaze and looked directly at her. In this dim light, his eyes were dark. Like Jack's eyes, Annie thought.

Then he was gone.

And then she heard them coming, too fast, a pickup on the county road, gravel spraying as the truck rounded the curve—and shouts, voices she thought she recognized, but raucous, blurred by the speed. "Hey teacher!" "Got any more stories?" "Yeah, give us another story, Teach!" "Here's one for you—" Annie heard the sound of breaking glass, a bottle shattering against basalt. Then a motor revving, shifting gears; squeals from the back of the pickup, red lights fishtailing out of sight.

13

Annie skimmed the pages. More notes: Whitman Mission, the Great Awakening. But hadn't Jack already written this story?

He had talked about it from the time they were first together: how schoolchildren in his part of the country were bused each spring to the Mission site to be told the gruesome story of a Cayuse warrior creeping up behind a gentle Marcus Whitman to split his head open with a tomahawk. "What I don't understand," Jack had confessed one night as they walked hand in hand along the sidewalk to the Fred Meyer grocery near their student apartment, "is how can we *not* imagine the pain they were feeling. A little over a decade of the Whitmans and already half their people dead? One of those Cayuse men had watched three of his children die *that day!*"

Annie turned over another page.

I've just been marking time with this so-called research, Jack had written. *And I know it. The real question, the one I need to ask if I'm going to write about this history, is how does all of this—the land grab, the missionaries and the killings, apply to us? To Dad and me? This land?*

And Bancroft? How does what he said apply to us? To Annie, even. Riley. After all, where does it stop?

What was he talking about? Bancroft had published Oregon's first written history, but . . . She lifted the next page from the stack and turned it face side up. "*The quick extermination of the aborigines may be regarded as a blessing both to the red race and to the white.*"

The rest of the page was empty, a white glare on the surface of Jack's desk.

Annie laid her forehead against the paper. Here it was, the story the people in that pickup last night had grown up with. Maybe even the one that had killed Sam.

Give us another, Teacher.

We grew up with this story, too, she thought. It's everywhere, in books and movies, advertising, jokes, all offering to soften what had happened. Dehumanization. Genocide. "This thing is so big," Jack had said once. "It cancels all our mythologies. No wonder we can't face it."

But he had been trying to do just that. In this room, at this desk. Every day, all summer long.

"Did you know they had the huckleberry feast yesterday?"

Annie jumped: Leona was standing behind her chair. How had she climbed the stairs so silently?

"Now we can pick." She held out a small plastic bucket. "And the women say they're good this year."

Annie stood up. "Oh, Leona, I haven't been able to tell you, we found Jack's notes. Alex guessed his password, but it was just before you came to tell us about Sam, and—"

Leona was smiling. "I know. Don't worry, it's all right."

"I can only read a little at a time," Annie said. She heard Leona's berries dropping into the basket at her waist, a sound muted by the layer already covering the bottom. "It's like being with him and then losing him all over again." Rose crashed through the underbrush and a Douglas squirrel chirred from a pine limb. The boys had headed down the steep slope; Mattie too was out of sight. "But I keep thinking if I look carefully enough—at first I rushed through the whole stack of pages, hoping something would stand out. A hint, some kind of clue. Why he would just leave like that. It wasn't like Jack. No matter how upset he was."

"No. No, it wasn't." Nuthatches called from the jack pines. Leona stood up and held out a huckleberry. "See this circle on the blossom end? My grandmother used to call it an eye. She said Creator told the huckleberry to watch us human beings. Make sure we were doing right. Following the Law. Tama'nwit, natural law." She looked around. "Over there, does that look like a good patch?" Annie followed through the thick undergrowth. She could smell the berries in the sunlight. They looked like dark freckles spattering the brush.

"Grandma said water was created first. Then land and people. She said land takes care of the people, and people take care of the land." Leona reached deep into the bush. "It sounds so simple. But sometimes it's not easy. To know how to do what's right."

Annie frowned. Why was Leona talking about the land? The older woman was picking silently now. "But he must have intended to do what was right," Annie said at last. "He always—I can't imagine Jack doing anything else."

Leona stood and pulled Annie up from her own kneeling crouch. "No, Annie, I meant me. I meant to do what was right, too. And I'd promised. I'd promised Mary. But Jack was so happy in his life with you and Riley, and I told myself he was okay now, he didn't need me. The truth is, I felt bad about those years when I should have been there for him. I could tell he hardly remembered me."

From below them came the whirr of a startled grouse and a faint burst of laughter.

Rose was barking. But the sounds seemed distorted. Annie couldn't make her mind focus. Leona was still gripping her hand. "Hardly remembered?"

"When I came that day to bring him the letter. Roy's letter." Leona let Annie's hand drop as she reached to brush tears from the corners of her eyes. "Roy wrote a long letter to Mary after she died. I thought it might help Jack to read it. To help him understand his dad. Why Roy raised him the way he did." Leona turned away, feeling blindly behind her, and took a lurching step before Annie could reach to guide her toward the fallen log. They were still sitting, Annie's arm around Leona's shoulders, when she noticed Mattie standing at the edge of the pines. When the girl caught Annie's eye she raised her hand to touch the bill of her red Trailblazers cap. Then she turned downhill, holding her pail high to avoid the branch of a whitened snag.

"Leona." Annie released the older woman's shoulders. "I haven't found a letter. Most of what I've read so far in Jack's notes is just his research into the history of the reservation land, but some of it seems to be a journal, or maybe a diary. About his father. And about the story having been right here all this time. He said, 'She kept him alive to raise me, and she made sure I survived him.'" Leona had closed her eyes. "Was he talking about you?"

Leona tipped her face toward the sky. Annie too leaned back, resting on her arms; the sun felt warm on her shoulders. Leona was breathing quietly now. At last she stood and looked down at Annie. "I don't suppose the boys will ever let us forget it if they out-pick us while we sit here." She said something else as they walked back to the berry patch, but her voice disappeared into the air.

By the time the boys and Mattie climbed onto the rear bumper and swung their legs over the edge of the pickup bed for the dusty, rough ride home, Annie had heard the story of Mary's death. By drowning, Leona said. No, her heart was fine. If anyone had ever had a strong heart, it was Mary. She had gone down to the river just at dawn that morning. She so wanted another child; she had lost two before Jack and another after he was born, and she—yes, she, Leona—had told her about something women used to do in the old days: lie in the river with your head downstream and let the current wash into you. It was a remedy her grandmother had taught her as a young woman. Rose hips and water, prayer—how do we know the right thing to do? Leona had asked, tears rising again in her dark eyes. No one really knew why it had happened. Mary had grown up swimming in that river. Hypothermia, a cramp? Or maybe she had just let herself float, forgetting about the broken cottonwood, the big limb that had fallen into the river at the bend just past the swimming hole where Roy had found her body trapped in a maze of underwater branches.

"I begged him to let me bury her," Leona said. Her voice had become a whisper. "It's so important. To let our bodies go back into the earth." She wiped her eyes again. "But he had her cremated. What I buried under that rock is only ashes. He did let me have those. 'Now stay the hell off my land,' he told me. 'You gave her to me and I'm giving her back. But by God the boy is going to survive. If you come near him, I'll kill you myself.'"

Annie had stood still, one hand beneath her berry bucket. "What had you promised Mary?"

Leona bent over the huckleberry brush, hiding her face.

"Leona?"

"To take care of Jack. She had made such a difference in Roy's life. But she knew how vulnerable he was. 'If anything ever happens to me,' she said, and I told her yes. Yes. I'd always be there for Jack."

⟿

You gave her to me. What had Roy meant? Leona would tell her, Annie knew. But only when the time was right. On the next trip to the mountains, Mattie and Leona picked side by side, sharing a comfortable silence, and on the one after that, Annie knew they were too close to the boys for such a conversation. Then it was time to enroll Riley in school. He would catch the bus to the high school in Athena. "I *would* rather be driving a Maserati," he grinned. "School bus. Kinda lame." But Mattie and Alex would be sharing that bus ride, and he knew she would need the Toyota to get to work herself. If she had work.

He had found a job, though, helping Gus with chores after school. "It's not that far, Mom. I'll get off the bus there, and I can just walk home." Alex would work at the tribal museum on weekends, at least until basketball season, and Mattie had already been recruited by the elementary after-school program.

I'm on the substitute list, Annie reminded herself when the moments of blank panic struck her. "Most administrators tend to call the same people over and over," the woman in the district office had told her, "but once they get acquainted with you, you'll be one of those people." Dorothy still wanted her to help with the reservation's own after-school program if she could find money in the budget for an additional employee. "Maybe as a temp. Sometimes it's possible to get a person on a three-month e-hire when I can't get them any other way. Have you put your name in at the college?"

Yes. Yes, she had. Adjunct work was what she had always done. "It's as much work as tenure track, sometimes more, at a pittance of the salary," Jack told her. "But you'll love it. And part-time will get you in the door."

Which wasn't true, she had discovered. Adjuncts were viewed as people who couldn't get the real teaching jobs. Granted an interview, sometimes, when a full-time position came open, but rarely hired. Of course, none of that had mattered when Jack was alive.

And her income had helped, of course. She and Jack had almost paid off their student loans; soon, they thought, they would be saving for Riley's tuition.

How quickly it had all disappeared.

Yet how familiar this new life felt to her. Applying for food stamps, scanning her cupboards. Counting the days until she would be able to flip the calendar picture to the beginning of the next month. Before Jack, and now, without Jack.

How would she ever help Riley with college? And Alex, and Mattie, all three of them, those young minds. It was so necessary and so impossible. She could sell the Portland house eventually, but there was so little equity. And it would need some work first, the property management company had written. Replace the roof, they said. Bring the old wiring up to code. Nobody buys a house with just one bathroom any more.

She could put her name in at the trailer plant. "They do hire a few women," the man at the employment office said. He had come around from behind the counter to stand beside her at the computer terminal. "It's a bit more than minimum, but—well, it's not a living wage, exactly." He had reached as if to put his hand on her forearm. Annie pulled away.

Had it come to this? That she needed to find Jack's body—a splintered rib, a knuckle bone, a matted tuft of his dark hair —so they could collect his life insurance?

Riley had looked over his shoulder before he stepped up into the yellow bus, and she had lifted her chin and smiled. See? I'm okay, I'm good. She watched him moving down the aisle, an off-balance shadow. Alex had spent the past few nights with Ruby; he would already be on the bus, and Mattie too, though the morning sun reflecting from the windows as the bus pulled away made recognizing them impossible. At her back, Annie could feel the empty house. A grasshopper whirred up from the steps. She closed her eyes.

What are you so afraid of? Annie asked herself. But she stood under the shade of the arbor until the faint sound of the school bus climbing out of the canyon had been swallowed by the low murmur of the river, itself almost inaudible.

⮹

"All we can do, Annie, is try to make things better now," Jack had said one night as they sat together on the porch steps.

Was that the afternoon he had written these words? He had sat here at this very desk. Looked out across the river toward the rim of hills, one hand resting on the back of his neck. And then his fingers had returned to the keyboard, feeling their way forward.

Sometimes, sitting here, she felt as if he were here with her. No. As if she were inhabiting his body. This was his spine pressed against the chair back. His lungs almost forgetting to inhale.

It was always about the land, he had written.

How do we see the land? History has its explanations, all neatly bound in books. I've read those books. Expulsion from the Garden is our guiding story even if we think we have rejected it; the idea of linear time takes us farther and farther away from some imagined Eden, so we're exiles in a wilderness we have to fight to manage and control. We've even written books about the Cayuse, who had no fall from grace. For the Cayuse, the relationship with the land was who you were.

But how can we bear to look at it personally? This land. Our own family. Me. Okay, hot shot. What now?

He was sitting at the kitchen table sharpening his knife. Those hard hands always so gentle with the whetstone.

Tits on a boar hog. That was the night he said it.

And now, reading his letter, I see that I've been running from something all this time. Telling myself that I was pushing that door open to face whatever was on the other side. History.

That tablet Roy had been writing on, Annie thought. The letter Leona had given Jack. Why wasn't that here with the other books and papers?

I almost didn't recognize her. How long had it been? It was smell that brought her back to me; smoked buckskin, the narrow thong tying her necklace. And her voice. That voice. Ona, I had called her. Auntie Ona. "It's good to see you, Jack."

Riley had done that too, Annie remembered. Shortened names he couldn't quite pronounce.

Afterward, I watched her climb back up the trail. And kept watching, waiting to see her again in the open places. Standing there beside the lilacs with that tablet in my hand, I remembered digging that hole. And thought, 'I'm glad Annie's taken Riley into town this morning.' Not a good reaction for a historian to have. But I wanted time to sort this out.

She had saved it. Slipped it out of the burn pile, she said, when he went back into the house for another armload of Mom's things, her clothes, everything it hurt him to look at, or smell. Or touch. I don't remember seeing Ona there that morning, but I can still see him dousing that pile with kerosene; it was when he tossed the lit match that I knew Mom was lost for good. She was never going to find her way home.

Of course it was Auntie Ona who had left their childhood treasures, hers and Mom's, in the coffee can for me to find. She was returning Dad's letter now because, she said, she'd heard I was researching local history, and she thought it might help me to know why.

When the phone rang downstairs it took Annie a moment to recognize the sound, and then to remember that there were other people out there in the world. Voices that might be calling to offer her a job, some way to make her legs carry her down the stairs and through the coming days, even though they would be calling from somewhere far away from this place where she was alone.

14

"I come up here sometimes to be with her." Leona was spreading a blanket on the dry grass beside Mary's marker stone. "The old people say to let the spirit go. Don't call your loved ones back; they're on their own journey. Don't make it harder for them." Leona lifted her chin, but Annie had already seen the corner of one eye, squeezed tightly shut. She lay back on the blanket. The September sun still felt warm on her own face. Today was the equinox, the day of balanced light. Those small strips of colored flannel fluttering in the nearest wild rose bush; why hadn't she noticed them last summer? And look, there were more than she had seen at first; most of them, in fact, were badly sun-bleached, their edges shredded by the wind. "Maybe it's wrong, bringing you here to talk," Leona was saying. "At the longhouse people mourn for a year, but then the family has a memorial. A giveaway. They re-join the community. The person is remembered, and later her name can be passed along to another young woman who shows some of her strength. Her heart. She's not forgotten. But Mary—"

Annie sat up. Leona had turned her head away.

"I miss her," Leona said at last. They were sitting cross-legged now, facing each other, their knees almost touching. "Roy wouldn't talk about her. Jack learned early not to ask about her. Even after Roy had softened enough to let me come around when Jack wasn't there, it was on condition that I never mention Mary." She looked down. "It was almost as if she had never existed."

Rose had trotted the length of the rose thicket, pausing abruptly now and then to sniff a low stem or bury her nose in a patch of yellowing grass. Now she settled on the blanket with her back to the women, staring out into the air above the river canyon toward the pale gold line of distant wheat fields as if she were keeping watch. Only the far edge of the canyon was visible from here.

Which meant, Annie realized, they couldn't be seen either. Not even from the barn loft.

"The last time I was here you said Roy wasn't a bad man. A monster, Riley had called him."

"Well, it's like I said, we don't always know what's the right thing to do. The good thing. I guess you could say what Roy did was bad, and it was. Seemed to me it was. But even then I knew Roy was trying to save his child. His son. And himself, too, I guess. He had gone back to the story his father had taught him about survival."

"Sink or swim, you mean. Roy threw Riley out into the river once, when he was small."

"I know."

She saw it happen, Annie realized.

"I just happened to be on the trail. I wanted to see Jack and his family one more time before you went back to Portland."

"So you did keep your promise to Mary, Leona. You kept watching over Jack, even if he didn't know it."

Leona looked down. After a while she said, "You made him happy. Roy too. Happier, anyway."

"I liked Roy. I'm not sure why; he wasn't an easy man to like. I used to think it was because I didn't have a father. Jack said I sure cut his dad a lot of slack, but he always smiled when he said it. I don't know. Underneath all that hardness Roy seemed so—"

Annie's voice trailed away. She didn't know, exactly, what he had seemed. Not soft, certainly. Not even vulnerable. No, he was steel all the way to the end. To that last reaching arm.

"He was different, you know, before she died."

"Was he?" Annie tried to imagine a different Roy.

"Meeting Mary had saved him. She was—like Jack. I don't know how to say it any other way."

Annie smiled. They sat in silence. In the shade of the brushy draw, the crickets had already begun their evening song.

"Why did Roy say, 'You gave her to me'?"

"That's what I brought you here to tell you," Leona said. She stood up, pulling Annie up with her. After a few steps they sat again, this time on the grass with the stone between them. Annie laid her hand flat against its warmth. Rose had stayed where she was on the blanket, her ears pricked. Now she lifted her nose, testing the air.

"Mary was my sister," Leona said. "By choice. Not by blood. We were in the same class at St. Jude's, the old Academy. Third grade. It wasn't a boarding school, exactly—you know, like Chemawa—but a lot of Indian kids were sent there, and the out-of-town kids stayed there." She stopped and looked away. *Local history is personal history,* Annie remembered. Even when people do want to know, it's hard to talk about. No wonder Jack's notes seemed almost incoherent. It was as if he were already lost, reaching for something that might give him a sense of direction.

But Leona was speaking again. "Mary's family lived down by the tracks. A big family. Irish Catholic. I think there were twelve of them, maybe thirteen, brothers and sisters. Mary was one of the younger ones. Her mother worked night shift at the hospital right next door to St. Jude's. Well, she had to, Mary's dad was so deep into drink no one would hire him. And a brawler besides. When things got rough Mary would slip out and I'd wake up in the night with her pushed up against my back. Those cots were pretty narrow. She'd always be shivering. No coat, sometimes not even shoes. She was a little waif, I guess you'd say."

Like me, Annie thought. Even if it was Mary's father who drank, not her mother; even if she was one of many, not the only one. Was this why Jack had sat down beside her on the bus that day?

"So anyway." Leona was looking over Annie's shoulder. Her round face looked almost golden in this light. What was she seeing? "That summer she came home with me and just never went back. I think her mother was relieved she was safe, and her father might not have even noticed she was gone. He was locked up in jail about half the time. And the older kids were in and out of the house, coming and going, finding their own shelter. Then Mary's mother got sick, and the young ones went to county homes. So Mary just stayed with us. She was part of our family."

Her voice was softer now. "To Mary living above the canyon was heaven. She told me once—we were almost teenagers by then, we were lying out in the grass watching the meteor shower, the old people were singing inside the house, they sang late into the night—anyway, she said she never wanted to leave this land. She wanted to just sink deeper into it until she became balsamroot. Or yarrow. 'What about cheat grass?' I teased her, but she just laughed. 'Listen to it, though,' she said. 'Hear how it whispers when the air moves? Cheat grass is part of the earth too. It must be. It has to be.'"

Leona looked out across the canyon. "When I'm up here with her, it's like I'm unwinding a time ball," she said at last. "Have you seen them in the museum? Indian hemp twisted into string, with knots or beads for the moments of their lives women wanted to remember. I want to remember everything about her. Everything we did."

Annie traced the chiseled letter with one finger. Mary. Mother. M for mercy.

Not to mention monster. If Roy wasn't a monster, she thought, he was at least mean. Not only hard but miserly, locking his own memories away. How could he have let Jack grow up without even hearing his mother's name? *All sorrows can be borne if you can put them into a story.* Annie remembered reading that sentence at the public library, sitting alone at the long wooden table. She had looked up at the shelves of books, all bound in rich library colors, tans and maroons, muted shades of green.

"Mary and I were quite a bit younger than Roy," Leona said. "Six or seven years, I guess. We knew who he was, of course, our places being so close. And we spent so much of our time out on that bluff, exploring, making brush houses, all the things kids do. We had to be careful not to let John see us, though. Roy's dad. He didn't like us."

"Two little girls?"

"Well, our family. Indians. But mainly our family."

Annie remembered the splintering gray slab she had found half-buried in the duff at the foot of the yellow pine. *KEEP OF.* Jack had tried to smile: *Guess he couldn't spell 'Trespassing.'* She had closed her eyes against the memory when she felt Leona's hand rest lightly on her knee. "But Annie, Jack was right. If we knew each other's stories, what people have been through— you've heard about the famine Irish? To John, land meant survival. He wanted our place because it was right next to his. For cattle range and water, but really it was because of that famine. The stories his grandmother had told him. Starving people turned out of their houses, crawling along the road banks. Eating grass. Seeing her sisters, her own mother lying dead with green stains around her mouth—"

Leona lifted her face: a flock of starlings spun through the air above them, lifting as one, turning, gone. A murmuration. "To John, my family was in the way. A threat to his family's survival. Kind of upside down and backward, but that's how he saw things." She brushed her hand across Mary's stone as if sweeping it clean. "Of course he didn't know our family's history. Our people's. Or even all the history of the famine. Do you know, Annie, the Choctaws raised over seven hundred dollars for the people in Ireland? They knew what it was like to be hungry. They'd seen their own mothers starving, on the Trail of Tears. A few years ago eight Irish people walked the trail themselves. To honor them. The president of Ireland, another Mary, she thanked the Choctaw people too."

"I remember, Jack showed me the story in *Indian Country Today*."

"Well anyway, Roy went to Korea. They still had the draft then. When he came back he was different. That war—any war, but that Korean War was a bad one for a lot of the boys. John expected him to settle down and get back to ranch work, but Roy was down at the Silver Spur more than he was ever at home." Leona brushed a piece of dried grass from Mary's stone. "Then he got the idea he could rodeo. Ride rough stock. People said he was a demon—taking out his feelings on the horses, I guess. He got broken up pretty bad a few times. He'd spend the winters limping around to help John with the feeding but every day about six o'clock he'd take off for town.

"And then John and his wife, Roy's mother—Nora was her name but we saw her so seldom I have to think back to remember it. She pretty much stayed inside the house; she was sickly, people said. Anyway, they were both killed at the Gibbon crossing. John may have been trying to beat the train or maybe he just didn't look. A lot of people forget about that crossing." Leona looked at Annie. "Of course there was talk. And none of that talk helped Roy."

"When did he quit drinking?" Annie had been trying to imagine this other Roy, this wild colonial boy, as she had already begun to think of him— slumped over the bar, his face hidden beneath a battered cowboy hat, his words slurring like her mother's—but she couldn't make this image blend into the Roy she had known, neither the quiet, straight-backed rancher tipping his hat to her that day or the grandfather jiggling Riley on his boot, his cowboy-shirted arms outstretched to balance the baby's horsy-ride.

"That night, I think. Gus and Audrey helped him deal with the funeral home. They'd been friends for years, they were real worried about him. After it was all over he wrapped a jacket and some dried meat inside his sleeping bag and went off into the mountains. He was gone a long time, two or three weeks. Gus took care of things at home for him." Leona glanced at Rose, who had raised her muzzle and was watching the women. "But when he came back he still wasn't right. Mary and I heard Audrey scolding him for not eating. She brought him part of their own supper over every night and a warm loaf of bread whenever she made a batch, but she carried away as much as she took in. We were watching all this from the ravine. We still thought of the bluff as our place, Mary's and mine. The ranch had always been just part of our view. We were curious, I suppose. And sad for him, too. Mary was, especially. By now we were seventeen and Roy was maybe twenty-four, and we felt connected to him the way young people do, even though we were sure he didn't even know who we were." Leona reached over to stroke the dog's head. "Turned out, though, Roy had always known when we were up there. We'd left pretty deep tracks in those early days, playing house and sliding down the trail on the seat of our pants. He'd watched us grow up."

"Anyway. What happened was this. Mary was hanging out the wash, she was still in her white nightie, for some reason, and she was singing. She had such a beautiful voice. I wish you could have heard her, and heard her laugh, too, the way she laughed." Leona tipped her chin toward the sky. "I'll never forget. It was one of the songs she remembered from her childhood, one of those sorrowful Irish songs that somehow sound so beautiful they make you happy anyway. *The minstrel boy has gone to war,* hmm hmm, something, *and his wild harp slung behind him.* Well, I don't sound anything like her, but she was singing and doing what we all called her willow-dance as she bent down and then lifted each shirt or sock out of the basket. I started over to help her but my father put his hand on my shoulder and looked up to the place where the trail breaks over the ridge between your place and ours. "Go to him. He won't come down here otherwise," my father said.

"What does he want?" I asked him. But I knew. I guess I'd always known I'd have to share her.

"I was halfway up the trail before I could locate him. Roy looked like he had been dropped out of the sky into that yarrow patch. His shoulders were slumped so far forward I could barely see the back of his head. In fact I wasn't sure he was still alive, but when I got closer I could see his back moving. I'd never seen a white man cry. It scared me a little. But when I could tell he felt me standing there I sat down beside him.

"He wiped his face in the elbow of his shirt sleeve. I remember smelling the yarrow and thinking how yarrow can take away the pain. I wanted to say things about being good to her, how she was my sister and—you know, all that stuff people say. But I didn't, and I guess it was a good thing, because Roy did something that surprised me. He reached for my wrist and brought my hand flat against his chest. I could feel his heart beating.

"So I pulled him up and we walked down the trail together, and he met Mary."

15

"It's different from Portland, that's for sure. Way different." Riley had set the table for three—Alex would be late, but he'd be here—and now he was ladling his special chili into bowls. Did he have any idea, Annie wondered, how good it felt to her to come home to find dinner already made? The trouble with teaching was that she spent so much time on the road, driving back from her late-afternoon class in the dark every Tuesday and Thursday. And last week she had been called to substitute in two high schools, one at each end of the county. "In a lot of ways it's better." Riley dumped a handful of grated cheddar on top of his chili and reached for the bowl of chopped onions. "Two hundred kids instead of two thousand. Everybody knows everybody else. I'm still learning who's related to who, the family stories and all that, but I know all the names. 'Course I already knew some people."

They sat down to the meal, their heads bent over the bowls. The chili tasted rich, warm. Sustenance, she thought. Something to fill the hollow place. "God, this is good," she said, finally. How could she be as hungry as a sixteen-year-old boy? She hadn't been this ravenous even as a teenager herself.

"And the teachers are, I don't know. More human, I guess." Riley stood up to refill his bowl.

"More human?" Annie thought of the faces in last week's faculty lounges. The man who looked no older than Riley laughing with two older teachers at the coffeemaker, and that gray-faced woman bent over a stack of papers, frowning. Were these people guides to the full spectrum of humanity, good souls who yearned to open all the doors of human possibility to their students, or were they—much more likely—people like herself, well-intentioned men and women limited by their own lives' circumstances, doing a difficult job as best they could? "Only human," she probably would have said.

"Well, you know. They know you, and you get to know them. Mr. Soderling even remembers having Dad in class. *That's* pretty weird, actually."

"But are they good? Are you—"

"Sufficiently challenged?"

Annie threw her napkin at him. Riley grinned and picked up her empty bowl. Now would come his specialty, the fresh-ground coffee he made a point of buying with his own money. The hollow place that had nothing to do with hunger was still empty, but the blue mug was warm in her hands. The mug had been Jack's last gift. On her birthday. It was her color, he said, and he knew the shape would fit her hands. And it was made with clay from Weston Mountain.

"Don't worry, Mom." Riley blew across the top of his coffee, his elbows, like her own, propped on the table. "This school did all right by Dad, didn't it?" He blew again. They heard Rose's short, sharp bark: Alex was coming up on the porch, then opening the door. "Besides, there's basketball. I'm nowhere near as good as Alex, but he thinks I can make the team. That never would have happened in Portland."

Alex bent to hug her with one arm as he laid his stack of books on the table. His jacket carried the cold October air. "Smells good. Where's the fry bread?"

Riley laughed. "Good question."

"He's better than he thinks he is," Alex was already crumbling crackers into his chili. "He must have done nothing but shoot free throws in that place. If he can get enough people to foul him we can't lose."

That place. Yes: she had seen a backboard at the edge of the asphalt parking lot. With a ragged chain net hanging from a blackened hoop. She stood up and turned toward the sink.

"Yeah, I was a regular Steve McQueen," Riley was saying. How many times had he watched that old movie with Jack? *Look, Dad! The Great Escape's on Channel 12!* "No catcher's mitt in the whole place. Had to make do with a basketball," Riley was saying. Suddenly she was being lifted from behind, his arms wrapped around her waist. "Bet you didn't think you'd ever be one of those parents screaming their heads off in the bleachers, did you?"

"Keep your grades up, kid." Alex's voice was a throaty growl.

Riley set her down and turned, laughing. "That's perfect! For a second there I thought Coach Samuels was in the room."

Annie reached for the dish towel. "I'll be the only mother grading papers during time-outs." She dried her hands, then turned and smiled at them. "And I can't wait."

Later, with the boys upstairs doing their homework and her own students' essays spread across the kitchen table, she remembered what Leona had told her as they walked back down the trail that warm September day. She had stopped to point toward an intricate spiderweb backlit by the low sun. *Remember, it's okay to let yourself feel happy.*

Rose was pushing her muzzle into Annie's lap. Annie cupped her palm on the soft fur. "I know," she told the dog. "But I have to get these papers graded. I'm the breadwinner, you know. Not to mention the provider of dog food."

Rose lifted her head against Annie's hand.

"Or, maybe you're right and it's these papers that can wait." Rose sneezed, sneezed again, then turned and trotted toward the stairwell, glancing back to make sure Annie was following. She was already curled beside the desk when Annie reached the top of the stairs.

How did a dog know Jack's words were waiting? "She's just reading your body language, love," he would have said. "It's you she knows."

At first I thought he might be out there watching me, Jack had written.

When he shook me awake that morning it was still dark, and I'd gone back to sleep in the truck, so when he stopped I had no idea where we were. The trees were bright green like they are in the first morning light.

"Head on up that ridge," he said.

Was I afraid? I don't think so. I didn't know what he had in mind, but that wasn't unusual. He wasn't one to waste words on explanation. We were probably out scouting for elk, I thought, and he'd meet me up on top. I took the packsack he handed me and got out of the truck. I was still bone tired that morning from stacking hay the day before, but he had worked right beside me, as always. Two bales to my one.

I didn't find his note until late afternoon. I'd made my way up the mountain and along the length of the ridge—it dropped down into some drainage I didn't recognize—and I'd been waiting in a clearing for him to show up. Daydreaming, mostly. Thinking about girls, wondering if one of them would ever look twice at somebody like me. After a while a doe brought her twins out into the open. The wind was right so I got to watch them for a long time before she saw me. Even then she thought about it for a while before she led them away.

By this time I was getting pretty hungry. We hadn't had any breakfast, or at least I hadn't. Dad always carried the lunch, but it occurred to me that he might have put a sandwich in my pack this time. He hadn't, though. Just my jacket and a box of kitchen matches, and his old Swiss Army knife. I'd always wanted one, so I was pretty tickled. Maybe I had done something to please him.

Then I found that scrap of paper. "Find your own way home."

Annie felt sick all over again. She knew this story; Jack had told her all about it—but seeing it in print, imagining him sitting here, in this room, re-living that day—

"God, I love being out here," he had said once, turning in the trail to face her. "And knowing you're with me, even when I can't see you." They'd been hiking up the Hurricane Creek trail, Riley still in the child carrier backpack.

"You need a rest break?" She had read his face, and knew.

"Not really." But he had sat down on the windfall anyway. "I guess it was passing that boulder field and feeling the cold draft that always comes out of there. Like something's alive in there, breathing. It kind of spooks me, even now." He passed the water bottle back to her. "That night Dad left me out on the mountain I saw and heard all sorts of things, once it got dark. And to tell the truth, Annie, some of them I still can't explain. I could feel something touching my face. Maybe just spider webs, but—" He shook his head and stood up. "Don't worry, little man," he'd said. We'll make sure you can find your way anywhere in the world, your mom and me." He had reached around to jiggle Riley's foot, though Riley was leaning against the back of his father's neck, his eyes fluttering shut. "See? That one up there's Sacajawea Peak. Yup, and pretty soon we'll be right under the Matterhorn!"

Annie laid the page back on the desk and stood up. Yes, here it was, in Jack's own words, the reason he had disappeared. She'd always known, really, why he had gone after Riley the way he did. If Riley were lost, he might be as frightened as Jack had been. What she couldn't understand was why he hadn't made her part of it. He was *our* son, she thought. Even in his blind rush out the door, hadn't he wanted to reach out to her?

"You know, just when I think I know everything about you," Jack had said once, "you surprise me. There's always more. You're a bottomless pool." He had smiled, touching her hair. They had been sitting on the driftwood log; he had come to her special place to find her, to ask her something, she couldn't remember what, nothing important. "I love that," he had said. "The mystery of you."

She sat down on the bed. They'd even talked about it. Deep as their love went, they didn't always know what the other was thinking or feeling, how they would respond to something. "But damn it, Jack," she said. She was hugging her own elbows now, arms locked beneath her thighs. Rocking. "Didn't you even *want* to talk to me?"

He wasn't here to argue with. He wasn't even here to explain.

When Alex and Riley opened the door a crack, she was lying on her back, her fists still clenched. But the keening sobs that had finally penetrated their headphones were over. Had they heard anything else? "Mom?" His voice was quiet. So deep now, almost as deep as Jack's. Alex stood in the doorway as Riley sat down on the edge of the bed and covered her fist with his own hand.

"I'm sorry," Annie said. "I'm sorry."

"S'okay," Riley said.

He looked down at the floor beside the bed, then lifted his face toward the ceiling. When he finally spoke, his voice was tight. "Even me, Mom. Even with everything that happened. Sometimes I'm just mad he's not here. That he left us."

Anger. Fury, in fact; the fury of—yes, betrayal. That's what had come out of her mouth. After all these months of careful grieving, focusing intently on the core of what she knew. Jack was a good man, who loved her. Who loved his son. This boy who was sitting on the edge of the bed. He had lifted her fist and cupped it in both hands.

"He left me you," Annie said when she could speak. "Thank God, he left me you."

"Kid'll do, won't he?" Alex was still in the doorway. He grinned. "Like I keep telling him, he's better than he thinks he is."

Riley stood. "Yeah? Well, not at genetics. Definitely not at genetics. So you'd better break down and help me with that biology assignment if you need my free-throw prowess to pull your sorry-ass team out of the dungeon this year."

Then they were boys again, hip checking each other in the doorway. She heard their bedroom door closing. Orion was already well above the horizon. Downstairs, the stack of her students' essays was still waiting for her to read, and think about, holding her fine-tipped pen above the page as if she knew the words to fill the margins of their lives.

And over there on the desk, more pages. *If I'm going to write about this land, I'll have to tell these stories.*

Rose had been sitting quietly, those pale eyes watching her. But now her tail thumped against the floor like any ordinary dog.

⌀

"I caught an elbow," Riley said when he came in. The bruise had started on the outside of his left cheekbone and was spreading through the area around his eye, which was barely open. The right eye looked red too. Annie felt her heart push against her breastbone. What kind of coach would send a player home without even an ice pack? Some of the cubes she twisted out of the plastic tray missed the ziplock bag and slid across the kitchen floor. "Wait—we should wrap the bag in something. Here. Use this." Riley took the clean cotton dishtowel and bag separately and turned toward the stairs.

"Are you sure it's worth it?" Annie hadn't meant to say the words aloud. But she had. "Riley?" Now she was standing at the foot of the stairwell. "Of course it is. I'm sorry. I was just operating on mother-instinct, I guess."

No response. Annie stepped up to the first landing, where she could see the crack of light beneath Riley's bedroom door. He hadn't heard her. Maybe he hadn't heard her.

It wasn't until later, when Alex opened the door and set Riley's book bag inside, met her eye and then stepped back onto the porch, that she knew something else had happened. Someone was sitting on the step beside Alex. A girl, bending forward, bent almost double. Mattie. Wasn't it? Then the girl was gone, even her shadow dissolving into the darkness. The watery glass in the front door pane distorted Annie's vision, but she knew that it was only Alex who was coming back now into the dim light from the house. He looked up toward the room he shared with Riley, and spread his arms, palms up. His hands were empty. Then the door opened and he was in the room with her.

"I'll be back down in a minute," he said.

Annie picked up the book bag and raised her left hand to balance its weight. It was too heavy to hold out to Alex when he turned back. He'd remember it, she thought. But he kept going. She set the bag back on the floor.

By the time Alex came downstairs Annie had reheated tonight's stew twice. She watched him dip the ladle into the blue enamel kettle. "I think you can help him more than I can," he said, still facing the stove. "This is one of those things where Mom is even smarter than a friend." When he turned to sit down he tried to smile. "If I could have gotten Mattie into the house I'm pretty sure they'd have it all sorted out by now. It was just—it just happened. Riley came up behind her in the library and put his hand over her eyes, she was reading, concentrating like she does, and he put his other hand over her mouth. To keep her from getting in trouble, you know, for making noise. Mattie just reacted from instinct, I guess. She didn't mean to hurt him, she didn't even know—"

"So it wasn't basketball." Annie felt as if her mind had gone numb.

"No. Not basketball. There might not *be* any more basketball. We both missed practice." Alex was pushing the carrots to the side of his bowl. "Coach isn't real big on that." Now he lifted his spoon and looked at her. "Something happened to Mattie."

"I know." Annie stood up. "Leona told me." She looked toward the door to the stairwell. "Does Riley—"

"I think so. Now. I'm not sure, though. He's feeling pretty bad."

Riley was lying on his back, the bag of ice cubes, mostly water now, on the floor beside the bed. He sat up and took the new ice pack from her, but when she sat down beside him and his body tipped against her, the ziplock bag was still in his lap. He let her put her arm around his shoulders. She wanted to rock him, just rock him, humming all the old lullaby promises.

"I can't believe I was so dumb," he said.

Annie squeezed his shoulder. "You know what the songs say about love. It's not easy."

Riley leaned forward, shaking his head. Annie let her hand rest on his back. "From what Alex told me, it sounds like a mistake anyone could make."

When Riley didn't answer, she felt her way onward. "Mattie seems to feel as bad about this as you do. Maybe worse. I'm sure she didn't mean to—"

"That's the thing, Mom. I should have known. I shouldn't have put her in that—Mom, how could I *not* know? Alex figured it out, apparently. And you?" Riley turned and looked at her. "You knew, too. I can see it in your face. *You* knew." He turned away. "And I was dumb enough to believe I was the one who loved her." Now he sat up, rigid, and Annie's hand slipped off his back.

"I knew because Leona told me."

Riley leaned forward again now, elbows on his knees, and Annie watched her son's back slowly softening.

"She said you were wonderful to Mattie when she was pregnant."

Riley lifted his head and looked straight ahead. "I just assumed. You know, that it was some jerk, maybe even an okay guy, after a dance, something like that." He turned and looked at her, tears in his eyes. "It happens." He looked away again, and when he finally spoke his voice was choked. "But my world was so good, so—perfect, Mattie called it, *perfect*—that I couldn't even imagine what had really happened."

Not such a bad thing, Annie thought. Not so long ago, all three of them, or at least she and Riley, had been—

"And then, this afternoon, when she wheeled around with that elbow— oh, Mom, how could I not have known? I'm—we hold hands, but if I—oh, Mom, I can't talk about this with you, you're my *mother*. I wish Dad was here. I'm sorry, I'm sorry, Mom, but damn it, I *need* him, I—"

"I know you do, Riley." *You'll have to be both mother and father to him,* those words slipping so easily from people's mouths, people who had no idea.

"Oh, Mom, I'm sorry. I didn't mean—"

This time Annie put both arms around him and pulled him close. "It's okay. It's okay." When his breath had steadied, still holding him, she said, "Here's what I know. Love is the only thing that heals a wound this deep." She waited, thinking ahead. How to tell him this? "You'll have to be patient. So will she. It's hard to trust, and even when you think you do, your body remembers, and tries to protect itself. When she—"

Riley had pulled back from her embrace and was looking at her.

"Love works, honey. It takes a while, but it does work. And it's the only thing that works."

"Mom?"

Her voice had broken. What was happening? Riley reached up to touch her cheek. "Mom, you okay?"

Annie pressed his hand between hers. This boy. No, this man, this man she had once carried beneath her heart, a life within her own. That strange, swelling joy.

They could hear Alex downstairs quietly washing dishes, glasses clicking against each other. After a while Annie said, "I'm guessing that Mattie's reaction surprised her even more than it did you. This isn't who she thought she was."

"What do you mean?"

"Remember what she said about time being a sphere? About everything being connected? That's why we have to acknowledge the past, she said. So we can heal. And forgive, even ourselves."

Riley nodded. "The only way out is through? That's what they always said at McLaughlin."

"Mattie is—well, you know her better than anybody. Striking out at you, the one she loves—she must be wondering who she really is. And horrified that she hurt you." Rose nosed the bedroom door open and padded in, her toenails clicking on the wooden floor, and sat in front of Riley. She cocked her head. "She's looks as if she's asking why you haven't gone looking for her," Annie said.

Riley stood up. "Okay if I take the truck?"

"The keys are hanging by the door. There's a flashlight on the porch, and Riley?" He turned back to accept the ice bag she was holding out. "Check down by the cove first."

"That place you go?"

"It's just a feeling. If she's not there she's probably home by now."

Riley jammed one arm into a sweatshirt sleeve and turned toward the door, then back again. "Mom—"

"She's so lucky to have you." Annie took the ice bag while Riley pushed his other arm through its opening. "And of course we're all lucky to have her."

Riley gave her a quick hug. Three leaps and he was down the stairs. "Find her," she heard him say. Alex's murmured reply, and the sound of the front door.

Annie looked down. She was still holding the ice bag.

16

She had been thinking of it as "the first Christmas," though the first Christmas, of course, was the one she had spent pulling sheets from sour-smelling motel beds and trying not to think. But imagining, in spite of herself, picturing Riley unwrapping the green Oregon Ducks sweatshirt, or maybe he would open the books first. *Ceremony* and *Wind, Sand, and Stars*, used copies, their covers worn, their passages underlined by someone else, someone he'd never known. Some staff member would be reaching out to take them from him, shaking them upside down to check for drugs tucked between their pages.

"This is nice," Riley was saying now. He laid the poker down beside the stove and pushed another piece of tamarack onto the glowing coals. "I always wanted to be here at Christmas time." He closed the stove door and they watched through the glass as flames licked up and around the thick-grained edges of the wood. The house was staying warm with both of them home all day. No need to open the doors under the kitchen sink and run the electric heater to be sure the pipes didn't freeze. Even the bathroom plumbing was safe. "Alex and I were talking about how good it feels to know we split all this wood ourselves." Alex. Was he having a good Christmas with Ruby? Riley put his feet up on the wooden stool and blew the small half-melted marshmallows across the top of his hot cocoa before he took a sip. Then he set the mug down on the wooden arm of his grandfather's old Morris chair and lifted his chin in a way that reminded Annie for a moment of Roy. "We didn't get it ourselves, though. That'll be a challenge next summer."

"One winter at a time?"

He grinned and hoisted his mug. "Okay. Sure, I'll drink to that."

"It would be easier in Portland, you know. Thermostats. Remember thermostats?"

"Weird little box on the wall, right?" Riley laughed. "It *does* seem weird, now. Press a button and warm air just—happens."

"There's something to be said for it, though." Annie set down her own mug. "You don't talk about it, but you must be missing your friends. And the library. Live concerts? The museums?"

"Not so much. Now dance clubs!" Riley grinned. "I do miss those. Those sexy smoke-filled rooms. And movies. The new ones! No, wait—not movies. *Films*. Remember waiting in line at the film festival?"

"And on the sidewalk outside The Cup and Saucer on Sunday mornings?"

"All of us huddled under Dad's umbrella. Makes me hungry all over again. And—oh, yes, small plates!" In his best Upper-class Twit accent, he said, "Damn and blast, Mother, you have deprived me of small plates!"

Annie laughed.

"It's still there," Riley said. "That world. Don't get me wrong, Mom. I do miss it sometimes. The library, especially. And Powell's. Remember how we used to lose each other in Powell's? And you know how much I loved the history museum." The flames were pink and orange now, with flickers of green. "Sometimes I miss all the people wearing Gore-Tex—and that Portland look, black tights, whatever, you don't see that much here. And oh yeah, bumper stickers."

"'Keep Portland Weird'?"

"I think my favorite was 'Come to the dark side. We have cookies.'"

"I saw one once that said, 'NATIONAL SARCASM SOCIETY: like we need your support.'"

"The best one I've seen around here was, 'EAT LAMB! a million coyotes can't be wrong.' Cracked me up. But of course that one has an agenda."

Annie kicked off her slippers and crossed her stocking feet on a corner of Riley's stool. "What about your friends?"

"What friends?"

"Well, Adam. Dante. And Jordan? The people from the chess club?"

"I left messages. When I was in McLaughlin. Out of sight, out of mind, I guess."

Out of sight and in treatment, he means, Annie thought.

"It's okay, Mom. Really." Riley set down his mug and pulled his feet off the stool. When he leaned forward, forearms on his knees, Annie thought: Jack, this is exactly what Jack used to do when he had something important to tell me. In so many ways—

"Alex is my friend. He's always been my friend. And this place, living here—" Riley turned his head, almost imperceptibly, feeling for the right words. "I'm glad you and Dad gave me that life. It felt—I don't know, rich, I guess. Like a thick book. There were Chinese kids in my class. Ugandans. Kids who spoke Russian. African-Americans. Geez, we even had a family membership in OMSI. It was kid heaven. I had the best of both worlds, summers here and winters there. I knew it even then. But, Mom, it always made me sad when we left this place. I felt like this is where I belonged. Where *we* belonged."

"I know," Annie said. It was the same feeling she had had the first summer she came here with Jack. How could it be true? she had asked herself. She had felt like an imposter, reveling in someone else's life. Yet, somehow, at last, she was home.

"I guess I never told you how grateful I was that you came here. When you came to get me." He looked down. "I don't know how I could have gone back to our other house." They heard a soft hiss as the burning tamarack collapsed into the glowing coals. "You know. Without him."

Annie couldn't answer. Riley got up to add more wood, his back to her, and she closed her eyes and heard him walk into the kitchen. When he returned he was carrying the plate of gingerbread men they had made that afternoon. "I heard them calling," he said. "But of course this means I need to make some coffee."

"You used to dunk them in milk."

"Good idea. That'll hold me until the coffee's ready. You too?" he asked over his shoulder. Annie shook her head.

While he was busy in the kitchen she stepped out onto the porch. Even between the bare vines of the arbor she could see the brilliant winter stars. Jack had missed them so much that every year he drove the family up the highway toward Mt. Hood, far enough from the filter of streetlights, flashing signs, and Christmas lawn displays that they could see them too. "December stars. Really, they're at their brightest in December," he had insisted. How could they be brighter than the stars of those August nights? Somehow, though, the freezing air always turned them to crystals of pure light. All three of them standing like stair-steps, Jack's arms around her, her own arms around Riley, their heads tipped back, and when they grew dizzy, swaying as one body.

Through the window the fire-lit room looked like a Christmas card. When Riley opened the door she could smell coffee. Dark roast, the smell blended with—"Cinnamon sticks! Oh, Riley!"

"Well, it is Christmas." He handed her the mug, then walked to the edge of the porch and leaned back against the wooden pillar. "December sky. For Dad, Christmas was really about the Solstice, wasn't it? Stars in the darkest night, and then earth turning back toward light?"

Annie put her hand on his shoulder. "I was just remembering."

"Those drives up Highway 26!" Riley sipped his coffee. "I loved those. Especially when I was little. Getting to stay up so late. It always felt late, anyway, since it was so dark. And then falling asleep in the back seat and waking up in my pajamas, in my own bed."

Annie wrapped both hands around her coffee mug and inhaled. But she was shivering.

"Shall we go back to the fire?" Riley put his arm around her shoulders. "Or should I say, 'What are you doing out here without your coat, young woman?'"

They had finished the coffee and nearly half the cookies when he handed her the Joy Harjo CD. Soprano saxophone and poems. Her present to him—it had been their Christmas Eve tradition to open the "stocking gift," something small enough to fit into a stocking, and always something fun—was a gyroscope. "Sweet!"

"And how did you know I loved Joy Harjo?"

"Oh, I have my sources." Riley grinned. "It helps that Mattie does, too." He was watching the gyroscope spin. "Mom, do you think Dad felt like he belonged here? You know, the way we do?"

When she didn't answer he looked up. "I didn't mean to make you sad."

"No, that's—"

"It's just, I've been thinking. He worked so hard to teach me about the land. Both of us, I guess. He said he wanted us to be at home on the earth.

Remember how he was always taking a bearing, and telling us which rock or tree would help us keep oriented, be our witness point? How to count the ridges by the morning fog lifting up from their canyons, and see the way the drainages converged into the river itself? All that stuff about the angle of the sun changing as the seasons changed, and which constellations we could find only in the summer?"

"And how they moved across the sky, where they would be at midnight and then just at dawn?"

"Yeah. I loved it. It felt so—scientific, I guess. But the thing is, I already knew. I've always known where I am. I don't know how, exactly. It's just a feeling. Like gravity, or—magnetism, or something. I just know." The gyroscope had finally begun to wobble, but it was still spinning. "I thought everybody was like that. That Dad was just sharing, I don't know, extra knowledge. Like his history stories. Or the way he taught me about the birds, and the trees, all the different grasses. How to tell rainbow trout from brookies. That kind of thing." Riley looked down. "Turns out most people aren't like me. Or so they said at McLaughlin. They made a big deal of it, in fact. When they were trying to get me to talk about Dad."

Annie felt her heart clench. She was still holding the new CD. Joy Harjo, with Poetic Justice. *Letter from the End of the 20th Century. The Real Revolution is Love*. Rose was curled in front of the stove, her chin resting on her paws.

"Naturally they were jerks about it," Riley said. "That was their M.O. I knew they were trying to break down our defenses so we would face how our drinking and using had hurt other people. But I already knew I had hurt you guys, understatement of the year, and drinking was so *not* the problem. If it hadn't been for the *idea* of drinking, you and Dad and I would have been going on with our lives. So I blew off most of what they said." He shook his head. "This too, at first. It took the other kids to wise me up. Only one of them said sure, he could do that, wake up in a strange place in the dark and know which way was north. Alfie. Who also claimed he could communicate telepathically with Seven of Nine." Riley reached for another gingerbread boy and slowly broke off an arm. "Anyway, it came as quite a shock, as they say."

"You do have a special gift," Annie said. "Your dad and I always knew that. Remember how we'd say, 'Which way, Riley?' when we came to a fork in the road?"

"I thought that was just a game."

"Well, it was, at first. But we couldn't help noticing how you were always right. Even as a toddler. You just knew." Annie smiled. "But we didn't call the Guinness Book of World Records. I'm sure there are other people who have that kind of spatial intelligence."

Riley leaned back in his chair, still holding the cookie.

"You know, Riley, Ray Bradbury says he remembers being born, and until he was twelve years old he assumed it was something everyone could do."

"You mean they can't?" He was inspecting the cookie, thoughtfully breaking off the head and now closing his eyes. Chewing.

"Riley?"

There it was, that grin. "Gotcha!"

"I was just going to *say*, I can remember pretty far back myself."

He looked at her. Then they were both laughing.

"But I'm confused," Annie said. "Just because you have a special sense of where you are, why would your dad's teaching you about orienting yourself on the land mean he didn't feel he belonged here?"

Riley looked down, and then lifted his chin and looked directly at her. "I didn't mean to talk about it tonight, but I have been trying to work up the nerve to tell you. I've been reading Dad's notes."

Annie felt her back and shoulders relaxing. Was it the fire? Wood smoke, ginger, cinnamon? As if she had been drinking wine instead of coffee, she was letting go, letting her body sink into the cushions of the chair. "I just couldn't wait," Riley was saying. "I—"

"No, it's okay. It's more than okay." Her elbows were wings, soft feathers on the arms of the chair. Like reaching the high lake at last and taking off the pack, her body suddenly so light she had always felt as if she could take flight. "I've been wanting to share it with you, but I thought—I've read through all the pages, but I keep going back over them, trying to understand. The history notes are clear enough, but the personal parts—there's just so much to sort out."

"Yeah, I know what you mean. I'm only about halfway through the stack myself. I read a while and then I kind of have to let it roll around inside me for a while."

Annie smiled. This boy.

"Anyway, Dad seems so—sad, when he talks about the land. Of course it is sad, the Whitmans and allotment and all that, the whole history of America when it comes to Native people, for that matter, but—"

"But he already knew that."

"Yeah. Yeah, that's it. And in these notes there's something—I don't know what, maybe I just haven't read far enough, but I've been thinking maybe he felt like he didn't belong here. You know. He in particular didn't belong here." Riley stopped. "I know he loved this place, though. That's the thing. He did love it. He couldn't wait to get back every summer. I guess I'm just grasping for something. I mean, I already know why he went up into the mountains: he was trying to find me. I just keep thinking there must be something more, something I didn't know about his life, maybe, that would make it easier to live with."

How to tell him? She knew, and didn't know.

But Riley was looking down at the last piece of his cookie. "What a dumb thing to say. I can't believe I *said* anything that stupid. Nothing can make it easier to live with."

"I knew what you meant." Annie felt the tears coming into her voice. "I kept thinking I had to find something too, that comfort, whatever it is we both need, before I talked to you. It seemed like too much to lay on you otherwise. But it's as close as we can come to being with him again, and I didn't want to keep that from you, either." She reached for a Kleenex. "And then things happened, and school, and—but I should have known. You were always trying to lighten my pack."

"Mom?"

"It's just such a relief. To know that you—that we've been reading it together."

Riley leaned forward. "I've been wanting to tell you. Audrey said it took Granddad a long time to get over whatever happened in Korea. Just being in that war, I guess. She and Gus kind of helped him out, it sounded like. They were friends. 'Went to school together,' is how she put it." He sat back. "I'm not sure how important that is, or if it's a clue to whatever it is we're looking for, but I think it might be."

"Leona's told me some things, too. She said she gave your dad a letter that Roy had written just after Mary died, and—" Annie picked up her empty mug. "You know, I think we'd better make more hot chocolate, Riley. This is going to take a while."

When Annie opened her eyes on Christmas morning, she was lying on the couch with Rose at her side. Riley was asleep under a blanket in the Morris chair, and he must have covered her too; this was the star quilt from Alex's bed. Through the glass door she could see deep, glowing coals, the kind that would quickly kindle fire. *Good Solstice, Jack,* she would have said if he were here.

17

He knew I couldn't accept his version of things, Jack had written.

He saw the earth as something to be conquered, subdued, controlled, through brute force if necessary. Like breaking a colt by snubbing him to a post and hobbling his front foot to his rear one. I knew there had to be a better way. But after that night out on the mountain, I thought, if the relationship to the land is who you are then maybe I don't belong here any more than he did. Maybe only the People of this place belong here, or will ever belong here.

And then white space. On the next page, nothing about Roy or the home place, just details about the agents on the early reservation, Moorhouse firing a superintendent for "brutalizing the students," the controversy over his own use of laudanum, those two men who brought word of the Ghost Dance being sent home on the train. The Bannock Uprising.

Where had Jack been going with this book? "I don't know, Annie, I'm trying to find some sense in it, some pattern, but the personal stuff, my own family. . ." He had run his fingers through his hair. How tired he had looked that summer.

Riley was leaving penciled question marks in the margins, too, but he'd been so busy with school and basketball, helping Gus and Audrey, and spending as much time as he could with Mattie, that they hadn't had much time to talk about what he was making of it.

Still, if anyone could find an underlying framework in Jack's notes, Annie thought, it would be Riley. She sat in the bleachers with the other parents, well behind the cheering students and slightly to the left, watching him. Alex was a starting forward but Riley sat on the bench as the game began, focusing intently on the visiting team's players. When Coach Samuels sent him in to sub for one or the other of the starting guards, Riley moved the ball past and through the weak places in the defense, feeding it to Jake or Gabe or—often without looking—to Alex, who was always where Riley knew he would be when the pass arrived. Then a whistle would blow, or a buzzer sound, and Riley would be back on the bench, a white towel around his shoulders, watching again. Up and down the court.

"*Call* that, ref!"

The man next to her had stood up, blocking her view, and now he glanced back over his shoulder at the scoreboard. Annie looked too: four red circles, and white-lit bulbs flickering into square-cornered numbers. Home. Visitor.

"Jesus," the man said. When he sat back down the woman next to him put her hand on his thigh, but her face was turned to follow the ball down the court, her chin raised. Alex's feet left the ground as the ball arced upward, his right wrist hanging in the air like a bent butterfly wing. Three points. He was already backpedaling, not quite smiling but—what? relaxed. Focused. "He gets in a zone," Riley had explained. "I have to think, but he's just *there*."

Neither of the boys seemed upset when the team lost or overly elated when they won, for that matter, though their banter on the ride home on such a night might be a bit quicker. They were playing to play, Annie had realized early in the season. Her boys. She couldn't take her eyes off them.

Riley had turned to reach behind him for a bottle of water, and when he turned back Annie saw him glance toward the parent section. Was he trying to find her? She lifted her hand to wave, but it was Mattie he was watching. Mattie, looking up to find the best path through the crowded bleachers, people leaning to let her pass between them as she climbed. Annie slid closer to the man to make space on her other side.

Riley was out on the court again when the referee's sharp whistle blew. "Yes, by God! About time!" The man hadn't stood up this time, but Annie had felt Mattie's flinch. They watched as Riley went to the foul line, rubbing his hands on his uniform top. The referee held the ball out, and then handed it to Riley, who bounced it once, twice, three times, and looked up at the basket. "Pock-ets! Pock-ets!" The basketball swished through the net.

"That Fallon kid's good for two points damned near every time," Annie heard the man tell his wife. The woman nodded without looking at him. Riley was taking the inbounds pass, moving the ball back down the court. Annie poked a gentle elbow in Mattie's ribs. "Fallon kid's okay." Mattie ducked her head to hide her smile.

The gym was too noisy for talk, but when the final buzzer sounded both of them stayed behind as the bleachers emptied. "Grandma wants to see you," Mattie said. "Can your truck make it up to our place?"

"I'm not sure. We're getting pretty good at putting on chains, but do you think Spike could pull us out if we get stuck?"

"With his teeth, probably," Mattie said. "If Grandma told him to." Annie laughed. Spike had turned out to be a gentle man, better at caring for children than any feat of brute strength that his name and body—he was, what, twice Leona's size?—might suggest. "But maybe we'd better come to your place instead. Tomorrow?" So Leona has more to tell us, Annie thought. That's good. Yes. Good. No matter what. "She can just bring her fry bread, I guess," Mattie was saying.

"I have plenty of flour. She can make it at our place, can't she? So it will be nice and hot? And I'll get some stew going. James left us some elk meat." The gym was almost empty now, though they could hear voices in the main hallway and through the open doors, the sounds of cars starting up. "Mattie, I haven't had the chance to say thank you for the Joy Harjo CD. Riley said you had a hand in that. I love it." The custodian was coming along the top row of bleachers, bending to pick up popcorn bags and candy wrappers, and they both stood up. Annie pulled her jacket on. When they were halfway across the gym floor, she said, "You know her poem about fear?"

"'I Give You Back'?"

"I wonder how many people copied that poem into their journals and carried it around with them like I did."

"What I wondered was, how? How did she do it?" In this big space, Mattie's voice was almost too quiet to hear.

"I guess I'm still working on that, too." Annie said. "But you know what, Mattie? If you were a flower, I think you'd be a dandelion."

"A what?"

"I like the way they keep coming back. No matter how short you cut the grass, by the time you put the mower away there will be a dozen dandelion stems standing straight up from the grass. Stems six or inches tall."

"You calling me a *weed*?" But she was smiling.

Annie crossed the slippery parking lot alone. The boys had already scraped the Toyota's windshield and had the heater running. "Free-throw Fallon saves the Tigers but not the Scots," she heard Alex say.

"'TigerScots,' whoever heard of such a mascot, anyway? It's too much for one basketball wizard, I tell you." Riley turned the heater fan up higher. "And anyway, what we needed was five three-pointers, not a measly four."

Annie laughed. "You guys hungry, by any chance?

"Raa-venous," they said together.

So many things Jack was missing.

⌖

"You can use yeast or baking powder, *or*," Leona grinned, "self-rising flour. I call it Betty Crocker Fry Bread. The real trick—" she was tossing the thin disc of dough back and forth between her palms now—"is letting the dough stretch. Real thin. And then some people make a hole in the middle. You want it to fry flat."

Mattie was standing beside her, turning the dough to let it brown on both sides, then lifting each piece with a long fork above the pan to let it drip before she added it to the growing stack. Annie had set the kitchen stool on Leona's other side, where she could watch this practiced team without being in the way. Aromas: bread, elk stew. Her favorites. Behind her, she heard the sound of the pepper grinder. "Adjusting the seasoning," Riley liked to call it.

"Not *too* much, you guys."

"It's only about a six."

But when they had gathered around the table and sat down to eat, everything was perfect. Riley dipped his fry bread in the stew while Alex reached for the huckleberry jam. "I like my dessert during the meal."

"Before, during, and after, more like."

Mattie smiled at the boys across the table, and later, when she stood up to help Riley serve coffee, Annie saw her touch his hip.

"James can take you hunting now, ennit?" Leona spooned jam onto her last corner of fry bread.

"He wants to, he said. Next fall." Alex laughed. "Do you suppose I'll be the oldest boy ever to give a first-hunt feast?" He stirred his coffee. "I just can't believe how good it is. To have him, you know. This way."

"Sober." Alex looked up, but Leona was still spreading the jam. "Yes, he can be a real uncle to you now."

And Ruby? What about Ruby? Annie hadn't even thought to ask.

No, she corrected herself. She hadn't dared.

"Do you *want* to hunt, though?" Riley had laid down his spoon. "I mean, I eat meat too, and I do know it doesn't actually come wrapped in plastic." Mattie was looking intently at her bowl. "But killing, shooting something that's alive, I'm not sure I could—" He stopped again, heat reddening his face. "I'm a real catch, aren't I?" Mattie had raised her head; he was speaking directly to her. "No blood quantum at all, and now I suddenly discover I'm a vegan."

They all laughed, and Alex put his hand on Riley's shoulder. "To be honest, Rile, I don't know how I'll feel. But it's my job."

"Your job?"

"My role, maybe, is a better way to say it. To provide meat for my family. And for elders. Families in mourning, or the ones who don't have a man to hunt for them."

"We all serve our families, our people, in different ways," Leona said. "You have a real strong heart, Riley. Strong as any hunter. You're like Jack that way." Riley's back stiffened, but then his body seemed to soften, settle in the air around him. "And Jack was like her. Mary. That's why he couldn't—"

They had all stopped eating. In the silence Leona's vision seemed to focus beyond the boys' heads, beyond even the cottonwoods outside, and the ice-rimmed river framed by the window. Mattie stood and quietly collected their dishes, then sat down again beside her grandmother. Annie felt her heart beating. Leona was here for a reason. Was she ready for this?

"I have a story for you," Leona said. "But first you have to try to understand. Roy loved her. He loved her. In that letter I told you about, Annie—it was a real long letter, he wrote night after night in those first weeks after she died—he told her he was going to keep Jack alive. He couldn't lose them both, he said. She had showed him a new way of looking at the world, the circle of respect you talk about, Mattie. How everything's connected, how we're all part of it. But he thought that way of seeing the world was what had killed her. Swept her right under that limb and taken her away from him, and from Jack, too. It was his fault, he thought. He should have taught her what his father had taught him. But he would teach Jack. He promised her. He'd make sure Jack survived."

"And what his father had taught him was . . ." Annie's voice trailed away.

"I can guess." Riley looked at Mattie and shook his head.

"It's just a different way of looking at the world. Ranking things, stacking them up. What's the word?"

"Hierarchy? Is that what you mean, Grandma?"

"Hierarchy, yes. With man at the top. Higher than the other animals. And different. Separate. From the earth, the trees, the rocks, the birds, everything."

"And in charge," said Alex. "Don't forget that part."

Leona's eyes were filling with tears. "I keep seeing Roy," she said. "He was hurting almost as much as Jack." They waited as she wiped her eyes with a corner of her napkin. "It's such a hard way to live. Yes, you're in charge. You have dominion, they say, over the animals. But the earth is against you. 'In the sweat of your brow you shall eat your bread.' Imagine a creation story that tells you the earth is your enemy. That your own mother is hostile to you. I've always felt sorry for people who were given this story."

"But Grandma, isn't this the story that destroyed us, or tried to?"

"It's certainly the story that's in charge," Annie heard herself say. "Still. I hate it."

Leona let the room fill up with silence. "Yes," she said at last. "It's hard not to. But I let hate take me down some dark roads for a long time. Too long."

Mattie looked down. She knows these stories, Annie thought. Mattie's father may not have been the only lost one.

"And if everything is connected, if we're all part of it, then all of us around this table are connected to that story too. Or to the people who believe that story. So maybe what we really feel is pity." Leona paused. "Even that day I knew I should feel pity for him. For Roy." Her eyes were filling again. "I do, now. I do. But it took me a while."

"That day?" Riley couldn't wait. His face reddened again as he focused on his coffee mug, encircling it with both hands, but the tips of Mattie's fingers brushed his knuckles.

"It happened the summer Jack was twelve. Lady had been gone for two days. Just disappeared. And he'd looked everywhere. He couldn't stop crying. That was part of what made Roy do what he did, I think. That dog was Jack's comfort, his soft place. He slept with her, he told her everything, the way kids do. He was grieving for her the way he would have grieved for his mother if he'd been old enough to understand when she died. So when the coyote came trotting along the fence line, Roy took down his rifle and held it out to Jack. 'That pack of coyotes lured her off and killed her.' Jack just looked at him. 'Do it,' he said. 'Be a man.' And then he stood over him— poor Jack was crying, couldn't hold still—until he pulled the trigger."

Riley looked as if he might be sick. Annie wanted to stand up and walk to him and hold him, but she made herself sit still. Did that make her like Roy? Honoring these customs of manhood, at such a cost? She felt Rose's head in her lap. Soft ears, warm. That strange bony crown.

"The coyote yelped and yelped—I heard it from up on the trail—and finally dragged itself off under the fence line. It's the worst thing that can happen to a hunter, wounding an animal and letting it get away to die slowly. Jack had already started after it, but he was sobbing. Like I said, it was that grief that got to Roy. Touched a place it hurt too much to touch. That's why he did it, I think now. Though like I said, it took me a while to get there."

Riley was looking at her, but this time he waited.

"He called out after Jack, 'Don't come home without the hide.' Jack stopped in his tracks. Just stopped. Like a big weight had fallen on him.

"But he didn't look back. He kept going.

"I had come to see Roy that day. We'd worked it out that way. I stayed away from Jack, like he wanted, but he and I needed each other, I guess you'd say. We both had the same hole in our lives. That day, though, he wouldn't even look at me. I was nothing but a drunk, he said. So I left. I left him standing in the yard. But I stopped halfway up the ravine and waited until finally I saw Jack coming along the trail beside the river. It was almost dark by then, but I could see he was covered with mud and blood. So was the rifle, and so was that mangled hide. He handed them both to Roy. Roy hadn't moved, just stood there like a tree in that one spot. Jack was still crying."

Leona closed her eyes and sat in silence for a long moment. No one moved.

"My sister's boy," she said at last. "The boy I'd promised to take care of. But Roy was right. I wasn't even doing right by my own boys."

"Anyway, three weeks later Lady met him at the school bus. Bone-thin, her fur matted, and her paws bleeding. The tie rope still knotted around her neck above the place she'd chewed through it to free herself."

Riley had laid his head down on his arms, his face hidden.

"They never did find out who took her. People steal dogs sometimes, working dogs like border collies. She may have been out by the road."

"Did she—was she all right?" Alex had glanced at Mattie.

"Yes, she lived another six years. Died in her sleep just before Jack left for college. It was as if Lady knew he couldn't leave her, and he needed to go."

⌁

"I never saw him cry. Not once." Riley hadn't spoken as he followed Mattie down the trail along the river. Now she dipped through the wide space between the barbed wires of the boundary fence; he was stepping on the lower wire and lifting the top one so forcefully she barely had to bend. "Dad was passionate. He cared about things. But he was always so—I don't know, positive." Mattie reached to hold the wires apart but Riley was already stepping over, holding the top wire down behind him with one hand. "He made me feel hopeful about things. You know. In the long run."

Mattie led the way to the fallen log and used her sleeve to brush away the snow. When Riley sat down beside her she took his hand and pulled it into her own jacket pocket. "That was a hard story for you to hear," she said.

Riley shrugged deeper into his quilted jacket. "Oh, there's more. Maybe your grandma doesn't know it, but a couple years later Roy—my granddad— deliberately left Dad out in the woods at night. With no food. Just a knife, and oh yeah, a jacket. And a note: "Find your own way home." Of course he'd gone out of his way to make sure Dad had no idea where he was."

He started to shiver, and Mattie took her hand out of her pocket and pulled his shoulder closer.

"Mom knew the story about shooting the coyote. I saw her look at me; she knew what was coming. But I'm not sure he'd told her everything about being left in the mountains. In his notes he keeps starting to write about it and then stopping, like he couldn't even face it himself." He shook his head. "What was it, last July? When your grandma showed us Mary's marker stone? That was my first hint that things hadn't always been so—perfect, you called us. Our family. Little did I know."

He heard the Toyota start up. Alex, checking on his mom. They heard the snow-muffled motor as the pickup turned the corner by the barn.

Then silence.

"I don't know how he did it," Riley said at last. "How did he get from that boy to the man who was such a good father? And teacher. He seemed so strong." Riley squeezed his eyes tight shut. "Maybe your grandma can be so forgiving because she doesn't know about Roy leaving Dad out in the woods."

Beyond the willows, a great blue heron lifted up from the center of the river, where the current had kept the channel free of ice. "Grandma did tell me about a deserted boy," Mattie said after a while. "It's one of the old stories."

Riley's breath was a white cloud in the air, mingling now with hers.

"The people go across the river to gather reeds, Grandma said, and when they go back home, they leave a boy on the other side. On purpose. 'He was considered bad,' the story says. But both of his grandmothers have secretly left him things. A small fire burning in a shell, five Indian potatoes, a short piece of hemp string. He makes a string net to catch magpies and uses their feathers to make a robe, and then catches fish and cooks them. It's a myth-story so everything happens in fives, and he grows to manhood in only five nights. The next time he fishes, he catches a bowl of roasted fish, which it turns out is a gift from the merman's beautiful daughter. It's like he's—chosen, I guess. Special. She also brings him a mountain sheep blanket, a beautiful tent, a never-ending supply of fish. The story says she has 'bracelets up to here.' And of course they marry."

A clump of snow fell from the cottonwood as kingfisher launched into flight and chirred upriver. Riley hadn't moved. "What about the people who abandoned him?"

"They're having a hard winter. Starving. In some people's versions of the story, the Nez Perce, I think, the grandmothers come back across the river to ask for help and he shares his food, first with those two and then with everyone. In other versions, he shares it only with the grandmothers, and calls up a Walla Walla wind, a cold wind from the east, so all the others capsize and drown."

"So." Riley turned to look at her. "It's either forgiveness or revenge. What Mom calls poetic justice. It has to be one or the other. Is that it?"

"I'm not sure. There's so much in that story. I don't understand it all." Mattie smiled. "But we can guess which version your dad would have chosen."

"Yeah." Riley stood up and shoved his hands into his jacket pockets, then kicked at the snow. "Yeah, we sure can." When his kicking uncovered a fallen branch he picked it up, lifted it above his head and drove it hard against the ground. Again, again, and again, until at last the branch hit a rock half-hidden under snow and broke. Mattie watched the shortened piece flying end over end toward the river. His back was still toward her when he spoke.

"I don't think I can be as good a man as Dad was. I mean, how do you forgive something like that? Your own *father*?"

"I don't know." Mattie's voice was so quiet it was almost a whisper.

Riley was by her side in an instant. "Oh, Jesus, I'm sorry. I'm such a— Mattie, I'm sorry. I'm so sorry." He was holding her, rigid as she was, against his chest. Finally her body softened and she leaned into his shoulder, the top of her head resting against his cheek. From somewhere downriver came the high, laughing music of coyotes. Neither of them moved.

"I don't deserve you." Riley's voice was husky.

Mattie didn't answer.

"Or any of this—good stuff that's happened. Since I came home." He closed his eyes. "The funny thing is, I used to think I was okay. It wasn't hard. You just did the best you could, and tried to treat people with—but my dad's father wasn't the one who led him out into the wilderness to die. *I* did that. No matter what Mom—and I try not to talk about it, I don't want to make her sick all over again, but—"

When Mattie pulled away and sat up to look at him, he looked down. Then he lowered his head and covered his face with his hands.

"Listen," Mattie said at last. "Are you listening?"

Riley nodded without looking up.

"Two things. One, you don't know everything about your dad's life. Most of it happened before you were even born. Sometimes we don't even know the right questions to ask. Maybe you'll find something in his notes that will help you understand."

Riley wiped his wet cheeks with the heels of both hands. "I know. I know that. I suppose that's why I'm so afraid to finish reading them."

When she didn't say anything, he looked up. Mattie had lifted her chin as if to check the sky over their heads.

"What's the other thing?"

"It's just—well, I'm starting to think you wouldn't recognize a merman's daughter if she were sitting right beside you."

18

It had begun as such an ordinary Saturday. Alex off to spend the long weekend with James and Ruby, Annie waving Gabe and Riley out the door without even thinking to ask when they'd be back. In time for dinner, of course. Or for a second dinner, even if the cab of Gabe's primered-out "Rez Ride" was overflowing with burger wrappers. All she'd been thinking about was the timing of Martin Luther King Jr.'s birthday: this early in winter term she wasn't rushing to catch up with student papers. *Yes, Jack, I am even more grateful to Dr. King for what he did.* She had smiled, remembering.

But now all she remembered was looking up from her book to realize that the fire had burned so low the embers were barely glowing and rushing to make sure she had a warm meal ready when the boys came through the door. Then the smell of baked macaroni and cheese dissipating as the crisp brown top cooled into sogginess. Finally, at 11:30, she called the hospital. No, a woman's voice told her. No one by either of those names had been admitted to the ER.

Rose's legs were twitching, and her muzzle wrinkled. *Where is he?* Annie whispered. *Tell me what you see.* But the dog's whine was small, cut off, smothered in sleep, like her own voice when she woke herself from a nightmare by trying to speak, sound mangled in her mouth.

It couldn't be as bad as last time. Unless she broke down and called the police.

Why didn't cell phones work in this canyon? She should have gotten him a cell phone. No matter how much it cost. Every kid had a cell phone now.

"Who would I call, Mom?" Riley had laughed. "My friends live in the canyon, too." Silly old bear, he had called her. Silly Mama Bear. Tousling her short hair as if she were the child and he the parent.

She wasn't even sure where they had been planning to go. "Just out," Riley had said. "Change of scenery."

What kind of mother has no idea where her child has gone? Annie envisioned blue-uniformed men exchanging a look before one of them scrawled the answer on his pad.

He could be freezing in a ditch. Trapped under Gabe's truck.

He could be dead.

It was nearly 3 a.m. when Rose's ears pricked forward. Annie kept the blanket wrapped around her as she stood up from the chair and stepped out onto the porch. "Shhhh!" she heard Riley say. "She's a light sleeper." Laughter. Then Gabe's voice, low and throaty, his words garbled, and the sound of a truck door closing, tires turning on gravel. Gabe's rig was pulling up onto the county road now, still without headlights. She heard the crunch of Riley's footsteps on old snow. At the bottom step he paused, then reached out to steady himself against the arbor post. The smell rose to meet her. Her mother's smell.

Was that what triggered her anger? Or was she was just another parent whose relief turned to fury the moment she knew her child was safe?

It was the coyote story that had gotten to him. When his dad was cutting up that coyote, pulling off its hide, blood everywhere—not to mention killing it *again*, having to shoot it again, seeing it suffer, thinking about it suffering—he'd have been seeing his own dog. He'd have been seeing Lady. Imagining her body, wherever it was. What was left of it.

Mattie had tried to comfort him—*had* comforted him, with her merman's daughter story. But he couldn't shake this vision, and the dreams he'd been having all week weren't the kind he could share even with Alex. He hadn't felt so alone since those first few weeks at McLaughlin.

But he and Gabe weren't looking for any trouble. They were just driving the gravel road up on top, the one paralleling the foothills, when Gabe pulled into a long rutted driveway. There was no house, just a travel trailer. With a window broken out, Riley could see as they got closer. No cars around.

"You know who lives here?"

Gabe didn't answer.

"Looks like they're not home."

Gabe slid out of the truck, keeping his back toward Riley. When he bent forward, hands on his knees, Riley got out too. "Hey. You okay?"

"Yeah. I guess." Gabe stood up straight. "Nobody lives here. It's a meth lab. It's where they cooked the stuff that turned Mouse's brain to permafrost."

"Jesus." Riley put his hand on Gabe's shoulder. "I didn't know." Mouse. Skinny, all ears and grin. He hadn't seen Mouse around for a long time. Not since he got back, for sure.

"We were tight. You know?"

Riley looked toward the trailer. "He was a lot of fun when we were kids." Mouse could stay underwater longer than anybody else. Come up shaking water from his hair, his face shining. Sometimes holding up a prize, piece of quartz or a spinner blade from a broken fishing lure.

Gabe packed an icy snowball and threw it hard against the trailer door. "Yeah, well, he's not much fun now."

"Who—?"

"White guys, Mexicans. Somebody from the rez." He kicked at the patchy snow. "Does it matter?" His leg swept sideways. There they were, half-hidden under snow. Rocks. Fist-sized rocks.

The first one went through the trailer's remaining window. They heard the sound of glass splintering, then silence. So much space. Nothing but sky, white fields with their rough whiskers of wheat stubble. Even the Blues were too far away to hear. When they stopped they were both panting.

But what had changed? Mouse is still damaged goods, Riley thought. And Dad's still out there somewhere. Yeah, and here we are, kids throwing rocks. He felt about six years old.

"Wait a minute." Gabe was rummaging behind his truck seat, his voice muffled. "Yeah, here we go." When he stood up again he was holding an M-80 in one hand and a yellow Bic lighter in the other. "All *right*. Duck and Dive!"

His throw through the broken window was hard and fast, a perfect strike, just like the ones he threw on the baseball field, and when the trailer lifted, walls exploding outward, metal twisting into wings above the ball of fire, splintered wood ribs rising, falling end over end, Riley felt the coil of fear and anger he had been carrying inside him all these months spring open like barbed-wire, sharp and dangerous. And free.

"Indian fireworks." Gabe was driving fast now, heading back down into the canyon, the rear end of his pickup sliding sideways on the corners. "The last-ditch weapon of the rez." He was smiling that hard white-toothed smile, his wet face smeared with dirt.

"Light my fire."

After that, the drinking part was easy.

⌁

"Do you have any *idea* how long I've been waiting?"

Riley turned toward her shape there in the shadow. "Mom? That you?" He took a step closer. That smell—beer and smoke. Campfire smoke. "You been waitin', huh? All day? A whole day? Yeah, you know, Mom? I got a pretty good idea how long a day feels when you're waiting."

Annie felt as if a bucket of icy water had been poured over her, hissing the embers of her anger cold.

"You couldn't even look at me, could you?"

"Oh, Riley, that's not—Riley, please."

"And you *still* can't admit it. *Can* you." Riley stepped closer, his breath a warm, yeasty cloud. "I tore up your letters. They tell you that?"

"Riley, it's okay, please, son."

"It was just too fucking weird." He slumped to the porch step. "My mother, writing me *letters* from across town. Can't look at me, so she writes me letters. That say fucking *nothing*." Annie sat down beside him. He was holding himself stiff. "What could they say? 'How are you, I am fine?' And you know what really gets me? It was all a lie. I see that now. We're just as screwed up as everybody else, but oh no, we don't admit it. We're the good guys. The Fallons. We're golden. 'Don't tolerate it,' he always said. 'If you tolerate prejudice, you're guilty of it too.' Well, I did what he taught me, didn't I? What you *both* taught me. And now he's dead." He held his head with both hands. "So, yeah, it's my fault. And nobody can even fucking admit *that*."

Annie tried to put her arm around his shoulders, but he pushed her away with such force that she fell sideways toward the edge of the porch steps, his body toppling too and landing against hers. She was trapped, tangled in the blanket, her left elbow and knee rising hard and fast against the smell of his breath, his wet coat. Riley kicked free of the blanket and struggled to his feet. Annie was on her hands and knees now, but her arms were boneless. Trembling. "You *knew* things, Mom," he said. His voice broke. Was he crying? "Like about that coyote. And Granddad. You knew him. I was just a little kid, but you—you must have known. How could you not know?" The words tore from him, ripped like shredded plastic in the wind. Annie staggered to her feet. "And Dad was *there*. It was his *life*, for fuck's sake!" There were snowflakes on his hair now, snow sifting through the arbor. In the dim light his face was a blurred ghost. "Why did we have to pretend we were such a perfect family?"

"Riley," she said, or tried to say. His name a prayer. But sound strangled in her throat, and his face was changing—he had Jack's eyes, Jack's mouth, but not like this, twisted in nightmare-anger. "You were fighting with him while I was in Juvie, weren't you? People talk, in those places. 'Look what you've made your folks do, kid.' Yeah, I heard all about it. So go ahead, Mom, blame me. Blame me all you want to. I know you do. But maybe it was *you* Dad didn't try hard enough to come home to. Hell, maybe he's in Mexico, you ever think of that?"

Annie felt as if a rock had hit her breastbone and gone deep beneath it. She pulled the blanket tighter, pressed her fists against her elbows to stop their shaking. Her teeth were chattering. Riley tipped his head back, staring upward. Then he lowered his chin to look directly at her. His voice more even now. "Maybe it wasn't me you couldn't look at. Ever wonder if your sickness was a cop-out, Mom? You couldn't face that it was your fault, too?"

Then he was gone, shutting the door behind him. Annie heard his footsteps on the stairs. When her legs gave way she sat down on the porch floor, hugging her knees to her chest. It hurt to breathe. She pulled the blanket over her head.

When at last she lifted the blanket, it was snowing hard. *Move,* she told herself.

Inside the house, she stoked the fire and added another chunk of tamarack. Even under the extra quilt it took her a long while to stop shivering. She shouldn't have let herself get so cold. She heard Riley throwing up into his wastebasket. After that the world was silent, snow-muffled. She lay without moving, eyes open to the darkness.

The roar came at her as if out of a dream, nearer and nearer until it hit the house with all its force and she heard trees breaking, the crack of brittle cottonwoods like gunshots. *Turn the damper down in a windstorm.* Yes, Jack, or Roy, whoever it was who had offered that wisdom. The last thing they needed was a chimney fire.

They. She and Riley. They were in this house together, no matter how he felt about her.

☙

By mid-morning the fence had disappeared beneath the snow, though in some places the earth was almost bare. It's as if a giant hand swirled through a child's sandbox, Annie thought. The driveway was impassible. And how would she ever get those fallen cottonwoods out of the road? At least it had stopped snowing. Out of habit, she flipped the light switch on the kitchen wall, but of course the power was out. Let the faucet drip, they had always reminded each other during cold snaps, but that was in Portland. Was that old smudge pot still in the pump house? "Don't let that pump freeze!" had been Roy's mantra, Jack had told her. No, snow days weren't something he looked forward to. She opened the cupboard doors beneath the sinks, refilled the woodbox, and stacked armload after armload of tamarack just outside the kitchen door. The river was already freezing over, but the ice near the bank was still thin enough to break. She should have filled the bathtub yesterday so they'd have water for washing, flushing—though if she had heard this storm forecast with Riley out there somewhere—

"You're using work like a drug, you know. So you don't have to face him." She had actually said that to Jack once when Roy was still alive, when Jack stayed in the upstairs bedroom for hours, claiming he'd lost track of time. ("You'd know about that, would you?")

Her lower back was aching but she had the driveway opened almost halfway to the barn when Riley took the shovel from her and turned away, bending over his own first deep scoop. "Is there another one somewhere?" she asked, but he didn't answer. Maybe he hadn't heard. This snow did seem to absorb all sounds. Take a break, she told herself. Warm up. Her fingers were stiff with cold.

He had thought to put a kettle on the woodstove. The water was lukewarm, not nearly hot enough for tea or chocolate. Still, it was something, wasn't it? She pressed her hands against the kettle's sides.

Power outages could last for days, Jack had told her, if enough trees are down. She opened a can of baked beans and set it on the stove beside the kettle. They had bread, and tuna. Two? No, three gallons of distilled water. Peanut butter.

Survival is hard sometimes. Leona hadn't been thinking about food, either.

⊸

Riley was up early the next morning—or rather, she had slept late. Slept, period. He had left a cereal bowl in the sink, so at least he was eating again. And he had the Toyota chained, ready to try pulling limbs out of the driveway. Choker-setter. That would be her role. Could they do that, a teamwork job if ever there was one? Shoveling snow with the heavy manure scoop from the barn hadn't left either of them much breath for conversation, but Riley might not have anything more to say to her. Once anger as deep as his gets out, Annie thought, it's hard to stuff it back inside.

Or maybe he was just embarrassed. And hung over.

Two days ago they could have joked, maybe even sung the lumberjack "whistle punk" song Jack had taught them.

"You have to play the long game, Annie," Dennis had insisted. "You can't give what you don't have." Trust the people at McLaughlin House, he said. Get well. Find a job, a place to bring him home to. But Dennis was her counselor, not Riley's.

She stepped out into the cold air and heard the snowplow. Bright running lights, a high white arc of snow thrown up from the big blade—and following it, yes, that was James's four-wheel-drive pickup, with Alex waving through the passenger-side window. They pulled into the driveway and James lifted his old Stihl chain saw from the truck bed. Annie could have cried with relief, but he just nodded. "That was some wind, wasn't it? We had to cut our way out, too."

By late afternoon the wood was stacked in white-barked rounds and the electricity had come back on. James accepted the coffee Annie brought him, warming his hands around the mug before he drank, but he wouldn't come in. What to feed the boys? When she pulled the untouched macaroni and cheese casserole from the refrigerator, she saw Alex glance at Riley—you left *this?*—and Riley look away. Tonight's homework session might take them a while.

If they got to it at all. She could hear their voices rising and falling even after she turned out her bedroom light. Somewhere beyond the river coyotes were talking too, a sound like human laughter, high and wild. She pulled the pillow up around her ears, but she could still hear them. She felt—hollow. A shell enclosing nothing but echoes of ancient tides, the hiss of dissipating waves. *Sorry sorry sorry sorry sor—*

"We're puzzle pieces," Jack had said once. Holding her body close against his, spooning her. "A couple of half-orphans filling in each other's empty spaces."

How could Riley have gotten the idea that they were perfect?

19

It was another one of Dad's lessons. I'd have to retrace my steps along the ridge and hope somebody would come along and give me a lift home. If anyone was out driving that back road we'd been on, whatever the hell road it was. Of course it would be dark before I reached it, and he hadn't given me a flashlight. That's what the jacket's for, I thought. A night out in the woods.

Touching a wound. Is this all she was doing? Annie had read these pages many times already. Maybe that's what she had been doing all along: not so much trying to understand what had happened as trying to bring him back. His voice. His breath, warm against her neck. Words, even if they were just words on paper—and not the polite, empty kind that she and Riley had been speaking. This morning: "Sure glad that cold snap's over."

"Me too. Good muffins, Mom."

"More coffee?"

"No, thanks. Have you seen my book bag?"

A responsible mother would have already talked to her son about the drinking, reminded him what a second offense could mean for him. Asked him what Alex's "Fourth of July in January? Sweet!" was all about, even if she didn't want to know. A good mother would encourage him to talk about his anger when he was sober.

But if she said the wrong thing—this is what that night had left her with, this fear so deep she was afraid to acknowledge it—she might lose him.

Even now.

I was a disappointment to him, Jack had written.

A rancher's son who couldn't take the branding and dehorning, the castrating or butchering, not even the weaning. Well, screw him. This was one test I was going to pass. How many nights had I sneaked out the window and climbed the trail up to the hideout? Lady had always been with me, so I knew I hadn't really been alone. But I was a heck of a lot more at home listening to the deer and owls than I was in my bed upstairs, directly over Dad's.

I wasn't scared. Just mad. Who the hell did he think he was? If I'd opened the packsack as soon as I got to the clearing instead of waiting for him—trusting him—I'd have been back on that dirt road, at least, before it got too dark. I was walking fast, thinking of all the names I'd never called him before but would from now on, to his face, by God. It didn't even occur to me that I might get turned around in the dark.

I'd always had a pretty good sense of direction. The school bus climbed the canyon from Thorn Hollow and topped out on the wheat fields; we could already see the grain elevator over by Adams. Or Dad and I followed the river down to Pendleton, and sometimes on to Umatilla and the Columbia. To Portland, if we drove far enough. If we headed upriver instead, the Umatilla split into its north and south forks, but both of them flowed out of the Blue Mountains east of us. I had hiked that nine-mile trail and looked out from Coyote Ridge across the valley all the way to Pahto, Mt. Adams, from up there. You could see Mt. Rainier, too, on a clear day. Sometimes on a school trip the bus climbed Cabbage Hill and drove east across the Blues to reach La Grande and Baker City, or went on through Ladd Canyon, all the way to Ontario and Boise. Walla Walla and Spokane lay north of us; John Day and Burns and that lonely, by-God-beautiful Malheur country were south. I knew where I was. Everybody did. But of course we were all just riding along.

Riley must wonder why I keep showing him how to find his way when we're out in the mountains. He knows exactly where he is. Always. It's as if he has a map in his mind. But even in buildings, parking lots, long corridors, I take conscious note now. Orient myself.

I don't think even Annie knows I do that. I've told her everything I can about that night, but our language doesn't have the right words. "A terror not to be described." That's pure hokum, I know. But it's as close as I can get in English.

Annie looked up. Something had flown past the window: dark wings, a flash of red and yellow. She laid the page face down on the stack.

Robins had been massing on the lawns in town, several dozen at a time; in fact, February had barely begun when she'd heard the first red-winged blackbird calling from the river. She and Jack had caught this bird's bright trilling song on a Sauvie Island trail in their first spring together, and he had turned to her and laughed. "Where's the smell? I've always associated that call with the smell of the barnyard in a February thaw." He shook his head. "Never thought I'd miss *that.*" There were farms on Sauvie Island, just across the bridge from Portland, but they grew mostly fruits and vegetables. Not many mucky barnyards.

"So what's it like?" she had asked him. "The smell?"

"Ripe. In a word. But full of hope."

A terror not to be described. How had he done it? Gone from the boy in these paragraphs to the man she had met, not—what, seven years later? Reading his notes and journal over and over wasn't bringing her any closer to the answer.

Maybe there was time for a walk before she had to get ready for class. Rose wagged her approval as Annie stood up from the desk.

Her feet left long tracks in the slush as she slid down the riverbank. Yes, there was the blackbird, shimmering in the bare-stemmed willows, a sheen of dark feathers and that wing-flash of color. She poked the toe of her boot at the thin rim of ice still clinging here at edges of the current. Winter wasn't over, no matter what promises the birds were busy making. And February usually brought wet snow this far upriver, Alex had said. March, too, some years.

Wasn't it strange. Here she was, living through the first year of these seasons so new to her, all the nuances of earth and air with which Jack was so familiar. Without him. Yet she had the feeling he was here too, lifting his head to listen to the redwing. Of course, that was because of the journal. Was she wise to keep reading it? Dennis might not think so. It was like reaching for him in bed at night the way she used to when he was having a nightmare, his cries muffled by sleep, it's okay, you're okay—and then remembering all over again.

Rose had gone sliding and splashing her way downstream, hoping to startle the mallards into flight. Night class, Annie told herself as she turned back toward the house. She still needed to prep.

And there he was. How could it be? But it was, it was Jack, Jack was sitting on the porch steps in his old blanket-lined Levi jacket and the Mariners cap, standing up now as he saw her, not Jack.

Not Jack.

It came like a wave through her body. She reached out for something to steady herself but felt her foot slip and then she was on her knees in the snow. He was striding toward her now, and now he was above her. Not Jack. Nothing like Jack.

"Had women fall for me before," she heard him say. "But not like this." The hand he offered her felt almost gentle, but his jacket had a strange, sweet-sour smell. One knee wasn't—wasn't right. "Steady there," he said.

"Who are you?" She had finally gotten both feet under her. Had her knee been torqued by the fall? Or maybe it had hit a sharp-edged chunk of basalt beneath the snow. But it was holding her upright.

"Friend of Jack's. We went to school together." The man took a step toward her and then stopped. "Lon Parsons. I just came by to see if there was anything you needed."

"Anything I—" Parsons, Lon Parsons. When had she heard Jack say that name?

This time when the knee gave way she didn't resist as he pulled her up, looping her left arm over his shoulder and gripping her waist tightly with his own right arm. *Roy would have crawled*, she told herself, though that had ended badly, and then *I shouldn't let him in the house, there's something's not quite right about him* but of course he was in as soon as she was, both of them out of breath.

"Thanks." She had reached for the back of the nearest kitchen chair. "You just came by, you said?"

"Yeah." He was looking slowly around the kitchen. "Looks like you got things pretty well under control here. I've been wondering, though, if come spring you might need some help. A man to help you run this place."

"I have a man. Two men. I'm sorry, Lon, this isn't a good time. I need to get ready for work."

"Thing is, neither of them boys can do for you what I can." Parsons's face seemed to be melting, dissolving in the winter light. *That's what it was, that's what she had been trying to remember. That woman in the teacher's lounge last fall: Watch out, Annie, there's a whole pack of them, they spend their days down at the Spur, sooner or later one of them will come sniffing around and they're bad news.* "I'm what they call an old hand," Parsons was saying. He had stepped into the living room and now he nodded at the full wood box beside the stove. "They're good boys, I can see that. Been a while, though, since you've had a man around. S'pose maybe you've forgotten."

Annie took a careful step backward. Then another. Rose was on the porch now, barking, clawing at the living room door. Barking, barking. "What the—?" Parsons had turned and started toward her, his hand outstretched as if to lead her somewhere, when he saw the ulu in her hand. "What in the hell is that?"

"It's a woman's knife. For cutting salmon. Lon, I need you to leave now. I told you, this isn't a good time."

He blinked, but then grinned, boyish. "Jack always said you were a feisty one."

"No he didn't. You weren't his friend."

"Annie. Girl." He hung his head and raised his eyes to her, disarming, the guilty boy caught stealing but confident in his ability to charm.

The curved blade was razor sharp, riding her knuckled fist like an attached scimitar. "If you don't walk out that door right now, I'm going to find out what else this knife will cut."

"Jesus *Christ.*" Still smiling, he spread his upraised palms. "Is this what you city girls call bein' neighborly?"

"Get out!"

His eyes flickered toward the kitchen door. Behind him Rose was still clawing at the other door, her bark half snarl now, and Parsons's face twisted into another kind of mask. "And just how the *fuck* am I supposed to do that? With that dog out there ready to eat my balls?" Annie let her eyes drop to his crotch. If he came at her she would push through his bleeding hands—the ulu would catch his hands and arms from any angle—push hard and fast into his centerline, strike from the belly down, split him to the—blood was pounding in her ears; she saw him flinch as she, too, heard the knock. Someone was pushing the kitchen door ajar. "Lon? You in here? Lon Parsons?" Through the crack of light she could see worn boots, Levis, a white-haired man wearing a gray Stetson. The door opened wider. Gus. It was Gus.

"Saw your truck there in the ditch, Lon, so we called Tribal. Make sure nobody was hurt. They'll be here in a few minutes." He looked at Annie, blinking in the dimmed kitchen light. "Audrey's in the car."

Parsons squinted at the old man. The dog had stopped barking.

"They'll help you get your rig out, I shouldn't wonder."

Now Parsons cocked his weight on one hip and hooked a thumb in his jeans pocket. "Guess I could use some help, at that." He touched the old man on the shoulder as Gus stepped aside to let him pass. "Thanks, Gus."

Then he was gone.

"He'll make tracks, I imagine," Gus said.

"Did you really call Tribal?" Annie's voice sounded strange in her own ears. Like a vibrating wire, thin and tight. *Tensile strength*. Could she have sliced him open like gutting a salmon? Watched him curl around his own intestines?

"We would have, if cell phones worked in this part of the canyon. Your dog was real upset. That man's no good, Annie." He looked at the ulu. "Looks like you were holding your own, though."

Annie laid the knife back on the counter. "He might have hurt you, Gus."

"Naw." Gus shook his head. "Guy like that leaves other men alone. Even old farts like me."

Annie reached for the chair back.

"Besides, he can always pretend I'm too damn dumb to know what he was up to." Gus was grinning now. "I don't think he'll bother you any more, and I doubt any of those other losers down at the Silver Spur will want to come around either, once he spreads the word about that fish knife."

"Good Lord, Angus McCrae, can't you see she's hurt?" Audrey pushed past Gus, then turned and handed him her cane. "Hold that. I've got my hands full here."

Gus winked over her shoulder. "Don't worry, Annie. She's a good horse doctor. Been doctorin' me for years, and I'm still hobblin' around."

"Mule doctor, in your case." Audrey balanced her weight on the table as she turned to shoo him back outside. "We'll need a little privacy now, Gus."

By the time they left two hours later, Annie was sitting in the soft chair nearest the fire. Gus had stoked it and added another chunk of tamarack. She was wearing a pair of Riley's old sweats, her foot propped on two pillows and her knee wrapped in an Ace bandage under the ice pack. "Looks to me like it's just a real bad bruise. If you stay off it for a few days you'll be right as rain," Audrey had promised. The crutches she had sent Gus home to retrieve fit perfectly. "I don't suppose anybody raises a family without ending up with at least one pair of these darned things."

"Not in this canyon, anyway," Gus had added.

They had stretched the coiled telephone cord to the end table so she could call the college to cancel her class; by Tuesday evening, Annie told the woman who answered, she should be able to drive. "Just rest," Audrey had cautioned. "We'll send Riley straight home if he stops by. You let those boys do for you, now. You hear?"

That fading rattle of loose gravel was their Buick pulling up onto the county road. In the silence Annie was aware of the ticking kitchen clock. The fire snapped and she felt her whole body jerk. Slowly, she told herself. Breathe slowly.

When she opened her eyes the coyote was framed by the living room window. He had been trotting down the fence line and now he turned to retrace his steps. He paused to lift his leg against a weathered post, looking back over his shoulder toward the house, and Annie remembered where she had first heard the name. Lon Parsons was the one who had written those words in Jack's yearbook, pressing on the ball point pen with such force that though Jack had scissored them out she could still read their indentations on the next page. RED MEAT!

"What did he mean?"

"I'd asked Emma Broncheau to homecoming that year. Not everybody in our class was as nice as I was, love. You got the cream of the crop."

Annie glanced at her hands. The heel of her right hand was scraped a bit, but she had stopped shaking. "I imagine there will be men wanting to meet you," Audrey had said as she was shortening the left leg of Riley's sweatpants. "They won't all be after this place, and they won't all be like Lon. You're still a young woman, and there'll be no shame in it, Annie, if you find someone."

"Someone like Jack, you mean?"

Audrey had looked sharply at her and then snorted, and then they were just two women laughing and crying at the same time. "I guess not," Audrey said at last, wiping the corners of her eyes with the kitchen towel she had brought to insulate the ice bag. "No, I guess not."

When Annie looked up again the coyote was gone.

⌁

Alex had re-wrapped her knee and banked the fire, and Riley brought the manuscript downstairs before he set her up for a second day of rest.

Crutches within reach, a pot of tea on the end table with her favorite blue mug. A sandwich wrapped in plastic. "Cookies? Where did these come from?"

"Must be his secret stash." Alex was pulling on his coat. "Audrey keeps him well-supplied, you know."

"Ah. Well, thank you, both of you. I feel like a queen, being waited on like this."

"A queen with a sore knee." Alex picked up his bag.

But Riley's voice was climbing to a pitch she hadn't heard since he was twelve. "Leona doesn't even have a *phone*. She won't know anything's *happened* until Mattie gets home!"

"I'll be fine. Don't worry."

"If he comes back—"

"He won't."

"Right." Riley shoved his fists into his Levi pockets.

She reached out as if to touch his forearm, but pulled her hand back and pointed at the phone and then at Rose. "I have a pretty good breastwork here. Besides, Audrey said she would let the Tribal Police know. For real this time. She and Gus will be keeping an eye on the place too, I'm sure."

"I wish we didn't have practice tonight." This time it was Alex.

"Please don't worry, boys. I'm sure he got the message." When they continued to stand there, she said, "If you two miss school and practice, then he's won."

"This isn't a game, Mom!"

"Not if we don't play it."

Alex's half-nod meant he understood. But Riley's face was reddening. "Really, son, I'm not afraid," she said.

"Well, good." Riley picked up his book bag and yanked the strap tighter against his shoulder. "That makes one of us."

The door shut behind them. Already Rose's head was in her lap. "Don't worry," Annie told her. "None of this is your fault." Should she have told them how she felt, holding that ulu? But she couldn't quite reconcile herself to it, much less help them understand all that she had suddenly known herself to be capable of.

By the time Rose lifted her head and she reached for the next page of Jack's manuscript, her hand was nearly steady.

Pre-history, Mr. Turner called it. Whatever happened before it could be recorded and become "history." History was the written word. Oral history? No such thing. "Those are just stories."

The oral languages had been burned out of children's mouths with lye soap or torn from lips pressed hard against freezing copper pipes, or beaten out of them with straps and rubber hoses. Words like Emma's grandfather's name, a word that she told me meant not just "Grizzly" but "Grizzly swinging his head from side to side, looking back over his shoulder as he walks."

No wonder the first Inuit man Frobisher took captive bit his tongue in two.

Naming. Or rather, renaming. N'chi-wana has become the Columbia, the river of Columbus, even though it was more than three thousand miles away from where he landed. The very name is a lie. The lie that led to the search for the—not a, but the—Northwest Passage. The straight route toward those spices of Asia. All those searchers looking for the wrong thing, missing what lay before their eyes.

They had maps. Travelogues and guides written by people who had never seen these places, lies put in print and passed from book to book. People of the Book. That's us, all right.

Ever since Columbus and his journal.

That's what I've been doing, too. Writing books. Fitting what I saw and heard into the shape of what I've always called "the real story." I was so sure I knew what the real story was, and until Leona handed me that tablet—the letter Dad wrote to Mom after she'd died—I didn't even know the story of my own parents.

I still don't, really. How did Mom come to know the Native way of looking at the world, the one Dad said had brought him back to life and then taken her life away from him? And brought him back from what? Korea, I suppose, but what happened to him in that war? Why did he blame the Native view of things for Mom's heart failure?

And Leona. Where has she been all these years? When I heard her voice so much came back to me. I remembered her sitting on the porch steps with my mother, drinking lemonade, both of them laughing. She taught me to skip rocks across the water, I remember now. And showed me how to hold a blade of grass between my thumbs to make it squawk when I blew on it. Auntie Ona. Why did she disappear? And then come back this summer to hand me Dad's letter as if she knew I couldn't write "local history" without it.

But I can't seem to write a local history with it, either. I know too little, and too much. I know what I saw in that canyon, and what I heard. But where are the words for that? I'll look up Leona before we go back to Portland, take Annie to meet her. She can tell us things we need to know, I'm pretty sure. But she can't help me understand that night in the canyon. No one could who wasn't there.

I keep thinking about Cecil. Cecil Frank. He'd learned to read just like the rest of us, but when we got to high school he refused to open a book. "Why?" I asked him once. We were sitting with our backs against the wall outside Mr. Soderling's classroom. Both of us had been sent into the hallway. Me for reading in class, a paperback hidden behind the textbook. And Cecil, of course, for not reading.

He stood up and turned the handle on the drinking fountain and looked at me for a minute, and then he put his hand in the stream of water and held it there. "There's nothin' between me and this," he said.

Is that why Dad tried to burn his letter? I wonder. A white nightgown? A song he heard her sing one early morning? All he had was words, and words left murky shadows between him and the clear water that was her.

Rose lifted her head and then pushed herself up, her ears pricked. A minute passed, and then another, before Annie heard the soft knock and then the sound of the door opening and the dog's tail thumping the kitchen floor. She reached down for the crutches but forced herself to wait until Leona came into the room.

"I got here as quick as I could," Leona said.

"How did you know I fell?"

"I don't know. I just did. But not till this morning. Not in time to help." Leona picked up the empty teapot and carried it back into the kitchen. When she came back she was still frowning. "Now Annie, you've got to tell me. Are you okay? Are you all right?"

Annie took the cup of fresh, hot tea Leona was holding out. "I think so. Audrey says if I stay off it—"

"Not your knee. The other thing."

"That business with Lon Parsons?"

"That's who it was?" Leona's face darkened. She walked to the window and looked out toward the county road, her fingertips resting on the wooden frame as if for balance. Rose had already settled into sleep. Even the fire was silent.

"Jack didn't like him. I remembered that."

But Leona didn't speak, or turn around. She's waiting for an answer, Annie thought. Am I okay? Yes, of course. Of course. I must be.

But she wasn't. That sound, something between a choking gargle and a groan. It was coming from *her*. And now she was shivering, not just her hands but her whole body was trembling, and Leona was standing behind the chair with both hands on her temples, singing. Strange, rising tones, this song in a language Annie didn't understand, though maybe Leona wasn't singing words at all but syllables, just sounds, yes, sounds swelling into the shape of human palms, their warmth seeping now into her neck and shoulders, softening her back, until she felt her body slipping gently into this current and then, for the first time since the man who wasn't Jack had stood up from those porch steps, she was asleep.

When she woke the room was lit only by the woodstove's glow and the shaft of light coming from the kitchen, where the boys were quietly making supper. Even in the darkness she could make out a shape she knew was Leona, who must have been here all this time. And that was Mattie by her side.

20

"Yeah, that boy of yours has been a real help." Gus winked as he scooped two more spoonfuls of sugar into his coffee while Audrey's back was turned toward the kitchen counter. "My hands have got so crippled up, some days I can't hardly lift a pitchfork."

"He talks like he's still feeding livestock." Audrey offered them both a plate of oatmeal cookies. "All we've got left, really, are the pets. He can't bring himself to send Polly and Babe to the slaughterhouse, and I'm a bigger softie than he is. Even so, we've needed help for a long time and that's a fact." She laid her cane on the floor and settled into a kitchen chair across from Gus. "Don't you think you're fooling anybody. You old sweet tooth."

Gus grinned and reached for a second cookie. "Truth is, Annie, sometimes we just make up excuses to keep Riley around. Audrey here had him sorting garden seeds the other night."

"Well." Audrey lifted her chin. "You wouldn't know, but someone has to count the early planters, radishes and lettuces, see if we still have enough peas. It *was* a help. I was busy cooking, as usual." But then she shook her head and laughed. "Besides, I thought you were too busy in there sleeping off the news to notice." To Annie she said, "It's like turning back the clock. He's so much like Jack when he was a boy."

Annie sipped her coffee. What was Riley like when he wasn't with her? "Was Jack—happy?" she asked. "When he was a boy?"

"Happy?" Gus threw back his head and laughed. "What was it you used to call him, honey? Irrepressible?"

"He was like his mother, that's all. He had her spirit."

"*Full* of questions. I never knew a kid so full of questions."

"But did he—" Annie stopped in mid-sentence as she accepted another cookie from the plate Audrey was offering. "I'll bet he liked these."

"Oh, yeah. I used to tease her that's what he came for."

"He came, as you know full well, for some mothering." Audrey reached for her cane. Making her way back across the kitchen with the coffeepot, she added, "That's what Roy sent him here for, too. No matter what excuse he used."

"Well, he knew what he was doing, then. You were an awful good mama to our girls."

"They were grown and gone by the time Jack was old enough to need someone to play with," Audrey told Annie. "That boy was so lonesome. I always thought it was sad, him not having any playmates." She blew hard on her coffee.

"Hot it up and then cool it down," Gus teased.

Children had come out of the woodwork to play with Riley, Annie thought. And the previous generation of those same families had been living there when Jack was growing up. Surely there would have been children roughly his age? "Didn't the Indian kids—"

Gus and Audrey exchanged a look. No children had come to the swimming hole, Annie realized, until Roy was gone, but that had been the summer Riley was old enough for playmates, and she had thought that was the reason.

"I wish Riley had been able to spend more time with Roy," she heard herself saying. "He was—well, Roy was just so tickled with him."

"That baby was all he could talk about." Audrey sipped her coffee. "He just lived for those summers."

Gus pushed back from the table, then hunched forward and leaned on his forearms. "Annie, do you remember when we called to tell Jack about his dad's heart trouble?"

She nodded.

"Well, we might've stretched the truth a little. Her idea, but I went along with it. Roy was having trouble, all right, but not the kind the doctors can fix.

"I told Gus, it was no lie to say his heart was failing."

Gus sat up again and brushed cookie crumbs into his palm. "She said, 'He thinks he's never gonna see that boy again.' I told her, well, he may not. They do grow up, you know." He grinned. "That's when she reached for the old rollin' pin."

But Audrey wasn't smiling. "He was dying of grief, Annie. It hurt to watch him." She looked at Gus. "We didn't blame Jack for staying away. But we both thought—we *both* thought the two of them deserved another chance."

Was that it, then? That was what had drawn her to Roy that first summer? But she hadn't sensed grief, really. And besides, there was everything she was finding in Jack's journal, whatever horrors he had experienced that night out in the woods, and why in the world Roy or any father would have— too much, there was too much to take in. But they were waiting, these two old people who had known Roy before he went to war. And afterward. The friends who had kept him going when his parents died.

"There's just so much to try to understand," she heard herself saying. "There's an awful lot of Jack's story I'm just learning about. I thought I knew everything about him, but—"

Audrey reached behind her for the Kleenex box. Gus stared into his coffee cup while Annie blew her nose. At least she had only teared up. It hadn't swept her away.

"I'm grateful you called Jack. So grateful. I can't tell you." Annie wiped her eyes and tried to smile. "And that you came by when you did the other day. That's why I came over today, to tell you that, and here I've been so busy with these cookies I almost forgot."

"I'm glad we came along just then, too," Gus said. "But you'd have handled him all on your own, Annie. You're a strong one."

"You've done a wonderful job with that boy of yours." Audrey patted Annie's arm.

This time Annie held the lump in her throat until it had dissolved enough to let her speak. "You know I wasn't able to be there for him."

"Oh well." Audrey picked up her cane again. "You'd had a shock. Besides, every parent falls short sometimes. It's a job, all right, raising kids."

Annie gripped her coffee mug with both hands to steady herself.

"The trouble is," Audrey said from across the kitchen, "we're just as human as they are."

"And then sometimes," Gus said, "the harder you try the worse you do. We've all been there."

"Like poor old Roy." Audrey was refilling their cups now. "I'll never forget him sitting at this kitchen table that day. 'I've lost him,' he kept saying. 'I've lost him.'"

"When he left Jack in the mountains, you mean?"

"Afterwards, yeah." Gus looked at Annie. "I think all that had something to do with Korea. Well, I know it did. Somehow or other Roy'd had to find his way back to his outfit, and he wanted to make sure Jack knew he could do something like that, too. So his boy wouldn't have to be as scared as he'd been." Gus shook his head. "But of course it didn't work out the way he'd planned."

Audrey lowered herself into the chair again. "That war hit Roy awful hard. Half the boys in our class had to go. Gus was 4-F, thank God."

"Flat feet. Yeah, I was lucky."

"And does anybody nowadays remember why we were there?" Audrey raised her palms.

"I'm not sure we knew why even then," Gus said. "They just said go, and if you passed your physical, you went."

⟽⟾

Annie was grading papers at the kitchen table when she heard Leona's pickup door. Maybe the snow had muffled the sound of her motor; they had awakened to four inches of fresh snowfall. Well, it wasn't even quite March, she had told herself—though of course the ornamental plum trees would be blooming in Portland by now, maybe even the first daffodils.

Outside the kitchen door, Leona was brushing snow from her boots with the old broom.

Annie stretched her arms above her head, then out in front of her. Teaching was hard on the back.

"Ready?" Leona stood just inside the kitchen with one hand still on the doorknob.

"Ready for what?" Had she forgotten something?

"Spring." Leona laughed. "I know, I know. It was awful cold up on the mountain Friday, too. Wind and hail, even a little snow. But they were there. Our little sisters, the longhouse people call them."

Annie looked at her, baffled. "What am I missing here, Leona?"

"The celery feast, if you don't put your coat on and get in the truck. Are the boys upstairs?"

"Celery?"

"You'll see." Leona let go of the doorknob and wiped her boots once more on the small rug before she walked to the stairwell and looked up. "Alex? Riley? Pocket-boy?"

Annie stood up. "I guess my brain isn't in gear, Leona. They're not here. Gabe came by this morning, and when they went out the door they were still debating whether to check out the 2-A tournament in Pendleton or go play in the snow, see how far they could make it up the Lick Creek trail."

Leona laughed. "Come on then. We'll leave them a note."

Annie looked at the stack of essays.

"It's time," Leona said.

Time to go? Well, yes, Annie thought as she pulled on her coat. But Leona probably meant more than that. Jack had explained that Native cultures recognized another kind of time. Not clock time, but appropriate time. People gathered, he said, when the time was right to do whatever was necessary that day, or in that season. Now was the time to give thanks for the first food of spring: celery, whatever Leona meant by that word. It wouldn't be the kind of celery sold in supermarkets, she knew that. After this ceremony, as after all the first food feasts, people would be free to gather as much as they needed. She and Jack had gone to a root feast once, at Rock Creek. That was a few weeks later in the season than this one. And another time they had driven upriver for the salmon feast at Celilo. Celery, though, was new to her.

"It tastes like spring," Leona said. The pickup slid a little on the corner but straightened back into the tracks. "Smell the river?" Annie rolled down her window. Cold air, the sound of blackbirds. And yes, the water smell.

"This snow is different, too." Leona smiled.

"It is?"

"Yes. It's softer. Full of water. I think it's saying good-bye to the earth. Till next year, you know."

"I hope so," Annie said. She rolled the window back up and held both hands over the heater vent.

Leona laughed. "See? You're ready. Me, too. We all need a taste of spring."

"Were you up on the mountain?" Annie tried to picture Leona with the other women dressed in what they called their "work wings," with black rubber boots pulled over her moccasins and a cornhusk bag hanging from her waist.

"No. But Mattie's helping today in the kitchen. She'll be one of the servers."

At the longhouse people were already finding places at the tables pushed end to end and set with thin white paper plates. The cups at each place held only a small amount of water. Water, the bearer and sustainer of all life, Annie remembered. *Don't worry*, Jack had said. *They'll show us what to do.* Across the table a toddler rose to his knees on the folding chair and reached toward the paper cup. His mother touched his wrist. "Not yet." He looked at her.

Was the room warmer? Annie felt as if her cheeks were flushing. She lowered her head the way some of the others were doing. Praying, or just clearing their minds? All around her, greetings, murmurs of laughter, babies passed to waiting hands, babies on laps. "I'm ready to feast!" someone said. When the song began they all pushed back their chairs and stood. Should she be waving her hand too, or would that be presumptuous, disrespectful? The spirit of this morning's Washat service filled the longhouse, and the drummers were singing their prayer for all the earth. But this religion wasn't hers to take.

"Chu'ush." Water. A kind of communion, Annie had always thought of it. Without the blood. She knew not to swallow all the water in her cup, to save a little for the end of the ceremony.

The servers were coming, young men in moccasins and ribbon shirts circling the rectangle of earth in the center of the longhouse to leave a small taste of salmon on each plate, circling again with roasted deer meat. Then came the girls in wing dresses, women with shell earrings and braids wrapped in otter fur. Mattie, looking straight ahead. They brought bitterroot, cous—and celery: soft peeled green stalks of early lomatium. Finally the berries, chokecherries and huckleberries.

Was there a signal she had missed? Annie quickly joined the others, lifting the small portions to her mouth. These first foods were sacred, Jack had said.

And then the feast. Platters of roasted salmon being set down at spaced intervals, platters of deer meat. Bowls of huckleberries and chokecherries, roots, passed up and down the table; and plates of fry bread, salads, a huckleberry pie. Leona smiled and pointed with her lips: look who's sitting on your other side. Makayla. Yes, and Cecelia, and Virgil. Was that Leann, beyond his shoulders?

"Do you like the celery?"

"It's good. Leona told me it tastes like spring."

"You gonna teach us again next summer?"

"I'd like to," Annie said. "If there's a job for me."

Makayla turned back to her friends without saying anything more. *Give us another story, Teacher.* Annie reached for the cup of red Kool-aid. Anything to help her swallow. The kids were laughing at something, their conversation lost in the blur of voices all around her.

A few people were still helping themselves to seconds when a woman came by to hand out ziplock bags.

"Take something home. Whatever you need," the man across the table told Annie. "We don't leave anything."

Leona filled two bags with chunks of roasted deer meat and handed one to Annie. "Those boys will come home hungry."

Finally they rose as one and turned to face the end of the longhouse, where a carved eagle rested below the high window at the roof's peak, for the last song and prayer. "Aiiii." Annie heard soft falling voices all around her, but she was watching the four young people as they turned in complete circles, their hands raised just above their heads. It was over. Cecelia disappeared for a moment as she struggled into an oversized hooded sweatshirt, but none of the others had jackets. Now they were making their way toward the outside door, each of them briefly touching her hand as they passed. It was Leann who told her, in a voice so soft it took Annie a moment to realize the girl had spoken, "Everybody misses you."

"There, you see?" Leona shifted the old Ford into second gear as she pulled out onto the Mission Highway.

"See what?" Annie was looking out the passenger-side window. Were those bare red stems red willow, she wondered, or dogbane? Jack had told her a Nez Perce story about a young man who follows the girl he loves on her vision quest and kills her—who knows why?—but even though he threw his bloody arrow shaft into a clump of willows, and mourned loudly and publicly, the bright red willow stems proclaimed his guilt. They still do, she thought. And they will, forever.

Time immemorial, Native people said when they were speaking of a past so distant it lay beyond memory. Someone had used those words today, one of the speakers in the longhouse. Time immemorial. Time out of mind.

From the beginning, in the hospital, it had seemed almost instinctive to count the days, and then the weeks and months Jack had been gone. But that too was a way of looking backward, wasn't it? Like flipping through the pages of last year's calendar. Did the longhouse people have a word for a future stretching forward, as distant as any ancient past? That infinite emptiness?

"Why it's important." Leona glanced in the rearview mirror, then concentrated once more on the highway.

Do I see why it's important? Annie too looked at the road ahead. Focus, she told herself. "The feast, you mean."

"Yes. The celery feast."

"It was lovely," Annie said. And then, "It's important to say thank you, right? To keep that relationship of—gratitude, I guess. That relationship with the earth."

"Ah, you sound like Jack." Leona turned to smile at Annie now. "Very professional. No, what's the word? Professorial."

But her head was too full. Seeing them again, Makayla, and Virgil, no Sammy—Cecelia, and Leann, the songs, the drums. The taste of spring, yes, and then this aftertaste. What did Leona want from her? What did she have to give? Was there something she hadn't salvaged? Something she hadn't uncovered, dug up? Something she could give back, give away?

"It's not my ritual," she heard herself saying. "I wish it were, you don't know—sometimes I feel as if I don't belong here. Or anywhere, on the same earth where he—"

Then the truck was stopped on the shoulder of the road and Leona had pulled Annie into the circle of her arms. "Girl, girl," Annie heard her murmuring, though these sobs were so deep they might have muffled every other sound.

"I'm sorry," she said when she had finally caught her breath. "I think I'm past it, and then out of nowhere . . . I don't know how to let it go. And now Riley—"

She stopped. She hadn't told Leona about Riley.

They sat for a while without talking.

"Grief is always with us," Leona said at last. "That's why we sing Washat, you know." She closed her eyes. "There's an old story. Real old. I'm trying to remember, my father told me. Yes, it happened at Priest Rapids, what we call Priest Rapids today, before the coming of human beings. In the time of the ancient people. They were happy there. Life was good. But when their leader died, those ancient ones forgot everything but grief. They mourned and mourned, they did nothing but mourn. They forgot to sing the songs that brought them food. After a long time the sun went away, and there they were, in total darkness. Damp, and cold. They were starving. Dying. Some of them wandered away and got lost. Finally one young man who could see into the future remembered, and he started to sing the song of thanks. And then, little by little the others joined in, the words came back to them. And the sun, too. It only came for half of every day now, and there would be winter as well as summer now, but that spring the salmon swam up the river again."

Leona pulled Annie's head onto her shoulder. After a while she said, "I don't think we're not supposed to grieve. We just have to make some room for spring, too. For life, you know. Joy."

"At the same time?"

"Oh, yes, Annie. Yes." Leona was stroking Annie's hair now. "It has to be that way. Otherwise, what's love about?"

They were nearly home when it struck her. No wonder, she thought. Of course Leona understands. Grief in one hand, joy in the other: all Native people have to live this way. Whatever it meant in time immemorial, that's what it means to be Indian now.

Then she thought, no. That's what it means to be alive, for all of us. To survive. Not every Indian did, any more than every non-Indian.

The boys had left their boots on the back step and she nearly tripped over the pile of wet jeans and sweatshirts inside the kitchen door. They could hear water running in the bathroom, a room Roy had added years ago just off the pantry, close to the kitchen plumbing. The murmur of low voices.

"They might have gone looking for snow, but they found something even more slippery." Leona lifted a mud-crusted sock with the toe of her shoe.

"Why are you whispering?"

Leona grinned. "That was a good feast, all right," she said loudly. "I couldn't eat another bite. Could you?" Now she was banging pots above the stove. "Mattie, would you mind making us some coffee?"

Silence from the bathroom. Leona motioned Annie into a kitchen chair.

"Mom?"

Leona banged the pots again.

"Mom? You there?"

"Hi, son. Did you find my note?"

"Could you bring us some clothes?"

Leona was giggling. "I thought so. They've got themselves caught in a trap."

"Sure," Annie called. "Sweats okay? Or maybe you'd rather have your—"

"Anything!"

Leona was still grinning when Annie came back downstairs with an armful of boys' jeans and T-shirts, socks and underwear on top of the stack.

"Okay, they're just outside the door."

Alex's long arm reached out from a narrow opening.

They came out looking scrubbed and fresh as—as little boys, Annie thought. Both of them had that sweet flushed look. "Where is she?" Riley was looking from Leona to Annie, then back to Leona, who twisted in her chair to look back over her shoulder as if she too expected to see her granddaughter.

"Oh, that's right! She stayed at the longhouse, didn't she, Annie? To help clean up the kitchen."

"You mean—"

Annie watched his face slip from disappointment to the first flush of embarrassment. "Riley, I—"

"You what?" His cheeks were bright now.

"Guess I'm just getting old," Leona said. "Forgetful."

Riley looked at Alex. Annie couldn't see his face now. Her heart was pounding. She should have told Leona. But Riley threw back his head and laughed. "Are you *sure* this woman is a good influence on you, Mom? Alex, help me out here. Think we should let these two have any more play dates?"

It took Annie a moment before she realized she and her son had crossed a boundary, and even longer before she thought, Fun. My God, we're having fun.

21

Classroom after classroom, Jack had written in his next journal entry.

I've said it over and over again, framing it from every angle I could think of. It's all connected: Marcus Whitman, Ira Hayes, the Vietnam War. Beethoven. Geology. The wind. That's what history's about, I tell my students. We're swimming in it, all the time: What happened? Why? And what might therefore happen next?

Everything touches everything else, I tell them. That's why history matters.

Imagine a spider's web, all those delicate vibrations, a web the size of the universe. But no one's large enough to take it in. So narrow the focus. Northwest. Narrow it again. The place where you grew up. Where you live now. This building, the earth it stands on. This room. Then I watch their faces open. This is what my life's about, I think. Speaking this truth as clearly as I can. Helping them see.

And yet I couldn't see the story I'd been living all my life.

"I miss having a boy," he told me after he threw Riley out into the river and I confronted him behind the barn. "You left me a long time ago." I thought he was justifying the way he'd treated Riley, and it made me furious. But afterward, sitting beside Annie on the couch, I realized he was talking about the day I dug the grave. Well, he was right. I did leave him that day. "Find your own way home"? By God, I would, and I told him as much.

But oh, I was justified. I was fighting for truth. The deeper story.

"It might help to know why," Leona said. I thought I did know why. I've been telling people why, for twenty years.

What helps is Annie. Walking beside her, sitting across the table from her, holding her. Would I do any better than he did if I lost her? Or Riley? My God, how does anyone bear losing a child?

She's sitting on the porch steps, reading. Waiting for me to come down. I think she knows I've been teetering all summer, and she's what's kept me from falling.

↭

Somehow it was the good times that were hardest. Moments like this one wore their beauty like a shadow, a poignancy that seemed almost unbearable. Even now Annie found herself blinking away tears of what she once would have described as joy.

Alex seemed to have his own cheering section. Ruby and James were here, and their brothers, Big Al and Petey B. Annie and Riley, Mattie and Leona. Another woman Annie didn't know was sitting close to Big Al. Children, at least a dozen. Cousins? Maybe, because Marissa was with them, and little Jesse. Cecil was playing, too, though he was on the other team, and Gabe. And here came Dawn with a group of girls she didn't recognize. They climbed to the top row of the bleachers. "That's Riley's mom," she heard one of them say. Nearly in front of her now, Alex stole the ball and drove hard down the court. "Alex! Alex!" shouted Ruby, pumping her fist in the air. A group of deep-voiced young men a few rows above her stomped their approval. Annie turned to look. Yes, they were the same ones who had welcomed Riley that day at the Mission Market. The bleachers rattled.

"Why aren't you out there?" Ruby elbowed Riley's ribs just hard enough to make him jump. "Makin' him do it by himself this time, eh?" Her voice was a little too loud, but then, the gym was awfully noisy.

Riley grinned. "He seems to be doing all right without me. But hey, thanks."

Smiling, Ruby turned back to the game. Trust Riley to get it right, Annie thought. At his age, or even now, she might have thought Ruby was reminding him that he was an outsider rather than reassuring him that he belonged. Mattie was smiling too.

Belonging. From the time they're born, these children are part of the community, Annie had often thought, watching their small faces at a powwow or a basketball game. And cherished as such. Treasured. Passed from lap to lap, beamed at, blessed.

She knew this wasn't entirely true, though, no matter how many times she had witnessed it. Or—well, no, it was true, but so were the statistics that filled the tribal newspaper: truants, dropouts, alcohol abuse. Children battered, their mothers bruised and broken. Incest, rape. Those suicides. "I don't get it, Jack," she had said once. "They try so hard." This spring break B.A.A.D. tournament was typical, really. Basketball Against Alcohol and Drugs.

"It will take a while, Annie," Jack had said. "A long time. The boarding schools are gone, but the effects of all that trauma are still being passed on to the next generation. And the boarding schools weren't even the worst of it."

She knew what he meant. A way of life, a good life, had been lost in a generation. Sometimes overnight. At the time, though, could she really imagine such a thing? Waking up with half of your world dead? Maybe that's what Leona had meant that first afternoon, nearly a year ago now, when she had sat stirring sugar into her coffee at the kitchen table: "I brought you fry bread because now you can understand." No matter how sympathetic she had been before—the swiftness of their little family's loss was the same, and the unimagined scope of it. A good life, gone. In a matter of days. A month, less than a month. Nothing they could have seen coming.

Was it wrong, to think this way? Appropriation of another's grief to help her bear her own? Or were they really all in this together?

Alex was driving to the hoop again, but Cecil stole the ball and rifled it down court to Gabe, whose lay-up crashed through the netting like a fist. Behind her, the young men were stomping again, this time for Gabe and Cecil. Alex stuck out his lower lip and held up two fingers, then shook his head and made it three. Even Ruby was laughing.

Riley and Mattie had linked arms, their hands in each other's jacket pockets. They were cheering Alex on, those two, but only when they remembered to watch the game.

⬧

Alex had pushed the seat back as far as it would go. Riley and Mattie would be coming later with Leona, so at least he could turn sideways to make room for his legs.

"Last summer you still fit in this truck," Annie said.

"Been feeding me too well, I guess." He crumpled the burrito wrapper into a ball and opened his orange juice. "You see that guy from Kamiah? Raymond White Owl? He's a foot taller than he was last year. Six inches, anyway. And he can jump, on top of everything else." He tipped the plastic bottle up and drained it in what looked like one continuous swallow. "He's gonna stuff it down my throat tomorrow."

"Do you care?"

Alex recoiled in mock horror. "Why, ma'am. Of course I *care*. I'm a role model, you know, ma'am, whether I like it or not. I play with a ball stuck in my esophagus and every kid in Mission will be wanting one."

"Let's hope they start with tennis balls," Annie said. "Work up to the bigger stuff."

They were nearly home, and singing at the top of their lungs—the Black Lodge Singers kids' powwow songs the boys had loved—when they saw the black Ford pickup on the side of the road.

"Suppose they need help?"

"He needs help all right. Pull in behind him, Annie. Keep the motor running. And stay in the truck."

The driver lowered his window and turned his face toward Alex. Lon. It was Lon. And this must be where he left his pickup the other time, too. Farther off the road to make it look stuck, but—

Alex had leaned closer to the driver and put his right hand on the top of the truck door. To hold it shut? Lon was looking straight ahead now.

"Alex!" Annie called. But the word came out like a whisper.

Then Alex took a quick step backward. Had Lon threatened him? Annie was out of the Toyota and at his side, though she couldn't remember getting there. "Leave him alone, Lon. Leave us alone. You hear me? *Leave*. And leave my family alone."

"I've just been sitting here waiting. I didn't come onto your place, Annie. But I wanted to tell you I'm sorry."

Was he drunk? Annie didn't think so. But something wasn't right.

"I know I came on strong." He ducked his head, then looked up at her. "I really was a friend of Jack's, you know."

"No you weren't."

"Yeah, I was. For a while, in third grade. He was the only one who'd talk to me after my mother left."

He looked down again, though out of the corner of his eye he was watching for a reaction from her.

"I guess I'll have to get a restraining order," she said.

"No need." He squinted, hardening his face as if he'd been about to cry. "Plenty of fish in the sea, as they say. You're not such a prize, anyway."

Alex made a noise—half gasp, half moan, Annie would think later that night as she lay waiting for the escape of sleep—and took a step forward, but Lon raised his hand as if to say enough. Okay. Enough. He started the motor and said something else over his shoulder as he pulled away, but the only word she caught was 'Jack.'

Rose was waiting by the gate, her ears pricked. "You weren't about to let him in, were you, girl?" Annie hid her face in the dog's neck fur for a long minute, though Alex was still holding the gate, waiting for her to get back in the truck and drive through.

"Okay, Rose. Hop in. You can ride down to the house with us."

Rose leaped into the cab and sat between them, but she didn't want to come into the house. She's out there watching from the front porch, Annie thought as she pushed the button on the coffee grinder. She had already set the mixing bowl on the counter when she heard Alex coming back downstairs. He still hadn't said a word.

"I needed chocolate," she said.

"*Oh* yeah." He slumped into a chair, then stood up again. "I guess it's not too warm to build a fire?"

"That would feel good."

She heard him crumpling a newspaper, and then the quick crackle of kindling. The mixer would keep her from hearing the sound of the damper, but he would remember to close it. By the time he came back into the kitchen, she was tipping the dark batter into the pan.

"Twenty minutes."

"Good."

She sat down across the table from him.

"Coffee smells good," he said.

"I guess it would taste good, too, if I'd pour it."

He smiled. "Oh, wait. I've got chocolate!" He pushed his chair back and stood up. Again Annie found herself listening for the comfort of familiar sounds: the squeak of the stairs, a bureau drawer opening and closing. When Alex came back, he was holding a box of chocolate covered cherries.

"Mom gave me these at Christmas. I used to love them when I was little."

Annie took one from the box he offered her and nibbled at the chocolate.

"They're pretty bad, I know. And sticky. Very sticky." He looked toward the sink, but reached for another chocolate instead. "The trick is to be brave. Put the whole thing in your mouth."

"And don't look back," Annie said around her own mouthful.

Even the coffee didn't mute the sweetness. "I think there'll still be brownies left when they get here."

The fire snapped. A hot tub, Annie thought. Sinking into a hot tub. Or just a bubble bath, heady with lavender. And yes, a glass of wine—though she hadn't had one for months, didn't want to keep it in the house now. But yes, wine would be nice. White wine. And a deep feather bed.

"I don't think he'll be back."

"No." Annie smiled. "He'll be too busy with those other fish. The ones with the glittery scales."

Alex looked down into his coffee mug. "I wanted to hit him." He looked up at her. "I keep feeling like I should have."

She shook her head.

"I know. I know. 'Use your words, boys.'"

"Did I really say that?"

"Well, no. We must have picked it up from the playground monitors." He smiled. "We used to have a lot of fun with it, though. We'd lie in bed and use every bad word we could think of. Damn. And *hell*. And words we didn't think you guys knew about."

"You didn't!"

"Yeah, we'd even make up our own. Riley was great at that. And then we'd dive under the covers so you wouldn't hear us laughing."

"Vocabulary lessons, Jack used to say whenever he heard you two giggling upstairs."

Alex laughed. "You knew?"

"Just the general gist. No details."

He put the lid back on the cherry cordials and pushed the box as far down the table as his arm would reach. Annie waited. A hot bath, a feather bed— but that was her list. What would Alex be thinking of?

"Annie, do you know who your father is?" he asked her.

"No."

"Your mother didn't tell you?"

Annie reached for her coffee. "I told the other kids they were divorced. And that he didn't know about me. He didn't know she was pregnant when he left."

She set the mug down without drinking. "Actually, that's probably pretty close to what happened, except that she never married any of them."

"So it could have been—

"I saw the men who came home with her after the bars closed. I wanted a father, but I didn't want any of them to be him."

"Yeah."

The fire shifted. Annie heard the low bark that meant Rose was waiting just outside the kitchen door. When she came back to the table Alex was still looking at his hands.

"Have you asked her, Alex?"

He sat up straight. He's such a warrior, Annie thought. He's had to be. A warrior without weapons.

"She can't talk about it. She was fifteen. It happened at a party." He paused. "James told me about it. Who knew which one was the father."

"Oh, Alex."

"All of them, he said. One after another. His little sister."

"Does he know—"

"Who was there? The usual suspects, I guess. You know the kind, Annie. They just take, and take, and take. Like they're entitled."

"Your poor mom," Annie said.

"Yeah, that's when she started drinking. I'm lucky I wasn't a fetal alcohol baby."

"I'm so glad you have James," Annie said.

He nodded, but didn't say anything. He hadn't always had James. He'd had Jack, in the summers, but that wasn't—

This afternoon, Annie thought. The way he had stepped back from Lon's pickup. "What did Lon say to you? Just before I got out of the Toyota?"

"He called me son. Probably just—you know how people say that sometimes. But it creeped me out.

"Alex, it can't be him."

"Why not? You've seen how he is."

"Because there's not a trace of that man in you." Annie reached across the table. "Nothing. Not one atom. You know that, right?"

Alex's hand lay still beneath her own. "It was one of them," he said.

"Well, there are two of us."

He looked at her.

"Whoever our fathers were, I'd say they're missing out on a good thing."

His smile was slow to come, but it was there. "Yours, for sure." He sat up. "You know, Jack said something like that once." He touched the handle of his coffee cup, pushed and pulled it back, an arcing half circle. "Remember the thunderstorm that time we were camped at Horseshoe Lake?"

"Thunder crashing off the mountains just above us, rolling around the basin right on top of us? I'd never heard anything like it." (*Dad?* they had heard Riley call. Jack had unzipped the sleeping bag and reached for his unlaced boots.)

"Well, Jack came to our tent that night and squeezed in between me and Riley. To keep warm, he said. Pretending he didn't know we were scared. And we weren't, really, now that he was there. After a while Riley went to sleep, but Jack just kept talking, telling me things. Like how Chief Joseph's name had something to do with thunder in the mountains, and how spirit helpers used to come to people when they came up to these high lakes, or went out on a mountain by themselves. Maybe my spirit helper would be thunder, too, he said. Or maybe a hummingbird, or a water-strider. Something special, like me." He looked away, then back at Annie. "I may not know who my father is, but I had Jack. I know how lucky I am."

Rose lifted her head, listening. Then they too heard the distant motor, and finally the sound of Leona's pickup turning into the driveway.

"Hungry?"

"Always." He looked at her. "Don't worry about Riley, Annie. I think Tribal's just glad that meth lab's gone."

Then Leona was holding the door open for Mattie and Riley, who came in bearing Papa Murphy's pizzas aloft as if they were waiters' serving trays. "Meat lovers! Gourmet vegetarian! Which one goes in the oven first?"

"Alex? You played hard, you choose." Annie stood up. The oven was already hot. Meth lab? *Don't worry.*

"Veggie gourmet, of course." Alex grinned at Riley's wrinkled nose. "Hey. Artichoke hearts and sun-dried tomatoes? What's not to like?"

Mattie shook her head. "We'd better bake the meat-lovers one first, or there won't be any artichokes left for the rest of us. You guys aren't real good at waiting."

"Reverse psychology," Alex whispered behind his hand. "Works every time." He had tipped back in his chair and was teetering, fingertips touching the edge of the table, looking every bit as relaxed and happy as he had out on the court this morning. Would the others be able to sense that something had happened? Annie wondered. Maybe pain hangs in the air like a spirit, invisible to all but the seer. How else did Leona always seem to show up just when people needed her?

Of course I've needed propping up on a regular basis these past few months, she thought. Any time was a good time for one of Leona's visits. Leona had sat down in a kitchen chair and was peering into her purse, her elbows rising as she dug through the contents.

Rose cocked her head.

Annie laughed. "She's hoping you're going to find *two* bones in there."

"She's a wise one, all right." Leona smiled at Rose and touched the dog's head before she bent over the purse again.

But it wasn't until the pizzas were nearly gone and Mattie had caught her grandmother's eye and stood up to wipe the table, then dry it with a kitchen towel, that Leona opened the square white envelope she had found in her purse. It took Annie a moment to recognize the young couple in the photograph: a slender cowboy leaning against the fender of a 1950s-era sedan, his arms wrapped around a dark-haired young woman and his hands clasped at her waist. She was leaning back against him, looking up and laughing.

"Mary," Annie said.

"This was in the clock," Leona said. "I don't know how in the world it got in there. That old clock has a glass door you can open, and someone must have put it inside, and it had slipped down into the crack at the back. Like at the back of a drawer, you know?"

"It's *Mary*," Annie said again.

"Of course I'd looked in all the drawers. I took apart every chest we had. I looked and looked. I wanted Jack to have a picture of her." She touched the corner of the photograph. "I remember taking this. With her camera, her little Brownie. I don't know how we ended up with it. Maybe she gave it to my mother."

Riley was leaning over his mother's shoulder to see the photograph, and finally Alex stood and joined him.

"That's your grandma," Leona said at last. "And your granddad. Roy."

"They look so—"

"Happy," Leona finished for him. "Oh, yes. Yes. That's what I wanted you to see."

Mattie came around the table and stood close to Riley.

"That car," Riley began.

"Roy's '52 Ford. They had a lot of fun in that car."

Annie felt Riley's hand on her shoulder and reached up to touch it. "I used to wish," she began, but how could she explain? The canning jars, the blue enamel kettle, the first time she had touched the recipes. A mother's things. She'd never told Jack how sometimes she imagined Mary was in the kitchen with her, they were just two women together, the aroma of whole grain rolls rising from the oven, their men would be coming down from the high field soon. And now—she looked so much like Jack, was that it? Annie could hold back the words only with effort. *Oh Mary, he's gone.*

"Thank you," Annie said at last.

"So what all was in that tablet you gave Dad?" Riley had looked up from the photograph. "Dad talks about it in his notes, but it's confusing."

For a moment Annie thought all sound had stopped. The blackbirds that had been filling the air with their bright, swaying songs, the rushing snowmelt current, even the breathing of the people around her table. But how was Riley to know? He hadn't seen Leona's face last summer when she told Annie about the tablet. And look, Leona was still smiling across the table at the upside-down photograph, her lined face softened by memory. Annie heard the clicking of Rose's toenails on the linoleum and felt the weight of the dog's head in her lap.

"Well, nephew, you can see how they were," Leona was saying. "And there was more to it, too. After Roy came home from Korea, and then losing both his folks at once—well, your granddad was like a drowning man who reaches up one last time and finds a tree branch floating by, or a piece of lumber, a beam. Something to hang on to. When he reached up and found Mary, he didn't let go. She was a survivor, too, and she pulled him back to the surface. And she showed him a different way to see the world.

"But then the shock of her death knocked him back out of balance. That's how I thought of it, anyway. He was so angry. With me. With the world. Even Gus and Audrey couldn't help him."

Leona looked at Annie. "And I wasn't right, either. It was a hard time." She looked down, then back at Riley, at Mattie. "I told myself I was worried about Jack—and I was, I was worried about Jack—but I think I kept coming around in those first few weeks, even after Roy had warned me to stay away, because I was still trying to find her. I couldn't make myself believe she was gone any more than Roy could."

Leona closed her eyes. Annie saw Mattie give Riley's hand a quick squeeze.

"So that's why I was there," she said, finally. "I was keeping out of sight, but I was there. I saw him getting ready to burn her things. We do that, too, burn the clothes, anything that might hold the spirit back. But when he put that tablet on the pile, I slipped out of my shadow place and took it." Leona shook her head. "Like I said, I wasn't right. When I saw it was a letter Roy had written to her after she was gone, I knew I shouldn't read it. I almost couldn't, his grief was so raw. So was mine, but I had medicine people to help me. He had nobody.

"About halfway through the letter, though, his writing changed. His heart hurt too much, so he moved into his head; that's the way I thought of it. Anyway, he started explaining things. He told her how he and his father had disagreed about almost everything. Land, mainly. How much was enough? He said his father would never have tolerated her because she had been part of an Indian family. He talked about watching her that morning when she was hanging out the wash in her white nightie, and he thanked her for everything she'd done for him. Given him back his life. Helping him find joy when he had thought there could be no more joy in the world. And he thanked her for teaching him to respect the spirits of animals, rivers, trees. The wind. She'd reminded him of the ancient wisdom of his Irish ancestors, he said.

"But it was that view of the world that had taken her from him. He should have stopped her, he said, that morning. He was awake when she slipped out of their bed and walked down to the river. He should have followed her. Told her it was all just primitive superstition. He should have listened to his father. The famine Irish hadn't survived the coffin ships by becoming water.

"So it was his fault she died. That's what he thought.

"*Jack's like you, Mary.* That was the last thing he wrote. *I can't lose him, too.* He told her he was going to make sure Jack survived. Whatever it took."

Riley was frowning. "So you gave Dad the letter because you thought it would help him understand why his father was so hard on him?"

Leona nodded. She looked at Annie and then down at her coffee cup.

"It did help, didn't it?" Alex reached for the photograph. "It must have."

Mattie was holding Riley's hand, but she was looking at her grandmother. *A healer,* Annie thought. But what could a girl like Mattie do about this?

"It seemed to make him feel worse, though." Riley frowned again. "Like—well, guilty. But he doesn't say what he feels guilty about. There's something about digging a grave—but that must have been—I mean, it's all kind of weird. I can't imagine Dad, you know, killing anything. Having anything to bury."

"A metaphor?" Mattie squeezed his hand. "Maybe he was burying the past. Or something."

Leona was still quiet, folded in upon herself.

What was she remembering? But she might not know, either. The drinking, those "dark roads" she had talked about. So we might never know, Annie thought. Why hadn't Jack just told her? *She's what's kept me from falling.*

"Metaphor," Leona said at last. "What's that?"

When their faces turned to her Annie answered. "It's a way of comparing two things that are different, but have something in common. Like saying Mattie is a willow."

"Or a dandelion." Riley was smiling now.

"I guess it was a metaphor, then," Leona said. "But it was real, too. I wasn't here—that was when I was with the Navajo."

Mattie lowered her eyes.

"But Roy told me about it. Jack dug a grave out there under the shade of the lilacs. Not just a hole, but a grave. He buried that old dried-up coyote hide. Roy had strung it over the barbed wire fence and left it there."

"Why?"

"To keep coyotes away. Even now some ranchers have five or six hides hanging along their fences."

Mattie shuddered, and Riley put his arm around her. "So what was he really burying?"

"Well, you know, Mary loved coyotes; they were real special to her. Jack had remembered that, out there on the mountain. That's what Roy thought, anyway."

Annie's memory came almost as a vision. Beneath the lilac that first day: those yellow-black eyes, watching her.

22

Osprey. A pair of them, in that cottonwood snag by the barn. But they had never nested this close before. Were they just hunting—fishing, really—before they returned to last year's nest, the one closer to town? Annie turned in a half circle. Binoculars. There, on the table. Better grab a jacket, too. April wasn't summer. Riley's windbreaker would do.

Which was how she discovered the gun. A handgun, a small one, in his pocket. Snub-nosed, with an outline of a bird on the short black barrel. And a stamped inscription: Raven Arms. She laid it down on the counter, pointing away from her.

"Careful now, it's got a hair trigger," the man had said. His arm swaying like a cobra, holding the gun just out of reach. Her mother's hands flailing the air. "Please, Randy. She's my baby." Her mother's words slurring.

Annie took a step back, then another, feeling behind her for a kitchen chair, the table edge. What was Riley doing with a gun? *There are gangs on the reservation. I'm not denying.* No. Not Riley. But there was something heavy in her stomach, burning its way toward her heart.

That thing about a meth lab—

She sat down, keeping her eyes on the gun as if it were a living thing with a will of its own. "See what you made me do?" Their trailer filling with a smell like the strings of red caps boys liked to pound on the sidewalk, only stronger. A jagged hole in the metal door. And something else: her mother's strangled laugh. Or had she been crying?

I should check to see if it's loaded, she thought.

She had a three o'clock class.

In the end, Annie laid the gun in a shoebox and pushed it as far under her bed as she could. She had left a note in Riley's jacket pocket: "We need to talk."

⊸

"He came back, Mom! Alex told me." Riley leaned forward, his arms braced on his knees. "You said he wouldn't but he did. And I wasn't even *here*. Either time."

Annie reached out to touch his hand, but he stood up abruptly. "I knew you'd say no. That's why it was still in my pocket." He was pacing. "But it was different when Dad was here, you know? Now you're out here alone. All day sometimes." He faced her again. "Do you know what can *happen*, Mom? Not everyone's good like you. Things can—you've got to be able to defend yourself."

"I know." Annie felt him looking at her.

"It shouldn't be this way, Mom." His voice was thin now, tight. "I know that. If I hadn't—you know. Dad would be here." He turned away. Annie waited. "The least I could do now is protect you myself. But I can't even seem to do that."

"Please, Riley, sit down. If you can." He looked toward the chair. "Better yet, let's take a walk."

"Walkie talkie?" His smile was closer to tears. Who had made up this game, she or Jack? Give the kid a chance to talk without looking at you. Both of you looking in the same direction: ahead. After all, Jack had laughed once, he can't drive.

"I'm not too old if you're not." There. A real smile. But when he pulled the sweatshirt over his head she saw that his hands were shaking.

Rose thought a walk was a grand idea. She ran down the driveway, then sprinted back to them and spun around to tear off again. Leading us onward, Annie thought. As always. But they were turning the corner by the barn before she could think of a way to begin.

"I should have told you."

"I guess that's what scared me, Mom. I mean, if Alex hadn't let me know— if he hadn't been with you, for that matter."

"I'm sorry, Riley. I didn't mean to scare you. That's what we get for trying to protect each other, isn't it? We end up scaring each other half to death."

"Were you scared when you found the gun?"

"Guns bring back some real bad memories."

"You never told me about those, either."

"Sometimes I don't remember until something happens to dig up that old stuff." Annie looked sideways at him. "You're right, though. It's not *telling* the stories that gets us into trouble. It's *not* telling them."

Riley was relaxing enough to smile. "Okay, I think I deciphered that."

But smile or no smile, she had to say it. "So here's the first thing I didn't tell you. I could barely face it myself." They had reached the county road now, mud and gravel. "I was ready to kill that man. If he'd come at me I would have. The ulu is razor sharp, and I'd thought it through, how to get past his arms to his—" She stopped. "This is hard to say, Riley. I would have killed him."

Riley was looking straight ahead. What was he thinking?

"I don't suppose it's any worse than shooting someone, killing a person that way," she said. "Maybe it's even better, because if you keep a gun with the intention of killing anyone who threatens you, it's calculated. I couldn't do that. Make that decision. But it felt worse. It was so deep, so—instinctual. No, not instinctual. Irrational."

"Defending yourself? Why's that irrational?"

"But I wouldn't have been just defending myself. It all happened so fast, it took me a while to understand. Lon was pushing himself on me. He's good at that, setting up situations where no woman will take him to court. She invited me in, your honor. She even put her arm around me." *She's been hospitalized,* Annie stopped herself from adding.

Riley's shiver shook his whole upper body.

"But do you see? He wasn't trying to kill me. That's not what he does. Equal force, you know? I probably could have stopped him with a kitchen chair. Discouraged him, anyway. Or the long-handled frying pan. That was within reach, too. He'd have known I wasn't going to let it happen. But I went for the ulu."

Walking helped. One step at a time, Dennis had said.

"It was only afterward that I understood why. Part of it was those old memories. You probably guessed when I talked with you about Mattie that I'd had to fight off some of Mom's boyfriends, or try to. But it was more than that. He had used your dad's name. 'I'm a friend of Jack's.' And he said things that Jack had supposedly told him about me. I knew they weren't true. But somehow it was like he was killing Jack all over again. Desecrating his memory. His life. Everything his life stood for."

They walked along, slower now. April chill in the afternoon shadow. Time to turn around.

"So is this a woman who needs a gun, you think?" Annie had made sure her voice carried a note of laughter.

"Well, mebbe not." Riley tried for a joke of his own. Then he added, "But—"

"That's the second thing I should have told you. I wasn't really sure Lon wouldn't come back. I didn't think he would, but if he was drunk enough—well, I just wasn't sure. Now I am."

"But he did come back!"

"To apologize. I don't think he was sorry for pushing himself onto me. That's who he is. Or who he thinks he is. But he wanted me to know Jack really had been his friend. For a few weeks in third grade, he said. After his mother left, when no one else would talk to him."

Riley let out his breath. "So." He shoved his hands into his jacket pockets and they walked for a while without talking. Then he swung around, blocking her way. "Mom, you do know what a line is, don't you? Like when a guy feeds you a line?"

Annie didn't let herself smile. "No, I think he meant it. He really wanted me to know. And he didn't get out of his truck. But you're right, he was definitely hoping I'd feel sorry for him. Alex probably told you, I didn't. And he got to have the last word. Soothe his wounded ego, you know. It wasn't a nice last word. No charm at all."

"He really won't come back, then."

"Nope." Annie kicked a rock down the road. "And I've put the ulu on the top shelf of the cupboard, so everybody else is safe from me again, too."

Riley tried to laugh. "I should tell you, Mom, it's a cheap gun. Piece of junk. A pawn shop special, Gabe's cousin called it. "I had the feeling he should have been paying *me* to haul it off. I've been about half afraid it would blow up in your hand."

Annie reached out and touched his shoulder. "Maybe we should stick to light sabers."

"We did have some cool duels, all right."

"I'd have won sometimes, too, if it weren't for that Darth Vader mask."

There was one more question in his mind, Annie knew. But it wasn't fair to make him ask it.

"This ulu business—I didn't want to scare you. I thought you might worry about my—that I might be on my way back into the hospital."

Riley was shaking his head before she had finished the word. "No, Mom. No."

"It's okay. It's taken *me* a while to trust myself." Rose had circled back to them. "And I have to admit that imagining killing a man with a knife isn't—well, I might not be crowned Queen of Good Mental Health this year. But as parents go, I'm back to normal. None of us are completely sane, as you know."

Riley grinned.

"It's been hard for us. Losing him, and not knowing. The whole thing, really. The way it fell on us—on our family, on Dad too—out of the sky. It threw me out of balance, is the way I think of it now. You've done better than I have, all along.

"How can you say that, after—you know, that night? My meltdown?"

Was he ready to talk about it at last?

"That was one day, Riley," she said. "One day. You spent six *months* holding yourself together. In a place that must have felt like—what? prison, a mental hospital? being scolded and prodded and poked—when you were hurting more than you could possibly have imagined anyone could hurt. When you needed to be with the people who loved you. I don't know how you did it."

Riley stopped walking. "If you knew what it was like, Mom, why didn't you come see me? I mean, after you got out of the hospital?"

"God, I wanted to. Just hold you, never let go. But I was afraid to take the risk."

"What risk?"

"Of losing you." Could he understand? "It took such a long time, Riley. And some of the meds—I was afraid if you saw your mother shuffling like a zombie—worse yet, if *they* saw me, those people at McLaughlin—if I wasn't a fit mother, they'd have sent you to a foster home. That's what my counselor thought, anyway. I didn't know how I could keep going if I lost you. I tried to explain, in those awful letters, but I knew they read your mail, so I couldn't be too obvious."

"I almost left, Mom. Did you know that? I knew I could hitch back to Pendleton. They had this tracker guy, but he'd have never found me on the rez."

"That's what I mean. I don't know how you did it. Stuck it out. Thank God you did."

Rose was pressing her side against Riley's thigh. He knelt to embrace her, patting her ribs, then burying his face in her mottled fur. Murmuring something Annie couldn't hear.

Finally he stood. His face was red. "I can be such a jerk. Alex says I'm a mean drunk, too."

"It hasn't been a regular thing, has it?"

"God no. Once was enough." He looked away, then back at her. "You could never lose me, Mom. I don't suppose you can believe that now, after—I don't remember everything I said, but I know I really unloaded on you."

"Mattie's right, though, isn't she? About forgiveness?" They had started walking again. "I hope so, anyway. You have a lot more to forgive than I do. I wish we had talked about this earlier. I should have told you on the way home that day instead of trying so hard to look put together for you." She bent down to toss a stick for Rose. "I was still pretty wobbly."

"You know what, Mom?" Riley shook his head. "Sometimes I feel bad for *not* cracking up when it happened. It's like there's no right way."

"I think that's what we both have to accept." They had reached the driveway. "I'm okay now, Riley. I know it doesn't always look like it. Grief has its own timetable, I guess. But you really can trust me. I'm here for you. I'll be here."

Late afternoon light on his face, the sky streaked with pink. She hadn't said it aloud: *You don't have to take care of me, Riley. I'm the parent.* She had left him, as Jack would have said, what every man needs: a place to stand.

But they weren't quite through.

"One more thing," she said. "You were right, that night. I did argue with your dad about LifeQuest. I was afraid, I didn't want you to go. If I hadn't—cried—" She stopped until her voice was strong again. "I just wanted you home. My boys, you and Alex both. It wasn't rational, I know. I knew it then. But it was true. Home was where you belonged. Where you'd be safe." She looked at him. "And your walking away from LifeQuest, getting as far away from Darrell as you could—that was true, too."

Riley frowned. "You mean—"

"He used to tell me sometimes, 'You are who you are, Annie. Some things you have to do because you can't do anything else. You can't *be* anyone besides who you are.'" She reached for his hand. "I don't think you can, either." She gave it a quick squeeze. "Not sober, anyway."

His half-laugh sounded almost like a cry.

They were turning the corner by the barn before she spoke again. "I wish I could tell you what happened. Why he didn't call me. Why nobody in the search party even saw him. Bad stuff happens, we know that. Random bad stuff. Bulls on the highway, and worse. School shootings." She stopped walking. "But Riley, this is different. There's something we don't know."

He nodded. This boy, this man, who wanted to protect her. For a moment—something about the hard squint of his eyes—he reminded her of Roy.

The one thing they hadn't talked about was what to do with that gun under the bed.

23

Sometimes, waiting for sleep, Annie had the sensation that the weight in that shoebox was pulling her into the darkness, a force heavier than gravity, armless but irresistible, like the shadow-monster Riley had imagined when he was small. Even at her sickest, she hadn't been suicidal, and she trusted the boys. But nothing good could come of that gun. What should she do with it? She and Riley would have to talk about that sooner or later. At least they could, she thought. They could talk about anything now.

Anything but Jack's notes. Except for asking Leona about that tablet, he hadn't mentioned them since Christmas. She knew he needed to, or would need to.

I'm here for you, she had told him.

She had been up since dawn. But even in this clear morning light, she was no closer to the answer. How could she bring the subject up when she was struggling so much herself? She had read the manuscript over and over and still didn't understand what she knew must be the most important part. It was obvious that Jack had been in anguish in late August when he wrote those last few pages, but why? What exactly had happened? And those references to his father. The two of them had talked so much about Roy. Why hadn't Jack told her whatever it was he had been feeling about him that summer?

For that matter, if she knew the answers, would it make any difference? Could she tell Riley why his own father had disappeared?

He was sitting opposite her at the table now, his hands cupping a mug of hot chocolate. Alex was awake. They heard a door closing, then footsteps coming down the stairs, and he joined them in the kitchen, still yawning. He stretched his long arms above his head, pulling on one wrist and then the other.

"Sweet." Riley's snorting laugh had spattered his hot chocolate.

"What's funny?"

Alex has a family, Annie. They're just letting us be part of it, Jack had said. But that family had been bigger than even Jack knew. Mattie was part of it, too. And Leona. The five of them had become melded together this year, a family within a family, each of them holding the others up.

"Just you, Gumby," Riley was saying. "You're pretty funny. How tall do you want to be, anyway?"

"What?" Alex yawned again. On his way to the refrigerator he patted the top of Riley's head. When he had settled into a chair, leaning over a bowl of Cheerios, he looked up. "Don't worry, Pocket-boy. You'll get your growth spurt one of these days." Around the first mouthful he added, "S'called puberty."

Riley grinned and reached into the bowl to flick milk in Alex's face, and Alex lifted the bowl out of Riley's reach.

"No food fights, you two!" Annie had lifted her hand as if she were stopping traffic, but she was smiling. How many times had they kept her afloat?

Could she? Yes, why not ask this family for help? Leona would be there for her, she knew. And having the support of his friends might be what Riley needed to hear the rest of his father's story. In a way, they were all part of that story, too. When he and Alex stood to put their dishes in the sink, though, and turned to look at her—those faces: Saturday, school almost out, you need us for anything, Mom?—she could have lost her nerve.

"Boys, I was wondering—"

When she stopped mid-sentence they looked at each other and then back to her.

"Sit back down for a minute, will you? I know Alex has to work this afternoon, but—"

"Mom?"

"But I was wondering if you two could see if Leona and Mattie would come over this morning. I think—"

Finish a sentence! Annie told herself.

"Mom? What's up?" Riley had slid into the chair beside hers.

"Well, we haven't talked about—have you finished reading your dad's notes?"

"Almost." Riley sat up straighter and pulled his hands into his lap. He looked toward Alex, then down at the table. "I don't know why I stopped. I got right up to the last few pages."

"Maybe you didn't want it to be over." Alex's voice was so low it was almost a whisper. "I wouldn't have."

Riley looked up. "Yeah. I guess. But all that stuff about his dad leaving him out in the woods, and then—well, when he started writing about being a history teacher, and doubting himself, I—that's who he *was*. That's who I thought he was, anyway, and I couldn't—" Riley stopped. "I wimped out." He looked at his mother. "Didn't mean to leave you high and dry, though."

Annie smiled. "You haven't, son, believe me. You haven't."

"And she's not biased in any way," Alex said. "Now, if you want a more objective point of view?"

Oh, bless him, Annie thought. Sure enough, Riley's face was already relaxing into the beginnings of a smile. "I think you had a sense of what was coming in those few last pages," she told him. "They're pretty hard going."

"Painful?" Alex sat down across the table from them.

"Yes, definitely painful, Alex. But also—well, so much of it I just don't understand. It's about that night he spent alone on the mountain, I'm pretty sure, but—something happened, and whatever it was—but he doesn't really say, and—"

Annie stopped herself. Riley had all but admitted he couldn't bear to lose his father twice. Floundering like this wouldn't help.

"And so I wondered, if we all read Jack's last entries together, Leona and Mattie too, maybe we could help each other decipher them." She looked at Riley. "What do you think?"

"Yeah. I like it."

"Are you sure? You don't want to read them first?"

"No. I don't think I—this way's easier."

Alex looked away.

৹

The child is father of the man, Jack had written.

That line keeps going through my head. It's Wordsworth, Annie told me last night. *She quoted the rest of it: "So was it when my life began; so is it now I am a man. So be it when I shall grow old, or let me die!" Of course she was using her best mock-English accent, which we've always joked is closer to Irish washerwoman than Oxford don.*

She made me laugh. Which is just what I needed.

Too much information? Riley had tipped his head back and closed his eyes. Mattie touched his knee. When he could look at her again, Annie smiled. "We liked to be silly," she said. "Sometimes I forget that part."

Alex grinned at Mattie. "You should've seen them burling."

"Burling?"

"Trying to tip each other off a log. Trying to stand up on it, actually. In the swimming hole."

"In our defense, Mattie, there wasn't much to stand on. It was more like a lodgepole than a log."

Riley was shaking his head now. "Yeah, my mom and dad. Mr. and Mrs. Lumberjack." Annie looked around the familiar circle of faces gathered at the table. How could she feel so—what? Exhilarated? Yet there was a calmness, too. Leona was sitting quietly, her vision focused on her own hands, folded on the tabletop.

Apparently Wordsworth and I aren't related, though, she read. *That's sure not what I thought it meant.*

Annie laid the page face down. Riley reached for the next-to-last sheet of paper. "My turn."

"Oh, son, I don't know." She watched his jaw line lift and set, exactly like his father's. "You're sure?"

But he was. "I need to do this, Mom."

Annie looked at Leona, but Leona had gone inward, and Jack's words were already spilling over them, Jack's words in Riley's young voice. And Jack had been a boy, too, when it happened. Whatever it was.

By the time I saw the old man, I was pretty much hysterical. It didn't help that he was wearing a coyote skin, so what I saw was a human face looking out from beneath Coyote's. But that voice. I felt it go into me. Into my bones. I could breathe again, even before he put his hand on my shoulder.

Riley paused, but when he read on, his voice was strong.

He walked behind me, singing. It was a weird, high song, like nothing I'd ever heard. But he kept his hand on my shoulder, and somehow my feet moved

forward. Once he stopped and wiped the powder-stuff off my face with his
handkerchief. Then he led the way down the ridge I recognized.

He had sandwiches in his pickup, cold venison hamburger on white bread.
And coffee in a dented Thermos bottle. When I woke up it was daylight. His
truck was parked up on the county road but we were standing just outside our
fence on the deer trail between the barbed wire and the river. How did we get
there? He couldn't have been strong enough to carry me. He touched the dry
coyote hide Dad had strung on the barbed wire. This time his voice was dry,
splintery. An old man's voice. "Grandson." Then he reached into his pocket
and pulled out a small bottle. He wet his fingers, the hand he had kept on my
shoulder. And then me. My clothes, even my hair. My face.

When I opened my eyes again, he was gone.

Leona was hugging herself, shivering as if the room had chilled. Riley
looked at Mattie, but she nodded. Go on.

The child is father of the man. I thought it meant the way I felt that morning
when I got the shovel out of the shed and started digging the grave. I was older
than my father now. I knew things he'd never know. And I was going to learn
more. But not from him. I told him as much when he came out of the house and
stood there watching me. "You got it all wrong, Dad."

I had remembered some things while I was out there. Like how Mom had
taken me outside one warm summer night when the coyotes were singing. "Listen,
Jacky. Hear that? They're trying so hard to talk to us."

Annie had folded her hands prayer-style, the tips of her fingers pressing
against her lips. Riley looked at her and then offered the last manuscript
page to Alex.

Alex's voice was a hoarse whisper.

Dad was quiet, maybe waiting for me to talk. I didn't, though. I was through.

If I had told him my story, would he have told me his?

I've tried to be a good father. But now I know I wasn't a good son. Not even a
good historian. How could I have missed it?

Alex turned the page over in his hand as if he expected to find words on
the other side.

No one spoke. Annie had left the kitchen door ajar, and they could hear
a car out on the country road. Then the sounded faded, leaving only the
small cries of swallows skimming the river, dipping down to touch it, rising
free.

Mattie was squeezed between them on the split bench seat. Riley shifted his shoulder to give her more room, though he wanted to lean even closer, somehow meld the three of them in this pickup cab into one whole. Anything to keep from being alone. His mother's impulse had been just the opposite. "I need a walk," she'd said, though she had hugged the three of them in wordless thanks. Leona had already slipped away. They had seen her from the driveway, nearly halfway up the ravine.

Mattie and Alex weren't saying much, though Alex had reached across the back of the pickup seat to squeeze his shoulder. Maybe they were as confused as he was. He'd heard stories about bad spirits, but—

And what exactly had happened that night, anyway? His dad hadn't been forthcoming with details. Weird noises, weird sensations?

Usually, Riley thought, Leona would have said something.

"Why was your grandma so quiet?"

"I don't know," Mattie said. "She wanted to come this morning."

Alex was looking out the passenger-side window. "Maybe this was the first time she'd heard this story."

Riley took his eyes off the road just long enough to glance at the back of Alex's head.

Mattie was nodding, slowly. "It did happen when she was gone."

"You think she feels guilty? Is that what you mean?"

Alex turned to look across the cab. "The rest of us do. Why wouldn't she?"

"But Dad did get help. He made it home." Riley braked lightly for a graveled corner. "I know Leona got off track for a while, but a lot of people get off track for a while. And this wasn't really her fault, anyway. Whatever it was that happened."

Alex had turned his face away again. "Sometimes it can feel like that, though."

"Yeah, but—" But what? He scanned the banks ahead for deer. Not too likely at this time of day but then again he hadn't expected a thousand-pound bull, either. That day seemed so long ago now. Eons. A couple of eons.

They passed Gus and Audrey's place, stopped for the crossing at Gibbon. Dust in the rear view mirror, catching up with them.

Why were they being so quiet? Didn't they understand how he was feeling? If his father were here he'd *talk*. "Let's think this through, son."

They'd figure it out. He'd keep talking until one or the other of them thought of something that would—

Except Dad hadn't. He hadn't even told Mom everything about that night.

Native people didn't like to talk about some things, though. Even with each other. And he wasn't. Native. He would never be native to any place.

Great, he told himself. Self-pity. That'll help.

Mattie had begun to hum, softly at first, and now her voice rose above the road noise, a clear rivulet of sound. Then Alex's rich, low voice had joined Mattie's, like currents braiding together in the river. A song they both knew.

"Irish, right?" Riley was missing something here. Were they just trying to distract him?

"Yes," Mattie said. "'The Fields of Athenry.' It's a song about the Great Famine. The Great Hunger, the Irish called it."

Alex grinned. "Football. That's where I learned the words. Mattie probably read about it in some history book, but I heard that song when I was watching ESPN. Irish fans sing it at every match, even if they're losing. Especially if they're losing. The whole grandstand."

"Oh, yeah. I guess I've heard something like that."

It was a beautiful melody. Riley had an image of soft black velvet spread with cheats instead of diamonds, the words sharp and penetrating as those awful seeds that stuck to your socks and did such damage to a dog's soft ears.

"It's pretty sad." Alex had stopped smiling. "But defiant, too. I guess that's why they sing it at the football matches."

"Dad said there were stories about the famine in his family. There's still a lot of bad feeling about it in Ireland, he said."

"*God sent the blight but the English made the famine.* See, Riley, we get that."

"It sounds like an old song, doesn't it?" Mattie was looking ahead now. Focusing on the empty road in front of them. No. Focusing on nothing. "But it wasn't written until the 1970s."

"Really? The famine was—it happened before the twentieth century, didn't it? He should know the date, but he couldn't think.

"Yes. It began in the 1840s. Things like that, the really bad things—well, you know. It can take a long time."

Her voice suddenly so quiet, as if she were whispering the answer to a question on a quiz in school. Riley felt the heat rising above the neck of his T-shirt. Okay. Okay, he got it. It was like Vietnam. Or any war, the Cayuse war, for that matter. Those five men hung in Oregon City. Or what happened to Chief Yellow Hawk. The concentration camps. Internment. People had trouble talking about the really bad things. Over a century had to pass before the Irish could sing "Athenry" at their football games.

So yeah, maybe his father would have told them about that night out on the mountain eventually. But now it was one more thing he'd never know. An important thing, obviously.

Cold comfort. An expression of his mom's.

Mattie meant well, though. So did Alex.

Now she put her hand on his thigh. "Riley, that last part, about not being a good historian."

"And missing something," Alex said. "'How could I have missed it?' Isn't that what he said? So it must have been something obvious, something he thought he should have seen."

Riley had glanced down at Mattie's touch, but he was staring straight ahead at the road when he felt Alex's hand on his shoulder again. "You with us, Pockets? I have a feeling this might be important."

His head felt so full. Thick. Had his brain turned to oatmeal? *Say something,* he thought, but his mouth couldn't find the shapes of words.

"It's all too much right now," Mattie said. "I know."

"It's just, there are three of us. You're not alone in this." Something about Alex's voice pulled Riley's glance across the cab.

"Like the three musketeers?"

Alex grinned. "More like the three history detectives. Hey, maybe we'll even get our own show. *History Detectives, the Sequel*!"

"Or," Mattie said, "we could make up our own name and avoid the copyright lawsuits."

Weird, Riley thought. Joking at a time like this? Indian people were famous for it, though. Whatever. Whatever it took.

The road to Tamastslikt Cultural Institute was one lane, winding into widening curves like the foothill canyons of the Blue Mountains just beyond the building. "It's to get people ready," Alex had explained the first time he took Riley to work with him. "Pull them in from the freeway and gradually slow them down enough to see."

The parking lot was almost empty. Alex opened the truck door and looked toward the building. "You two coming in?"

"In a minute," Mattie said.

"I'm not sure I—" Riley shifted away from her to reach for his wallet.

"There's no charge for tribal members," Alex said. He looked toward the stone entryway again. "I'd better go on in. Can't keep the eager public waiting."

They watched him walk across the asphalt parking lot and up the curving sidewalk. He makes pulling open those heavy doors look easy, Riley thought. He looked at Mattie. "Tribal members?"

"We're a tribe of three, aren't we?" She pulled his arm around her shoulders, pressing his hand between both of hers. "There, see? We've found our name already."

✧

Annie was breathing hard. She had climbed the rocky road as if she thought Jack might be waiting for her beneath his yellow pine. A good father. And a good son, too, at least he'd tried to be. To a father who left him alone on a mountain. Among other things. She bent over, hands on her knees, to catch her breath.

The old hayfield was thick with seedling pines now, and orchard grasses, fescue, the wild rye native to this place. "We're not raising cattle," Jack had said. "We live here."

Her heart was slowing now. But no matter which way her brain turned, the story Jack had left dissolved like smoke. Fish shadows in the river, there and not-there. It was nothing but a shell, a ghost of a story. Why had she let herself believe that sharing it would be a good idea? With the boys, and Mattie? Even Leona had been frightened. Maybe even angry: she had left without a word. Leona, who had been so good to her. Saved her, really, in so many ways.

"We're in this together," Leona had said.

Or was she the one who'd said that?

"Whatever you do, don't ask to touch the hem of their garments," Jack had teased her once. They had been watching the older women dancing at a powwow, and Annie knew her own face must be glowing, the words pulled from her in an involuntary whisper: "*Look* at them!"

"I have to remind myself sometimes," he had said as they walked back to their car under the summer stars, "Indian people have to work as hard as the rest of us for their spirituality." He had squeezed her hand then, but when he spoke again his voice was tighter. "Whatever peace you saw in those women's faces, believe me, Annie, they've earned. I know that. Sometimes I find myself wishing—but they sure as hell don't *owe* us anything."

Her arms could reach only halfway around the trunk. Golden bark shaped like pieces of a puzzle, already smelling summer-sweet. The dark-edged ridges pressed against her skin.

Even in the hospital she had not felt this alone.

Maybe—yes; she half-slid down the sidehill toward the river, pushing her way through service brush and willow shoots toward her own place. Mary's place. The earth gives birth, the earth is woman, if she could connect with the women of this place—

But the circle of the cove around the windfall log was silent. The cottonwood, bleached white, felt smooth under her hand. And warm, though it was dead. A broken tree. Finally Annie waded out into the current, the icy water slowly filling her shoes, swirling around her ankles, then her calves, the backs of her knees. A kingfisher left his branch and swept upriver. That hoarse, dry rattle. Tunneled into the riverbank somewhere, his mate would be cocking her head. Hearing him, and understanding.

How could she not have known? She knew Jack. The patterns of the lines around his eyes, the way he leaned back slightly when he was puzzled. The small sounds he made in his sleep. She knew things about him that he didn't know himself. And now that she had these words he'd left behind, the words he had struggled so hard to write, wresting them out of the silence of those hot afternoons, how could she still not know?

Annie tipped her head back. Two small white thunderheads rising against the blue. Only two? No, more. Higher, and behind her. Dizzy now, she felt the current pulling her off balance, she was tipping, her arms flailing, and then Leona was there, holding her upright.

⌇

"*Jack and Annie Fallon.* There it is. About ten feet up, maybe three feet in." Riley was pointing at the metal salmon leaping up the painted falls, each fish engraved with a name of a donor to Tamastslikt. "Funny how long it always takes to find it."

"Look, Riley. Here's yours."

"You're kidding. I was, what, three? When they were building this?"

"Somebody donated in your name?"

"Hey, you don't know. I might've had a piggy bank." But Riley had shoved his hands into his pockets and hunched his shoulders. He had never noticed the fish engraved with his name. When had it joined the migration up this river?

When Mattie touched his back he flinched.

"Sorry," he said. "It's just, everything's so weird today."

"It's okay." She waved at Alex as they passed his admission desk. The counter was so high even Alex was nearly lost behind it. He was cradling a telephone on his left shoulder, nodding at an invisible caller. The doors opened on the long hallway and a wall of windows that seemed to pull the Blue Mountains even closer. Then the Coyote Theater, still closed for repairs.

"I never got to see it," Mattie said. She stopped beside the first placard, a backlit shadow-image of Coyote. "Did you?"

"Yeah, quite a few times, actually. We were practically first in line on opening day, I swear. Dad was pretty psyched about this place. The room was dark, I remember. A circle, like in a tepee. There was a fire glowing, and stars on the ceiling. Coyote was funny. And there was something about a monster?"

"That must have been the story about Swallowing Monster. iSpeelyi— Coyote—gets sent to make the world ready for people, the two-legged ones. He has to rescue all the plants and animals from the belly of the Swallowing Monster so they'll be there for us when we need them."

"That's right, I remember. Coyote gets himself swallowed, and then builds a fire inside. And all the animals go out the openings." Riley turned back toward the shadow-coyote blocking the theater entrance. "I wonder why it's taking them so long to get it running again?"

"The equipment, Grandma said. It's complicated. And expensive." When she spoke again her voice was so soft he could hardly hear her. "So you got some of your first stories from Coyote, too."

"I wish you'd been here then." I wish I'd known you all my life, he meant to say. I wish you had been sitting cross-legged on the floor next to me. But what came out instead was, "We'll just have to have a kid of our own. Bring him."

He felt the touch of moving air against his neck. She had turned away. Of course. What an idiot! Who knew what would come out of his mouth next? "Mattie, I—"

"Something wrong with *girls*?" She was already leading the way into first room of exhibits. "We Were." Was she asking him, or was she talking to the birds whose recorded songs filled the airy space above them? She was looking up, and her long black hair was a shimmering waterfall.

"The earth and myself are of one mind," said a voice from the wall. Hinmatoowyalahqit, the sign said. Chief Joseph, in the history books.

Mattie turned just long enough to smile and he reached for her hand, but she had already lifted it to the beaded necklace at her throat.

How many times had he trailed his father through this room? "The Seasonal Round" of living on this land, the recognition of kinship with all living things, the intricate cleverness of what Dad called the technology for hunting, fishing, plant harvesting—while his own ancestors had been starving, he thought now, somehow living through The Great Hunger, those fields of Athenry. How did it all connect? Or did it? But if time is a sphere, as Mattie had said all those months ago, if time is a pink-striped beach ball— no, it was too much. Too much. This whole day had been too much. When Mattie led him into the tule lodge and pulled him down onto the bench beside her, the voices of the elders seemed to be settling over him from somewhere in the lodge, and he felt his heart gradually slowing. "We were taught to listen. To water, rain, wind."

"Everything is a story," Mattie said as they ducked out of the lodge and followed the circular design of the museum past the first horses, the first European-American trade goods, drawings of the forts. "Or part of a story, anyway." She stopped to study a beautiful bone and bead and brass-coin wedding veil, but Riley remembered what waited around the next turn, the place where you had to choose which door—Catholic or Presbyterian?— and the long dark ramp down a dirt floor strewn with castoff junk from the Oregon trail, heavy trunks, a fainting couch, an organ—with the haunting life-sized photograph waiting at the bottom, all those miserable little boys in soldier suits, the sad-faced girls in aprons; then a row of desks on wooden runners, a bright pennant and a trumpet in the glass case, the replica of an old-fashioned schoolroom you could think might be nostalgic unless you listened to the recorded voices of the elders who had been sent to Chemawa, "taught to be ashamed to be Indian," and "spread-eagle on a table, whipped with a rubber hose" for speaking their language. Kill the Indian and save the man. Then another turn and that tall green pyramid of tin cans, the herd of twenty-thousand horses made into dog food after the Allotment Act and settlement. "Re-settlement," Dad had always made a point of calling it.

As if he didn't feel bad enough after this morning. Why had Alex wanted him to come inside, today of all days?

He was looking toward that doorway when he felt Mattie's fingers lacing through his own. "Some stories are hard to hear, I know."

At last they reached the part of the museum that showed contemporary life on the reservation. "We Are." Salmon restoration, first food and powwow celebrations, language preservation, Native participation in the Pendleton Round-Up. Riley sat down on the bench outside the small, dark theater where the movie was playing. *Chawna mun ma amta.* We will never fade. Was anyone watching the movie? In the dim light he finally made out the shape of a man holding a sleeping child. Maybe there were more people in the front row. It was nearly over. "Coyote is still here, still teaching," said a woman's voice. "We have a lot more to learn. Listen!"

Mattie had left the salmon display and slipped onto the bench beside him so lightly that Riley realized she was there only as he felt her fingertips brush the back of his neck. No flinch this time, thank God. Did she have any idea how much he wanted her touch? But she was leaning forward now to start the Veteran/Warrior display screen. Together they listened to the story of the woman who killed her captor with his own weapon and escaped to become a warrior herself, then of a veteran who had served in the Vietnam war. "Try 'Korea,'" said Riley. "That's Wish Patrick. I'm pretty sure I remember him."

"My grandfather told me never to point a rifle at another human being. 'Thou shalt not kill,' he said. He didn't know I was going to be in a war." There were fourteen boys in foxholes, Patrick continued. All of them scared. Yes, that was a war dance song I was humming, he told the boy next to him. No, I don't have to sing it again just for you, it will take care of all of us. When the Korean soldiers charged toward them and the Americans' machine gun nests, he said, "I picked up my rifle. Pointing it out there. Squeezing the trigger. Three clips."

There were five rifles in each foxhole. "'When this one's hot, grab this one,' they told us."

"It's still there. It's branded in my mind."

When he felt Mattie's involuntary shiver, Riley put his arm around her and pulled her close. "I pray every day, ask Creator to forgive me," Wish Patrick was saying.

Quiet now, they rose and turned toward the third and last section of the museum. "We Will Be." Young voices from the video spoke about preserving traditional ways and passing on this wisdom to the next generation. "Messages from the animals are nothing to be ignored," one man said. "Sometimes it takes years to understand." Coyote placards, each backlit with orange light, had guided them through the circle of the museum, Riley realized. Each one bore a different inscription, some wise, some foolish. "Everything you can think of, the Coyote did it. We try to find the middle road."

Was there a middle road for him? Funny, Riley thought. He'd told his mother that he always knew where he was, but if he had to draw a map of where he was going—where all of them were going, Mom, Leona, Mattie, Alex too—he wouldn't even be able to pick up the pencil.

24

"My father lives somewhere else now," Leona was saying. She had led Annie back to the fallen cottonwood. They were sitting side by side, both of them looking up into a snow of cotton seed-fluff floating in the breeze, settling on their hair, collecting in drifts against the fence line. Once she and Jack had been caught in a blizzard, Annie remembered, snowflakes swirling up out of the dark against the windshield, making them both dizzy. Where was the road? But this time she could feel Leona's shoulder against her own, and there was another human voice, steadying even if Annie wasn't sure just what Leona meant. "He's not always here with us. He's traveling, I guess you'd say. Getting ready."

Was everything a mystery? Why did she always feel so dumb? Not just ignorant, but unaware. "You're a survivor," Jack told her long ago. "You know more than you think you do." So how had she missed learning so much of what she needed to know to survive?

"But it was him. When I heard that word, 'Grandson,' I knew. I just needed to be sure. That's why I left. I went home to ask him." Leona tipped her face up into the falling cotton fluff. "And he remembered. Remembers."

"Your father. Your father was the one who came to help Jack?" That day in Leona's kitchen, someone sleeping on a red couch beyond the beaded curtain. Thin white braids, a soft snore.

Leona didn't answer, and Annie could no longer see her face.

"You knew because he called Jack 'Grandson'?"

"Mary was part of our family. My sister. So she was his daughter, too." Now it was Annie's turn to steady Leona. The two women rocked slightly on the sun-bleached log.

"How did he—" Annie began, but she didn't even know how to ask the question.

Leona let her hands drop to her lap. "He just knew. He can see things."

"So he knew where to find him?"

"That was how he knew Jack was in trouble. He saw where he was."

P'lay' ni' wash. Spirit Mountain. Zinc Mountain, some people call it, Leona was explaining, because a compass doesn't work there. A sacred place, but strange, and frightening. If you get lost there, you might not be found. Annie could feel her heart racing, then stopping. Starting up again like a car jammed into gear. She put her hand on her chest. Jack had been a boy lost in this place.

"My father used to tell us stories about white people going into that country and coming out, the ones who made it out, half-crazed," Leona said. "The old people always warned the kids not to wander away from hunting camp, he said. And if they saw I shuwi' shapa, a bird with no feathers sitting in a tree, they were in real trouble."

Focus, Annie told herself. She looked at a pile of cotton fluff gathered at the base of a boulder. It was shifting slightly, as if it were a blanket some small animal had burrowed under. Leona's voice seemed different somehow.

"And Chief Clarence Burke—I'm sure you've seen his picture, seemed like it was everywhere, used to be painted on the doors of all the county rigs—when he was a young man he got lost on Spirit Mountain, and when he finally came out people said he was covered in a real fine white dust."

The kingfisher plunged from the broken snag into the river. That flash of silver was a small trout, clamped sideways in his beak. Still quivering.

"So your father—"

"I didn't know. Oh, Annie, I didn't know." Leona had turned her face away; her voice small now, almost inaudible, the words melting into the sound of the river's current.

Didn't know what? Annie's brain felt numb. Would anything ever make sense again? When Leona finally turned back her face was wet with tears. All Annie knew to do was pull Leona's head against her shoulder and hold her in her arms. And even that wasn't knowing. It was automatic, it was human instinct. What any woman does for another woman.

It wasn't until they were back at the house and she was pouring Leona a cup of fresh dark coffee that it came to her. The weight of it was like invisible hands pressing on her skull. She carried the cup out to the front porch where Leona had sat down on the steps in the same spot where she had waited so many times for Jack.

"This place," she said. But couldn't make herself go on. Leona was holding her cup perfectly still. Annie looked out toward the river. Cottonwood leaves, moving in their gentle dance. "This place where Jack got lost. Where is it?"

Leona didn't look at her. "Near the Oregon-Idaho border. Mill Creek drainage, Tiger Creek. South Fork of the Walla Walla."

"So that's—"

"It used to be our land, our people's land. We can still hunt there, fish. Pick berries." Leona looked at Annie now. "It's protected."

"Wilderness, you mean."

"Yes. It's part of the Wenaha-Tucannon Wilderness." Leona set her cup down and turned to face Annie. "If I had known—I didn't know this story, I was off with the Navajo, and then when I got back—" She looked down, but raised her eyes to meet Annie's again. "I couldn't have saved him. But maybe someone could have. A medicine person. There might have been time."

Annie reached for Leona's hand. *We're all in this together,* she thought. Each of us blaming ourselves, Riley and Alex, James, Leona, all of us. Even Jack had been feeling guilty; whatever that mystery was about his father, and his not being a good son. No wonder Mattie thinks it's about forgiveness.

And stories, too. Not telling the stories, or not hearing them. "I didn't know that story," Leona had said. Jack hadn't told her everything about that night in the mountains, or told Roy what happened. He had carried that story all by himself, all those years.

"So Jack went there to look for Riley," Annie said. Leona's eyes were filling again, but Annie felt a strange emptiness. "On purpose," she said. "That's why he left in such a hurry and didn't tell me he was going. He must have just rushed back to that place where he'd been lost and scared. 'A terror not to be described,' he said. He'd tried to write about it that last summer, in his notes. My God, Leona, he went back on purpose."

"He had to try," Leona said. "He thought that's where Riley might be."

⌒

The three of them had squeezed into the blue Toyota, but Alex was driving this time, and when Riley put his arm on the back of the seat, Mattie pulled his hand over her shoulder and leaned against him. "Let's stop at Gus and Audrey's," she said.

"Why?" Alex pulled the visor down and leaned to squint beneath it. "I don't know about you guys, but I'm starving."

"Cookies. Think cookies." Riley would have jabbed him on the shoulder, but Mattie was still holding his left hand. "Oatmeal. Chocolate chip."

"It's just that Jack said something about Roy having a story. Gus and Audrey knew him his whole life, so maybe they'd have some idea what it was."

"Yeah. Okay." Alex slowed to turn in at the black mailbox. His face was blank.

It's always there, Riley thought. That distance. He'd felt it too, just walking into a café with Alex, sometimes. Even Walmart. "Code Blue, that means us," Alex had said. "Sorry, bud. You're under suspicion, too." And what about it? Could he guarantee that these people who were so good to him would not pull back from his friends? Surely they'd remember Alex. Wouldn't they? He liked Gus and Audrey, loved them, even. But no, he wasn't sure.

Audrey opened the door the same as always, her smile spreading even wider than usual. "Wake up, Angus," she called without turning around. "Look who Riley's brought to see us!" Then she was hugging him, and then Mattie, and Alex, who looked like a tall pole squeezed in her embrace, and then Gus was there, too, reaching to shake their hands.

"Well, it's about time," he said. "So this is Mattie. Alex? Lord, boy, I almost wouldn't have known you." Audrey was already motioning them toward the kitchen table. "And just for the record, people, I was not asleep. This woman thinks that's all I do in that chair."

Audrey snorted. "Thinking. He's thinking with his eyes closed, he says."

Riley smelled something good. Not quite sweet. "Cornbread about done?" Gus settled into his place at the head of the table. "These young folks look hungry. Especially that tall drink of water over there."

Don't overdo it, Riley thought. He'll think you're trying too hard. And in fact Alex was smiling that thin, cool smile, which meant he was uncomfortable.

But Mattie was already passing the bowls of Audrey's split pea soup and by the time Alex looked up from his third piece of cornbread, honey dripping onto his fingers, to see the others watching him—"Now there's a man who appreciates good cooking!"—he grinned right back at them. Was it the food, or the joking conversation? I shouldn't have worried, Riley thought. I should have trusted them.

They had gathered in the living room around a tray of Audrey's gingersnaps, Alex shaking his head, no room, but taking two anyway, when Mattie asked about Korea. "We know so little about it," she was saying. "Truman and MacArthur and the Yalu River, that's all they teach in school. We know Riley's grandfather was in that war, and my grandma says he had some trouble afterward. Today when we were at Tamastslikt we heard a story about something that happened in Korea, and I thought—"

Audrey looked at Gus, who had swiveled to look behind him as if he were waiting for someone to come through the kitchen door.

"Grandma—Leona—she says you helped Roy when he came home. And that you were there for him when his parents died."

"We felt bad for him." Audrey's voice, always so strong and cheerful, was shaky.

"He was our friend," Gus said. "We grew up together."

Enough of this, he means. Riley tried to catch Mattie's eye, but she was still looking at Audrey. "This morning Annie shared some of what Jack had been writing just before he—that last summer, the book he was working on, his research. She needs to know, but we don't know what to tell her. The last thing he wrote was something about his father. About Roy. There was something he missed, he said. 'How could I have missed it?'"

"Whatever it was had something to do with history," Alex said. "He questioned whether he was a good historian."

"Mom asked for our help," Riley said.

Audrey was looking at him.

"He said he knew now he wasn't a good son. Because he'd missed this thing, whatever it was."

Audrey looked at Gus, who looked back at her this time. But neither of them spoke.

"At least that's what I think he meant," Riley said.

Gus cleared his throat. "I always felt guilty that he had to go and I didn't." He waved off Audrey's lifted chin. "'Course, then there would have been two sick bastards instead of one."

Audrey sucked in her breath, and Gus ducked his head. "Sorry, Mattie. It just slipped out of me."

"He doesn't usually say things like that, you know."

"It's hard to talk about some things," Mattie said softly. "We wouldn't ask if—you were the only ones who knew him then, and I just thought . . ."

"I wasn't there. I guess that's the point. If I'd been in his shoes—"

"Any of us," Audrey said.

"Atrocities," Mattie said. "I know. They happen in every war."

They heard a soft thud from the stove, and Gus stood up to add more wood. He poked the fire until the coals blazed and a shower of sparks rose in the chimney draft. He's upset, Riley thought. Maybe even mad.

"Especially if you're in some other people's country," he said when he sat down. "And you can't tell who's your enemy."

"Like Vietnam," Riley said. "Or now, in Afghanistan."

"Or North America," Alex said. "Washita. Sand Creek. Like what happened to the Modocs."

Gus looked at him. "Yes. Same thing. Same damned thing."

This time Audrey didn't bother to correct his language. "We don't know any details," she told Mattie. "Roy just talked in generalities, usually when he'd been drinking. Sometimes he cried. So many innocent people getting hurt, he said. Suffering."

"Dying," Gus said.

"Well, yes, of course." Audrey looked at Gus. "And it wasn't your fault, Angus McCrae. Any more than it was his."

⌁

When they turned the corner by the barn the Toyota's low beams reflected off Leona's truck. Strange place to park, Riley thought. And there were no lights on in the house. His throat felt tight. *I should have stayed with Mom. No matter what she said.*

Mattie looked at him. "Hey. It's all right."

Well, maybe. There was no one in the kitchen, and a strong smell coming from the living room, where the two women were only dark shapes, sitting side by side on the couch. Sage. That's what he'd smelled. They'd been burning sage. Mattie went to them and touched their hands in greeting—his eyes were already adjusting to this dimness—then picked up the shell bowl where the bundle smoldered and waved the smoke toward her own face. Now over his face, around his head. Now Alex. She was cleansing them, he knew that much.

Something was happening.

It was his mother who spoke first. "We were right, Riley. There was more to it, a lot more. It wasn't that Dad didn't trust you. He thought you might be in the same place where he'd been, that night out on the mountain. That's why he left the way he did. He hadn't told you about that night, what happened. He had never told anyone the whole story. But Leona has helped me understand."

Riley could barely see her face, but he knew she was looking directly at him. She sounded—what, calmer? Or was she slipping away from him again?

"The important thing," Annie was saying, "is what we've both known all along. He loved you. He went because he loved you so much. And what happened to him wasn't your fault."

How could both of those things be true at once? This was the same story he'd been living with all these months. It *was* his fault, even if she couldn't let herself admit it. He wanted to shout. Scream. Stand up and throw things. Starting with that shell and that burning sage. Would his head explode before this day was over?

But Mattie was lighting the leftover Christmas candles, and Leona's voice had already begun to explain. As much as could be explained, he would think that night, lying in bed across the room from Alex, who wasn't sleeping either. When they heard the coyote, somewhere close, they both got out of bed to look. But there was nothing.

"'They're trying so hard to talk to us,'" Alex whispered. "She knew, didn't she? Your grandma?"

At last Riley heard Alex's breathing steady into sleep. Would it be any easier if Dad had written something in his journal about him, about the accident? He was still staring at the ceiling, his eyes burning, and then Mattie was reaching toward the coyote under the branches of the overgrown orchard, but when the coyote lifted his head to her touch, it was his father's face beneath a tanned fur skin and Alex was pulling him away. *Not yet,* Alex was telling him. *Not yet.*

"He was in the Seventh Cavalry," Riley whispered. No need for whispering, really. They had skipped the end-of-school awards ceremony to meet in the library, and everyone else was in the gym. "I don't know what battalion, but Dad did tell me his father had been assigned to the Seventh Cavalry. 'Just like all the others,' he said. I thought he meant his dad had been a murderer, like the soldiers who'd massacred all those people at Wounded Knee, but he said no, he just meant Roy had no choice. They still had the draft then. He said a lot of the soldiers at Wounded Knee were not there out of choice, either. They were mostly immigrants, men desperate for work."

"Work," Alex said.

"Food." Mattie leaned closer to the computer screen. "He meant they probably didn't join the army because they hated Indians. Any more than—yes, here it is. I knew I'd seen something somewhere. July 26–29, 1950. No Gun Ri. In 2001 the Pentagon officially denied it, but the reporters won a Pulitzer Prize for their investigative journalism anyway. And it wasn't the only place, apparently."

"The only place what?" Both Riley and Alex were leaning over her shoulders, trying to read the screen, but she had already clicked the back arrow.

"They had orders. At No Gun Ri it was the Seventh Cavalry, Second Battalion. But there's evidence in the National Archives that it happened in a lot of places. There were so many refugees, thousands of them, tens of thousands. Maybe as many as two million. The UN forces were being fired on from behind their lines—there were North Korean forces behind them as well as in front of them—and the generals panicked, I guess. They thought infiltrators must be coming through with the refugees. It was a double bind, even more than in most wars, because it was US troops who were evacuating villages to the north and pushing people toward the south. Anyway, the Second Battalion was given orders: don't let the refugees through your lines. Some of the soldiers testifying for the Pentagon said they were told to shoot them all. Kill anyone in white."

"In white?"

She opened the story again. "See? White was the color of the peasants' clothing. Like in Mexico, I guess. Except theirs were quilted."

Riley felt sick. "So what's No Gun Ri?"

"It's the name of a village near this bridge." She pointed to a picture, two underpasses in a wall of stone, or concrete, he couldn't tell which. "They had herded the refugees onto the railroad tracks and were checking them for weapons when our Air Force planes strafed them. The survivors ran under the railroad bridge, and when the American soldiers fired into the tunnel they dug into the sand and rock with their hands. Piled up bodies to hide behind. The shooting went on for three days."

She was still reading. Riley slumped into a chair and laid his head in his arms on the scarred library table. Alex touched her shoulder, but she didn't notice. "Years later, President Clinton said the US regretted the loss of civilian life, and offered to set up a scholarship fund. But there was no government apology. No record of such an order at No Gun Ri, the Pentagon said. The Seventh Cavalry log book's missing from the National Archives. So there was no compensation for the families of survivors."

"Did they all follow this order?" Alex asked, glancing at Riley.

"According to the ones who could talk about it fifty years later, some didn't. Some men went wild with killing, some hid from it. But of course they couldn't stop it. And either way—"

Alex was squeezing her shoulder harder now, and pointing with his lips toward Riley. Mattie closed the website and sat down across the table, taking Riley's hands in hers. Alex pulled out a chair and added his hands to the pile.

After a while Mattie said, "I'm sorry, Riley. I get carried away sometimes."

"We don't know Roy was there," Alex said. "He would still have been in boot camp that July, wouldn't he?"

"But it sounds like it happened a lot." Riley shook his head. "He must have seen it."

"Yes." Mattie's voice was softer. "Or something just as bad. That's why some tribes have ceremonies to help the people who come home from war. They all need help."

"I wish we had it now," Alex said. "For every veteran of Iraq, and Afghanistan. And Vietnam. Those guys are still having problems, some of them."

"Roy didn't have anything like that," Mattie said. "I don't know if Jack—if your dad thought he'd missed something specific, like the No Gun Ri Massacre, or if he just realized he should have figured out what had made Roy react the way he did to losing Mary."

Mary. Mary, in her white nightgown, hanging out the laundry. Singing. And doing her willow dance, Leona had told his mother. No wonder he had thought Mary could help him, Riley thought. She was a dark-haired woman dressed in white, and she was still alive.

⌁

More than ever, Annie wanted to talk with Jack. Now that she wasn't afraid of going back into the hospital, she could sometimes let herself do this. "You were right," she told him. "The past is here with us. The stories, too. They're then and now and will be. And we're all part of the story."

Though maybe that part is more my specialty, she thought now, driving to her last class of the term. Writing 115. A motley assortment of people with stories of their own, all of them touching hers.

But she hadn't really done them justice this term. Maybe she could get Mattie to ask them to forgive her.

Dorothy wanted her for summer school again this year, though. She would do better now.

"I'm worried about Riley," she said out loud. "These last few days have been so hard for him."

Riley's tough, Annie. He's strong, like you. He'll get through this.

It was only memory. She knew that. Still, it was a comfort. "He's like *you*, Jack, and you know it," she told him. He could always hear the smile in her voice. "That's why I'm worried."

The boys were already out of school and at their summer jobs, Alex at Tamastslikt and Riley off before dawn to change sprinkler pipes for a friend of Gus and Audrey's. He'd been promised work in the wheat harvest, too, in mid-July. "That's real money, Mom," he'd said.

"You'll earn it, too," Alex had told him. "I've got to get you a tribal ID so you can sit behind a desk, like me."

"Yeah, life's easy if you're Indian," Riley said, and they both laughed.

"I may be worried," Annie told Jack, "but I'm so proud of him. You would be, too."

Riley was in his stocking feet when she got home. He'd left the knee-high irrigation boots outside the door, but he was still wearing his mud-streaked jeans. There were sandwiches on the table, though, and iced tea.

"Don't worry, I washed my hands," he said. "Granted, they're the only part of me that's clean."

"Hey, no complaints from this corner," she said. "Any time I come home to find lunch waiting."

But the table was set for only one.

"Mom, I need to know where you put the gun."

Annie shivered. One quick, involuntary spasm, but he knew.

"Don't worry. I'm getting rid of it."

She heard him grunt as he struggled to reach the shoebox. Only his fingertips could touch it. Now he would be turning it, tipping a corner toward himself until his hand found purchase. She heard the sound of the box sliding on the wooden floor. Chew, she told herself. Now swallow.

Trust him.

She had carried the dishes to the sink when she heard the sound of the pick. He was loosening the soil under the lilacs, then spading turf and dirt into a neat pile. The gun lay on the grass on the other side of the deepening hole.

"I took the firing pin out," he said when she joined him. "Threw it in the river." He pushed his Blazers cap back on his head and wiped his forehead. "At least I think it was the firing pin. Might've been the trigger, for all I know."

Annie smiled. "You learned all you know about guns from me."

"Yeah, I thought about that later. Mom with a gun. I must have mistaken you for Annie Oakley."

The hole was deep enough for him to step into. Seventeen. His back and arms were thickening so quickly. "Want me to spell you?" she could have asked if they had been digging out the roots of a dead rose bush or planting an apple tree.

"I keep thinking I'll find the coyote skin," he said, pausing for breath. "Which is nuts, I know. It's gone by now."

"Part of the earth," she said.

He dug until he was thigh-deep in the hole. When he straightened and looked at her his voice was quiet. "Maybe not, though. Maybe not completely."

"I know," Annie said, and would have tried to say more, though what could she have said? But he had already sat back against the rim and was pushing himself up out of the hole.

"You want to do the honors?"

The gun lay on her palm, a foreign thing. Not nearly as heavy as she remembered. Small. A manufactured object. She knelt and leaned over the hole, reaching until she could lay the gun on solid ground.

Afterward, they sat together on the front steps, Riley accepting the glass of iced tea she brought him with a wince. "Blister. Damn. I should've used gloves." He drained the glass and set it on the porch. "I hope it's deep enough that no one plows it up."

"It'll rust," Annie said. "It's harmless now."

"Yeah, but I'd hate to have to explain." He rubbed his elbow, twisting his arm to look at it. "I might as well have hung a sign around my neck that said, I'M AFRAID. When people try too hard to control things—oh, I don't know."

"Like what happened in Korea? The thing you told me about?"

"Yeah, that's an obvious one, all right. All those people killed because somebody was afraid of what *might* happen. You know?"

"Yes. And Roy. Granddad. I've thought so much about him, clinging so hard to that rigid toughness the way he did, trying to make sure he didn't lose his boy."

"Which is why Dad ended up in that place where—well, that's why I knew I had to get rid of the gun. Whatever it was that scared Dad there was nothing he could shoot."

25

They walked single file, James in the lead. Then Riley and Annie, trailed by Rose. On this narrow section of the trail Alex had had to leave his mother's side but he was close behind her. Leona was here too, and Mattie, who wanted to be last.

"We have to try, Mom," Riley had said. "Now that we know where he is."

"Uncle James can help us find him, Alex told her. "He's—he picked up the drum. He's been going to the longhouse ever since it happened. He sings Washat."

"And he's talked with the men who used to hunt there," Riley said.

"The elders have told him it's okay." Alex was holding himself so straight he seemed even taller than he was. "He wouldn't do it without their permission."

"I know," Annie said. "He told me."

James and Ruby had stepped down from their old truck a few days earlier, and Annie had walked to meet them, holding out her hand. "It's good to see you." This time they came in. They had finished their coffee and the applesauce cake Riley had made the night before—fortunately there was still some left in the loaf pan—before they told her why they'd come. "He needs to be buried," Ruby said. "James can help."

Leona hadn't offered any guidance. No, that wasn't true. It's just that her guidance was ambiguous this time. "Look into your heart, Annie. Listen to the river."

And what had it told her? The same thing it said that day when she was churning though the current, unable to get to Riley in time? If everything Leona had told her about this place was true, not to mention the things Jack had written in his journal—

James held up his hand and everyone behind him stopped to listen. Annie had spent enough time in the wilderness to recognize the sound of the canyon below them: wind and space. Sometimes, waiting in her Portland classroom for her students to arrive for their first class of the fall, she had closed her eyes and heard that sound again. It's still there, even if we're not there to hear it, she had told herself.

But James was gathering them in a circle. They had all sweated the night before to ready themselves for this journey. Now James was burning sage and juniper, singing as he waved the smoke over their heads, and when he said a prayer it was in a language she didn't understand, the Umatilla or Walla Walla dialect of the Sahaptin language family. They were all carrying a bit of loose tobacco tied in a square of red calico, a pattern Annie thought she recognized from one of Leona's aprons. James looked at each of them in turn. Was he checking for signs of fear, Annie wondered? When he stood in front of his sister, he reached out and touched her shoulder, bowing his head for a brief instant.

Then they were on their way into the canyon.

The earth beneath her feet felt different. And the air. Yes, it seemed thinner, though they were going downhill. One narrow shaft of light filtered between thick branches, the firs rising on both sides of the trail nearly blocking out the sun. Had they left the trail or had the trail left them, narrowing to nothing the way so many game trails did? A doe rose up stiff-legged from her grassy bed, her fawn still emerging from her womb. James touched his forehead and dropped to one knee. The fawn fell to the earth and the doe turned to meet its wet muzzle, licking it clear for a first breath. Annie felt air rush into her lungs.

"Mom?"

But Annie couldn't make words come, even in a whisper to match Riley's. The doe was licking, licking, licking her newborn alive. The fawn shook its ears.

James rose and took a slow step backward, then led them in a wide arc around the deer. Were they spiraling into the canyon? It's a matter of paying attention, Jack had said, but in this darkening light anything that might be called a bearing point shifted and disappeared. She would never find her way back. But when had she felt this free? Was she still a small girl, spinning in circles until even tumbling to the grass felt like flying? She could stay behind, stay here forever. She stopped walking. Yes, that was Jack's whistle—he was calling her, come, walk hand in hand through these blue shadows, hand in hand forever and ever, no end, how could there be?

But Riley was reaching back to take her wrist and pull her along.

All the others were leaving their tobacco offerings. Ruby tied hers to a twig of something Annie didn't recognize, not serviceberry or current but brush of some kind, and now Leona laid hers on a white branch of a dying spruce. "You'll know where to leave it," Leona had told them last night in the sweathouse. "You'll feel it."

But she had felt nothing. Nothing. Was she unworthy? Yes, she always had been unworthy. Hadn't she always known that? She'd tried to hide from it, deny it, but—

The fear came in crashing waves, gray and dizzying. Salt water breaking endless against rock. The small bundle felt heavy in her fist, and something was pressing hard, insistent, against her back. She reached behind her to touch the dog and felt nothing. Empty air. Whatever had pushed her wasn't Rose.

The next push was a shove. She stumbled forward. Someone was calling her name.

"This way." Alex had been holding back a branch for her. She ducked under it and followed the others down a steep slope, James's loose-kneed descent reminding her of Jack. The forest closed around them, branches hanging heavy overhead. Single file again, they skirted the root-tangle of an old windfall. Yes, there was Rose, and something—a fluid movement— just beyond her. Did the others see it too? It looked like an old man, or the shadow of an old man, a gray-white shape dissolving into darkness. Leona's father? But how could it be? The dog was nosing at the base of a huge pine, the only yellow pine in a swale thick with spruce and tall cedars. A Ponderosa. An ancient fire had hollowed out the cavelike shelter in its trunk. James was kneeling, touching his forehead again.

Leona stepped aside to let her pass. But where was her son?

"Riley?"

"Mom!" She put her arms around him. He was trembling. Shaking. "Mom, I don't—"

"I know, honey." Annie's voice was jerky; she felt her teeth chattering. But the others were gathering around them, encircling them, and somehow they were moving toward the pine tree, Alex's hand on Riley's shoulder, Leona and Mattie pressing close behind her, and Ruby too, as if they were one body and she and Riley chambers of this body's heart.

Inside the hollow place what remained of Jack's body was slumped against the dark interior as if he were still listening to the pulse of the heartwood.

James's voice rose high above the others' answering echo. Were they singing or just crying with her? If it was a song it was the right one, sounds of keening grief, waves of sound she could fall into without falling. How could a shoe last longer than the foot inside it? He had pulled his knees toward his chest; a thin, tough band of ligament still holding them in place. Riley was sobbing. "Oh Dad oh Dad."

Yet it was the moment they had wanted, the one she had searched for even in her dreams, an endless waterfall of pain, timeless as childbirth. When at last the singing grew softer, Ruby spread a soft buckskin on the earth and they all knelt behind it. Riley's face was a pale sheen. James reached into the opening and then sat back oh his heels, Jack's body in his arms. Jack's bones, bits of tissue, rotting remnants of his blue plaid shirt. But how could that be Ja—Annie heard a cry and reached to comfort Riley before she realized the cry had been her own. Riley's head was bowed now; she couldn't see his face. Mattie and Alex had begun to sing, their gazes unfocused, Mattie's hand on Riley's back. James laid the curled body on the buckskin. In the places where they showed clean, the bones looked like bleached cottonwood. Delicate. Light.

Leona had carried a red Pendleton blanket draped over her arm. The blanket, Annie knew, was to fold around the buckskin. James would carry out the body.

But first, crawling on her knees in forest duff, Annie laid her tobacco bundle inside the hollow place. Jack had huddled here alone. She closed her eyes. A cave, a womb—had he felt something like earth's arms around him at the end?

The forest light had dimmed by the time they turned back, and even as her eyes adjusted, Annie knew that it was growing darker. How would James see where he was going? She didn't know, but she followed on his heels as if an invisible cord were pulling her along. She could feel Riley's hand on her right shoulder, and she knew that behind him the others were probably linked this way too. Step by step. It seemed a long way. But now James was singing again. Did Riley feel this way, too? Weak, and strong at the same time?

The moon that met them as they topped out of the canyon seemed sunlike after that deep darkness. There was the pickup. Leona climbed into the back and James handed the blanket up to her. When Annie was seated on the pickup bed, Leona laid the bundle in her lap. So light. Almost weightless, what remained of Jack. Ruby had slid closer to her brother to make room for one more in the cab, but the others were already hoisting themselves into the back of the pickup, and as the truck motor started up they pressed closer, sheltering Annie from the cool night air and keeping her upright.

James drove slowly, letting the tires climb gently as he could out of each rut. The truck bed tilted as the wheels crawled across the rocks caught briefly in the headlights. Finally they reached the gravel. Annie cradled the weight in her arms as if it might be wakened by the vibration of what Jack had always called washboards: small, hard ridges in the road that jolted her spine. Had he felt them this way too, riding in the back of Roy's pickup when he was a boy? She looked out at the headlight beams piercing the darkness. No matter how much she and Jack had talked, there was so much left unsaid. So many things she hadn't asked him about. And now talking with Jack—imagining that they were talking—even that was gone. Now that she'd seen.

Then the lights went out.

James stopped the truck. No headlights, no dash lights. The truck had gone completely dark. As her eyes adjusted to the moonlight, Annie could see that Ruby was feeling for something in the glove compartment. Jockey box, Roy would have called it. Yes, she had found a flashlight. Two flashlights.

In the moonlight now Annie could see Leona holding Mattie, gently rocking her.

"It's not a fuse." Alex' voice was coming from somewhere beneath the steering wheel, and then she made out his shape beside the driver's side door. "How about if Riley and I walk ahead with the flashlights? One on each side of the road?"

James murmured something and started the truck again. They crawled along, the boys' flashlights sweeping across the road to meet in the center, then pointing at the graveled edge again. Annie glanced at Leona. Her arm was still around Mattie's shoulders, but they were both looking at the road ahead.

Something white—an owl, rising up from the darkness into Riley's flashlight beam. Silent, quick. Riley threw up his arm as the owl's flight cleared his head. James stopped the truck.

"What?" Riley had turned back toward the truck, keeping the flashlight beam low, out of their eyes.

"Behind you." James's voice was quiet. "Where the land slopes toward that little draw. Looks like the earth gave way over there, just at the edge. And there's something—Alex, shine your light there too."

The flashlight beams were weakened by moonlight. "Don't see anything," Alex said.

"Go closer to the edge. Look down in that gully, in the brush."

How had he seen it? It was only a pale sliver, one corner of the Chevy's silver roofline. Jack's car, nearly buried in the thick overgrowth of the gully. Had he been in it when the wheels slipped over the edge, or had the earth given way after he left the car? Riley pushed through the brush and stood on Alex's braced knee to pull open the passenger door. Annie waited, the blanket in her arms, as the others rose—Mattie on tiptoe—trying to see. At last the flashlights jerked in thin lines toward the sky; the boys were climbing back up the embankment. And Riley was holding something white: Jack had wrapped Roy's letter in a handkerchief. "He'd left this on the dash, I think. We found it underneath the seat."

When James started up the truck again, the headlights flickered on. The boys climbed back into the pickup and they all huddled even closer around Annie, Riley between Mattie and Alex, their arms around each others' shoulders, a many-headed creature swaying with the turns.

They were all spent, but Leona said they would need to sweat again. When the women emerged from their turn in the willow-frame sweathouse, the sun was just rising over the Blue Mountains. Her body immersed in the river's current, strong with melting snow, Annie felt warm all the way through.

They would bury him next to his mother, but only after officials released the bones. The county sheriff, medical examiners, the death certificate. The insurance people again. But she could face them now. Jack had left her a note, after all.

My dear Annie, he had written on the back of Roy's letter.

When Dad left me alone and I got lost, it was somewhere close to here. Things happened that I still don't understand and never really faced. Riley might be in there now. I'm going to try to find him. Annie, I'm so sorry. I thought they were taking him into the Eagle Cap. I know you won't see this note unless I get lost again, and I don't have time to say how much I love you. But I do, Annie. I do.

"Now we need to rest," Leona had told them as she and Mattie left for home. "Sleep all day, Annie, if you can." Riley and Alex were both asleep upstairs, but Annie lay on top of the bedcovers, Roy's letter on her chest. Roy's letter, and Jack's. Both of them had been saying good-bye to the woman they loved.

"Coyote went to the land of the dead, too." Leona had spoken into the darkness of the sweat, her words wrapping like steam around Annie's body. "His wife had died, and he missed her. If he hadn't touched her, my grandpa said, he could have brought her back, and then no one would have died forever. Death would have lost its power. But Coyote—well, he just loved her so much."

"So he's like us," Annie whispered. "Like people."

"Aiiii." Whether Ruby's soft cry was assent or the sound of her own pain, Annie couldn't be sure.

"We're like him." This time it was Mattie's voice. "Creator knew. We're all his children."

26

"Here you go." Audrey settled heavily into her lawn chair and Riley looked down at the empty bowl in his lap. "Gus picked these before sunup, so they'll be sweet. 'Course the first peas are the sweetest anyway." Riley heard the shelled peas falling into her bowl. A sound like huckleberries falling into a pail. No, huckleberries made a softer sound. It would be time for huckleberries— when? After wheat harvest. Which could start as early as next week if this weather held, Jim Helgeson had told him. When he and Alex were little, summer was one long day that lasted forever. It wasn't divided into weeks and months then, much less these seasons within seasons. "Two peas in a pod," Audrey was saying. "You and your dad. More peas went into his mouth than the bowl, too."

"Now, Mother, he's a growing boy." Gus had come around the corner of the house with another milk bucket filled to the brim with green pods. He shelled peas into his palm and funneled them into his own mouth, winking at Riley from under his cupped hand. "I don't know why she has to cook these, anyway."

"Someone around here loves creamed peas and new potatoes, that's why." Audrey tossed an empty pod in his direction.

"How's that girl of yours? Now there's a keeper." Gus's hands were so big the green pods seemed to disappear between his fingers. "Pretty *and* smart. Like Audrey here."

Riley glanced up in time to catch her smile. What had she looked like when she was young? No, wait. Gus thinks she's pretty now.

"Good. She's good, I guess. She's been babysitting Spike's kids all week, so I haven't actually seen her since—" He looked down at the peapod in his hand. The words stopped in his throat. Body. Bones. Remains. The thing they'd gone in search of, needed to find. Found.

"It's hard," Audrey said quickly. She reached across the space between them to put her hand on his knee. "It will get a little easier, now. But for a while it will be even harder."

Riley nodded, still looking down. All that sweating, before and after, and the eerie darkness of that canyon, thin beams from the flashlights feeling their way forward like the antennae of some creeping bug—it had been so intense, their immersion in the journey itself. And then—what they had found. What was left of him.

No one else had said it this simply, this plainly. It's hard. And it will get harder.

He had come with a message from his mother. They'd have a ceremony of some kind at the house, because Annie knew Audrey couldn't make it up the trail to the gravesite and she wanted these two to be part of his dad's memorial. But he couldn't trust his voice to speak.

Gus cleared his throat. "We were talking last night, Audrey and me. It feels real good to think of you and Mattie living on the Fallon place someday. Maybe raising a family of your own."

Riley felt heat rising to his cheeks. Home. The ranch. The Fallon place. The way Gus pronounced it, though, it sounded more like felon place. Fell-in. The fallen place.

Audrey laughed. "I suppose we are getting a little bit ahead of ourselves here. You're both still in school, for heaven's sake. And there'll be college after that. Who knows what else."

"I guess it's obvious," he said at last. "How I feel about her. But I—" He looked down at the peapod in his hand. "The thing is, I always thought we were different. Our family, I mean. You know, innocent. Trying to do good. Tell the truth about what happened, all that." How to say this? "But now—well, Granddad, whatever it was that happened in Korea, and all that silence about Dad's mother after she died."

Audrey and Gus were quiet. Looking at the work their hands were doing. But they were listening.

"And Dad. It turns out he'd been lost in that canyon when he was a kid, and some old man came and led him out. He never told me. Never told anybody, the whole story." He shook his head. "I don't know for sure why. But—if there were things he couldn't face, or—let himself believe . . ."

Gus bent over to scratch Chubby's ears, the old Aussie not rousing from his sleep; Audrey was frowning at the peapod in her hand. Riley took a breath. "See, it's not just other people, it's us, too. Our family. Even where we live—the Fallon place is only ours because somebody was cheated out of it." He looked down. The peapod was mashed flat. "I've already screwed up once, big time. Mattie's says not to worry, she trusts me, but—"

"Gus leaned forward. "Indians. That's what all this is about? You're all worked up because Mattie's Umatilla-Cayuse and you're not?"

Riley nodded. He had poured it all out, stumbling and inarticulate, but it was out there. "What if I make things worse somehow? I could—I mean, I'd never hurt her on purpose, but—oh, I don't know."

Gus stood up and walked to the edge of the grass, hands in his pockets. The shelled peas were mounting faster now in Audrey's bowl. Finally she sighed and set her bowl down on the grass. She was pushing herself up out of the lawn chair when Gus turned. "Sit yourself back down, Mother," he said. "Riley, let's walk a spell. I need to check that gate in the upper pasture."

His boots left soft prints in the dirt path to the barn. Riley followed, stepping into the older man's tracks the way he once had his father's. God, what had he done? Ruined their whole day, for one thing. "Sorry," he said into the silence. "Guess I shouldn't have said all that."

Gus turned and put his hand on Riley's shoulder. Then he tousled Riley's hair as if he were still a little boy. "What we're doin' here is, we're just giving me time to think of what to say to you. And if we're lucky, Audrey will have time to get into her kitchen and stir up something for the oven." They had reached the draw now and he was panting a little, using the fence posts to pull himself up the hill. "She does that when she feels bad. Makes her happy, she says." He pulled himself up one more step and turned to look at Riley. "Steep as a cow's face, isn't it?" When he'd caught his breath he added, "Lucky for us, she bakes when she feels good, too."

Riley tried to smile. "Win-win."

"As long as I keep climbing this hill, it is. Otherwise I'd be as big as a barn. You'll get there someday, too, kiddo. Place where you have to think about these things."

Kiddo. Dad used to call him that.

At the top of the ridge they walked the fence line, Gus making a pretense of checking the tautness of the barbed-wire gate before he settled back against a tepee-shaped, rough board enclosure, letting the chunks of basalt that anchored this corner-post rock jack serve as a makeshift chair. When he raised his arm, Riley turned to look where he was pointing. Canyon air, and then the dark rim of the Blues, their foothills creased with gray-green shadows.

"I didn't know if you'd ever seen it from here," Gus said. "My God, no wonder the Sho-Bans wished it could be theirs."

"That why they used to come raiding?"

"Maybe. I don't know. Might've been to get horses and captives, women and kids. Or just to keep their fighting forces strong, the way we do today. 'Pray for war.' The Marines used to chant that in boot camp, you know. Between wars."

Pray for war. My God. Riley closed his eyes against the vision. Mattie had told him more about Korea, how bridges were blown while refugees were crossing them, prisoners on both sides executed, about the mass graves, and men whose lives were scarred with trauma and with guilt. Soldiers. Korean survivors, too.

Lose-lose.

"Sit down, why don't you?"

Cross-legged on the earth, Riley felt the warmth of rock through the June grass. A magpie flew from the small pine behind them and settled, long tail bobbing, on a fence post.

"You know, a few years back the tribes invited the Burns Paiute people to come for a reconciliation ceremony. They'd fought against each other in the Bannock War, and a whole lot of bad stuff had happened in the hundred years since then. Drinking, kids on drugs. Domestic violence. That kind of thing. And it kept happening. Like you said, the stuff that happened in the past keeps affecting people now, even if the people now didn't experience what happened."

"Like Dad, when he was a kid. Not knowing about Korea."

"Yeah, like that. Well, anyway, when I read about it in the paper, I got to thinking. Look, you could argue neither of these people was to blame. They were both caught in the trap we'd put them in. Our people, yours and mine. There was no "right" way to get out of it, really. So they could have blamed us, and only us. With good reason. Or they could have kept blaming each other for another hundred years. Like I said, they'd been enemies for a long time before we got here."

Riley nodded.

"But they knew. Both of their peoples were suffering, and they needed both of their peoples to heal." Gus bent forward to pick a grass stem and pulled it between his fingers.

"So did anything change?"

Gus put both hands on his knees and pushed himself upright. Riley would have pulled the words back into his mouth if he could, but they were out there, hanging in the bright June air. He scrambled to his feet. "I didn't mean—"

"Yeah, you did. We all give in to it, from time to time. Even Jack. Even your dad." Gus stood looking out across the canyon. "But then he came back home and tried again."

Riley wasn't sure what he meant. They'd always come back home, hadn't they? Every summer?

"It's hard to know what to do sometimes, Riley," Gus said. "I guess all we can do is just keep trying."

Riley nodded, but he couldn't speak. Was this all there was?

"That girl of yours, Mattie, that's what she's been doing. Her level best. And that's pretty much what I've seen from you since all this happened, too. A person's best, it's about all anyone can do." Gus rocked back on his heels and looked down, then up at the cloudless sky. "Oh, dammit, I'm not good at this. I wish your dad was here."

"Me too. Dammit."

They both laughed, so long and hard that Riley wasn't sure, after a while, if they were actually laughing; he could see tears in the corners of Gus's eyes. Finally he had to pound the old man on the back to help him catch his breath.

Halfway back down the hill, Gus stopped and turned to face Riley. "Okay, I'll tell you what I think about this Indian business. For better or worse, we're all here now, and if we're going to make things better, we all have to be part of it. Like the Umatilla Basin Project. Not everything's gone wrong around here, you know. Salmon can come up the river now to spawn, and that's because everyone worked together to get water back in the river all year long. Irrigators too." He braced his arm against a fence post. "I guess that's the gist of what I've been going all the way around the barn to say, and you can take it or leave it, but I'm pretty sure Mattie would tell you the same thing." He turned his head to look behind and below him, where the barn roof glinted in the noonday sun. "Lucky for us, women don't wait for us to get perfect before they take us on. Audrey, she's still working on me."

Riley laughed. He did feel better; talking helped.

But it was the words Gus tossed back over his shoulder that made him want to spread his arms and run downhill as fast as he could, run until his body was airborne. "Hell, we've just been making chin music up here, anyway," Gus said. "You got a little shook up from that trip into the canyon, but you're a Fallon, and once a Fallon finds the girl he loves, he don't let go. Not for love nor money."

27

They burst through the back door almost as one, though Mattie was clearly in the lead and it was only Alex's arm reaching over her shoulder toward an imaginary finish line. Riley was a few steps behind them, but when they collapsed into the kitchen chairs, panting, he was the one who still had breath enough to navigate the tangle of extended legs between him and the sink. "See?" he said. Alex was gulping his glass of water, trying to nod at the same time. "She can run a hole in the wind."

That old expression. It had been one of Roy's, Annie remembered. Alex held out his glass for more. "To Mattie," he said, lifting his refilled glass. "Fleetest of the Tribe." Mattie laughed. They were all still catching their breath. "What I don't understand," he said as Riley sat down in the chair closest to Mattie and put his hand over hers, "is how someone as slow as you are ever caught this girl."

Then they were out the door, Riley hard on Alex's heels. Through the open door Annie could see them rolling in a fierce mock wrestle down the riverbank. Mattie shook her head, but she was smiling. "Boys." She was half out of her chair now, straining to see. "Looks like they're going to get wet."

"Want to make sure?"

In seconds Mattie was knee-deep in the river, scooping water toward the boys with her hands. When the two boys advanced on her as a team, she turned and dove out into the deeper channel, surfacing with a quick look toward the porch. Annie watched as Riley pulled Mattie underwater.

They came up laughing, shaking water from their hair. Alex lost his balance and tipped over backward. High voices, shouting. Annie closed her eyes, remembering a Zuni poem she had showed Jack a long time ago, the one about the Kachinas returning to the Zuni people on the Winter Solstice to offer their world-renewal blessings, *that shelled corn may be spilled before his door, that beans may be spilled before his door, that in his house children may jostle one another in the doorway.*

But though they sounded like small children just now, they were growing into manhood, these boys Jack had loved. Their lives were going on. And Mattie, this girl who might become the mother of his grandchildren—how well had he known her? She had probably been only one face in a classroom the day he visited her school.

Annie sat down on the porch steps. The three swimmers were wading out now, water dripping from their clothes. The Tribe of Three, they called themselves. She belonged to something too, a circle that included Leona's family now, and Alex's. Gus and Audrey. Even Rose. It had taken all of them to find the stories that led them to Jack's body. To bring him home. But Jack's life, his own story, would always be unfinished. Those anguished questions in his last journal entries—what would they have led him to, if he had lived? Even after the comfort of the ceremony—the songs and prayers, the house and yard filling with his colleagues and her students, Riley's friends, so many Native people—Annie had awakened in the dark with her heart racing, the dream already fading to its own ghost. A letter someone had forgotten to mail, tools left outside turning to rust.

She clung to this, though: in the days since that trip into the canyon, even the hard things she had been left to do alone seemed almost trivial. Retrieving Jack's car was just a matter of locating a wrecker. He would have dealt with Jim Casey himself, but she could do it, too.

⤙

"So now we're even. Is that what you think? Listen, this don't even begin to make things even."

Annie took a step backward into the darkness of the barn. *He's with the horses,* Maxine Casey had told her. *In the barn.* Annie had waited for her eyes to adjust to the dimness and was moving slowly toward the smell of horses and hay dust when she heard his boots on the wooden floor behind her. Now he was standing between her and the big open doorway, backlit by bright sunlight. She couldn't read his face.

"I—"

"Your boy's been comin' around. Did you know that? I told him to stay the hell away. He's done enough damage." Casey lifted his hat and wiped his forehead with the back of his wrist before he pulled the cap down, hard. "So he waits until my truck's gone and then leaves his envelopes behind the screen door. Dollar bills. Kid could scatter dollar bills from hell to breakfast and not come close to paying for that bull."

Annie handed him the check as she pushed past him toward the open door, toward light and air. When she turned to face him he was staring down at the long white envelope. He hadn't opened it.

"I've been paying you too, Mr. Casey. And you've been cashing those checks, small as they were. Now that I've been able to claim Jack's life insurance, I'm paying off the rest of what we owe you. The amount set by the court." She could see it, the row of numbers at the bottom of the column in her notebook, the figure growing only infinitesimally smaller every month. But smaller. Good people pay their bills. Don't get their power shut off or skip out on their rent.

"Court don't know cattle," Casey was saying. "That was a prize bull your kid hit." He turned his head to spit into the darkness. "Look, city girl. Here's how it is. It took me a while to find another bull, which meant the calves were late. Which meant less weight at the sales yard. Time is money. *Jack* knew that. Least he did before he got too high and mighty for ranchin'. Makes me sick the way he let Roy's place go to hell."

He means the hayfield, Annie thought. The way it's seeding itself back to pines. The has-been and the now, and the will-be, touching each other like water in a lake.

Behind him, a horse shifted in his stall.

"What really galls me is, we wouldn't even be havin' this conversation if you and Jack hadn't let the boy of yours run with—I seen him with that girl of his outside Mission Market the other day. Leanin' over a Coke so close their heads were touchin'." He shook his head. "You know anything about her? About her family? I'll tell you somethin'. You'll be lucky if head lice is *all* you get from that bunch."

It was like the sudden plunge of a carnival ride, that pressure on her breastbone, a fist pushing her heart into her spine. A grasshopper buzzed in the grass beyond the open door. Casey shifted his weight, flipping the envelope against his thigh.

"You're right. We're not even." Annie hardly recognized her own voice, this thin, sharp blade slicing the air between them. "We'll *never* be even. Jack is dead—Riley's lost his father, do you understand that? Forever, for *all time*, because someone else said something like you just said." She took a step toward Casey. "Words have power. They matter. Don't you *know* that? You're a grown man!"

She had reached the Cayuse junction road before her heart stopped pounding. Casey had ducked as if he thought she was going to hit him. But yelled something after her, too, whatever it was lost in the bawling of a calf. At the gravel turnout to Kanine Road, she pulled over and shut off the motor. A pheasant cock flew up from the high bank, crossed the highway and sailed down to disappear into the summer grass.

What would Riley do the next time he heard Mattie insulted? And he would. She couldn't shelter him, any more than he could shelter Mattie, from the Darrells and Jim Caseys of the world. There were too many of them.

A car was coming, slowing for the curve. No, it was pulling in behind her. In the rear view mirror she could see Gus getting out of his dust-covered Buick.

"Everything okay?"

"Yes, I was just—" Annie felt her face flushing. Here came Audrey, too, her cane slipping in the gravel. "Jim Casey's bull. I wanted to pay him in person. Not too smart, as it turned out."

Audrey was frowning. "That man's a real pill, Annie. Don't you take him to heart."

Gus tipped his hat back and leaned down to rest his elbows on the window opening. "He did me some good, though, once. Long time ago. I heard him going on about the dirty Siwashes the way my old man used to do. It's the way we were raised back then, most of us. But Casey—I never did like him. He just set my teeth on edge. And I thought, 'I don't *ever* want to sound like that.'" Dad had told some stories about Scotland, too, how the Highlanders were hunted down like animals and killed, one at a time, after the Battle of Culloden, and how they wrapped up in their tartans for camouflage when they slept out in the open like they had to do. Anyway, that was the day I thought, seems to me we Scots have a lot in common with these Indians. Might be we oughta be on the same side."

"Now don't you give Jim Casey too much credit," Audrey said. "Jack was the one, and you know it. We listened to his stories all through his high school years."

"That's true." Gus grinned. "His first classroom was our kitchen. He cut his teeth on us."

"We learned a few things, too."

"You two," Annie said. "Bless you."

"Stop by for some iced tea, can you? Or lemonade?"

"No, by God. She needs something a whole lot stronger than lemonade after a run-in with Jim Casey." Gus raised his arm to fend off Audrey's imaginary blow.

Annie laughed. "Can I take a rain check? They're waiting for me at home. Leona's promised us frybread. And I think my backbone's back in place now."

"Well, good. We all need pickin' up from time to time."

"It's like we tried to tell Roy," Audrey said. "No one finds the way alone."

Annie reached down to start the truck. In the rearview mirror, Gus was matching his gait to Audrey's, one hand under her elbow. He would love her "'Til all the seas gang dry," as his fellow Scot had written, "and the rocks melt w' the sun." These two loved each other the way she loved Jack, loved him still, "while the sands o' life shall run." And beyond. Even after both people were dead, she knew now, their love could drift like a winged seed on the current of a child's breath or rise up from the pages of old letters. *Oh, Mary,* Roy had written. *I reach to hold you in the night and you're not there. My arms so empty it hurts to breathe.*

Would love shelter them, her Riley and Mattie? It's all we have, she thought. All any of us have.

It was cooler in the shade of the cottonwoods. The blue truck was all but steering itself now, the turns of this road familiar as the river itself. She passed the turnoff to Iskuulpa Creek and then the black mailbox. McCrae. Hand-painted white letters. And here came Chubby, rising from his low, ground-hugging crouch to race the pickup down the length of Gus's fence line, the game he had been playing all his life. She took her foot off the accelerator. On the other side of the road, the coyote was loping alongside her too, a mottled shadow in the rising wake of road dust, disappearing now into the land.

ACKNOWLEDGMENTS

A wide circle of story-makers contributed to this book.

I am indebted to Dr. Ron Pond's article about Spirit Mountain in the August 2011 issue of the *Confederated Umatilla Journal*, and to Annie Smith for her careful vetting of the manuscript from a tribal perspective.

Jeannette Cappella believed in this story even before it was written—a gift, as was her perceptive reading. Ursula and Charles Le Guin, Judy Klein, John Lynch, Hannah Thomassen, Judith Quaempts, and Barbara J. Scot also read earlier drafts and shared valuable insights. Much gratitude goes to Tom Booth, Micki Reaman, and Marty Brown at OSU Press.

Joyful thanks to Josh and Cecelia, whose marriage inspired this story, and to Dean, who knew it would.

Most of all I am grateful to Molly Gloss, who told me, "You have to write a novel," and was both mentor and friend throughout the process. This book is for her.